Seneca Ray Stoddard

The cruise of the Friesland

Seneca Ray Stoddard

The cruise of the Friesland

ISBN/EAN: 9783741127014

Manufactured in Europe, USA, Canada, Australia, Japa

Cover: Foto ©Andreas Hilbeck / pixelio.de

Manufactured and distributed by brebook publishing software
(www.brebook.com)

Seneca Ray Stoddard

The cruise of the Friesland

"IN MEDITERRANEAN LANDS"

The
Cruise of the Friesland
1895

By S. R. STODDARD

GLENS FALLS, N. Y.
Published by the Author
MDCCCXCVI

PRESS OF A. V. HAIGHT, POUGHKEEPSIE, N. Y.

INTRODUCTION.

"Now, look pleasant, please."

CONTENTS.

(Subject Headings of Chapters and Illustrations.)

ix

MALAGA—page 35.

GRANADA AND THE ALHAMBRA—page 43.

ALGIERS—page 55.

HISTORY OF FOUR DAYS—page 63.

THE NILE DELTA—page 65.

CAIRO—page 69.

x

A Nile Boat.

Natives of Palestine.

xi

CONTENTS.

A Street in Jerusalem.

xii

At Beyrout.

ATHENS—page 221.

CONSTANTINOPLE AND THE TURK—page 231.

NAPLES—page 251.

MOUNT VESUVIUS—page 258.

HERCULANEUM AND POMPEII—page 265.

ROME—page 277.

xiii

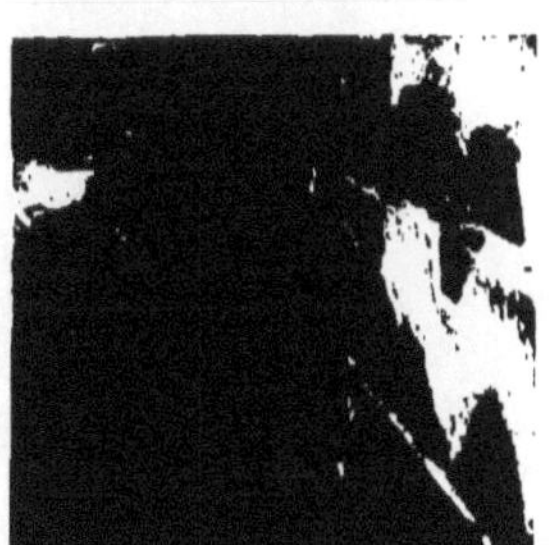

A Columbarium, with Ashes of Two thousand Romans.

Basilica of
Constantine.

CONTENTS.

THE STORY OF THE CRUISE.

THE

CRUISE OF

THE FRIESLAND.

THE START.

Wednesday, February 6, 1895.

NEW YORK is icy and drear. Like sharp needles the piercing wind cuts and stings. "The coldest day of many a year" says everyone as the Red Star liner "Friesland," with long continued straining finally breaks the fetters of ice in which she has been bound and, butted by a pair of sturdy, puffing tugs, backs slowly out into the frozen stream. Like brilliant Autumn leaves, starry flags are waving on ship and shore and white handkerchiefs flutter as snowflakes in the winter's air.

"Good bye, good bye," goes out from the straining throats of a thousand friends who have

1

Off at Last.

braved the Arctic cold of the bleak, wind-swept pier that they might see the pilgrims off, and "good bye" is shouted back from the crowded decks. "Good bye friends. Good bye, dear shivering old New York. Good bye all. Sorry are we to leave you in the dreary North but the time has come to part and we are off for Summer seas."

The great ship swings slowly around ; the swiftly turning screw kicks the water into foam at her stern ; she parts the ice floe with her sharp bow, and gathering headway stands for the open sea.

Clark's Mediterranean cruise has begun.

From the water goes up volumes of steam as from a sea of smoking lava. The piers along the city front are half hidden by drifting fog. Spires and sky-climbing blocks float in billowy clouds, now appearing in bursts of frosty sun-shine, now blotted out and lost.

Liberty—unlovely under the garish light of day and a thing of beauty only when night makes her gracious mission plain—shivers as we pass, lifting her naked arm and quenched torch high up into the pitiless air, as in dumb protest against her useless martyrdom.

The frowning forts are passed, the white gates of the harbor open and close behind, and at last we are on the broad Atlantic. Then the pilot goes down

3

the uncertain, swinging ladder to the icy boat that has waited out there to take him off, and with his going the last link that binds us to the shore is broken.

Around us, the writhing water steams in the frosty air as a seething caldron, sending up white mists like the smoke of a burning prairie. Incoming craft are sheeted with crystal, their bows hang heavy with glittering diamond fringe, their spars are as icicles, their cordage like spun glass in the sun-shine. Sluggishly they sink to the hollows of the seas and slowly gather to the oncoming wave. The hand of the Ice King is heavy upon them, but *we* are light of heart, for we are bound for lands where birds are singing and fragrant flowers ever bloom; where Poetry and Art go hand in hand; where Chivalry and Faith had birth, and History began.

Thursday, February 7, 1895.

MORNING, and the air is no longer wintry. For twenty hours we have been moving steadily southward, yet while we have left the frost behind the weather is not altogether satisfying. The wind is full of moisture and at times fitful. At noon comes a dash of rain followed by stronger blasts.

Now the waves come up out of the south and doff their white caps to us and the Friesland—staid old Friesland that she seemed, and on her good behavior when in town where she lay beside her dock as steady as a rock—becomes kittenish out here and bridles like a young girl, welcoming the playful advances of the gay white waves with many a bow and courtesy, swinging jauntily from side to side and bobbing up and down in anything but a dignified way, so that many who are novices in the art of sailing begin to wear a troubled look.

As the day wanes wild Boreas changes his pleasant pipings to notes of fiendish glee and rushes with wild shrieks and shrill whistlings through the straining cordage. Then Old Neptune, tyrant that he is, clasps the big ship in his arms and flings her like

5

a leaf on the rushing stream. He tosses her up on high and throws her down into the depths; he stands her on edge; he plunges her sharp nose into the big waves; he holds her down and pours tons of water over her shuddering stern; he rolls her over on her side until her taper yards drag through the foam, for he is King and she but a plaything in his hands.

And they that are on board hasten to pay tribute.

Many who have taken possession of their steamer chairs, and their places out on the upper deck, keep them all through the day, fearing to move. Locomotion has perils aside from the danger of bruised heads and broken bones. With coming darkness the gale increases. The ship labors heavily against the pounding seas that send clouds of spray, and sometimes considerable masses of water, over the decks, until at last the most

determinedly uncertain are constrained to go below however much they may fear the result. The attempt usually precipitates matters. Many are in condition to welcome death, for they are certain that the hand of the fell destroyer is already heavy upon them.

Between decks also the pilgrims are not happy. At midnight

6

Tribute.

Ah! Then came the rolls
That uplifted our soles,
And all that we valued took wings;
While the midshipmite,
Like an angel of light,
Brought comfort, and crackers, and things.

a monster sea comes over the bows and rushes along the upper deck, carrying with it settees supposed to have been bolted fast; wrenching from their fastenings boats lashed in their places on a level with the bridge and, uncovering a hatch which has been insecurely battened down, pours a flood into the cabin, followed by other waves which sweep at intervals along overhead to find unguarded openings through which the water goes so that many state-rooms are flooded and their occupants driven out to seek drier quarters elsewhere. Great seas which do not go over strike with mighty force against the sounding sides and the ship careens at times so that she seems literally on beams end. Small articles play tag about the state-rooms, trunks race wildly across from side to side, life-preservers, boxes, bags and bundles unattached hop about like kernels of corn in a hot popper, while occupants of bunks are tumbled unceremoniously out, to make unexpected calls on their neighbors across the way. Fear adds a distressing element to the situation; many do not undress all through the night. The public saloons are steaming with an aggregation of uneasy numbers who are in doubt whether it were better to go down, if go down they must, on deck, or under cover like rats in a trap. Below in the public spaces are congregated clumps of timid ones who, like masses of swarming bees, cling together in frantic fear, thinking that every plunge the vessel makes may be her last, but holding firmly to the "united-we-stand divided-we-fall" idea, although in fact visibly and often, demonstrating the exception. It is too moist even for jokes to crack, although dismal attempts are occasionally made in that direction and while there are more than two score of clergymen on board, temporarily out of a job, even they bring little consolation, and amateurs who feel the need take a hand at prayer on their own account. Uncertainty as to actual danger adds another element of fear. It is impossible to learn exactly what has happened or what is being done to avert disaster. The screw has stopped its revolutions—an uncommon thing at sea—two or three times. "Disabled," some one says. "To ease the pounding of the great waves against her bow" is explained semi-officially. "Mutiny in the fire-room" is a current report, and it is whispered that an officer has been stationed at the entrance to the shaft by which the fire-room is reached, with instructions to brain the first man who attempts to leave his post. "The worst storm the ship ever passed through" said the captain later.

Accidents were common. A deck steward received injuries which shelved him for several days. As a result of a sudden lurch of the vessel early in the evening of the storm, a group of twenty or more in their steamer chairs got away in a bunch *a la toboggan* down the slippery deck to the rail, where the leaders found themselves at the bottom of a promiscuous heap of struggling humanity. When the pile was sorted it was discovered that several had been damaged to a greater or less extent. Mr. Edwin Palmer, of Albany, had serious injury done to his face, but stuck pluckily by his party to the end of the cruise, shedding by degrees and in different parts of the world the bandages in which he appeared the day after the storm. Mr. H. M. Taber, of New York, had a broken leg when resurrected from the crush, and as a result was carried ashore on arrival at the Bermudas, where he remained until near the close of March, returning thence to his home. At latest reports he was in a fair way to almost complete recovery. Subsequently Mr. William A. Wilson, of Kansas City, had his arm broken and suffered most excruciating anguish from being unable to use it during the rest of the voyage (as he personally explained) with so many charming widows on board. Aside from the above no accident worthy of note was known to have happened to any member of the party on the trip.

The storm was a notable experience. No one complained that the voyage so far was monotonous. It was full of sensations of various kinds, and new sensations were a blessing to many. It was also satisfying in a certain sense, for we all felt that the Friesland had proven herself good for almost any kind of weather that might be expected on the trip.

THE BERMUDAS.

Saturday, February 9.

THE DEVIL'S ISLANDS, is what the old Spaniards called the little group which is known to us as the Bermudas, for—were they not known to be inhabited in those days by demons and vampires and dragons of horrid mould, as vouched for by certain venturesome sailor-men who had risked their lives there among the sharp-toothed coral reefs which guard them round about? Later, pirates made their homes there when they were not engaged in cutting throats or looting rich merchantmen, and during the late rebellion blockade runners found welcome and assistance in their ports, over which then, as now, the British flag waved.

The distance from New York is about 675 miles in a southeasterly direction; the time required to get there, according to schedule, about forty-eight hours, but the storm had delayed us so that it was Friday evening when the lights of the islands were sighted, and we lay at anchor outside the entrance to St. George's Harbor all night.

Saturday morning all went ashore in tugs. The sea was still running high and although we were in

Willing Hands.

12

the lee of the main island, the commotion was considerable and the transfer from the big to the little ship attended with some little risk. But experienced hands were there to render necessary assistance, particularly if the need was emphasized by a pretty face, and there being so many pretty faces in evidence, notwithstanding the rough experience up to this time, the willing hands above mentioned were kept very busy while the transfer was going on. The run to land and up through St. George's inlet to the old town of that name was delightful.

Green as the green on the peacock's neck are the surrounding waters; dark green and olive the shores and semi-tropic trees; white as snow the lines of box-like houses along the water's edge and against the terraced hillside. At the landing we were met by a delegation of native

citizens with axes to grind, and made welcome about the town. Hardly had we exhausted interest in the quaint, curious things of the place when—the news of our arrival having been wired to Hamilton, twelve miles away—there came in twos, in threes, in squads, in caravans, the flower of the Hamilton liveries, and with wild dash and shout; with beaming face and whip in hand these black Jehus of the sea corraled our people and carried them, willing captives, away out over the gleaming white roads that stretched through garden lands and lines of flowering trees.

There are, it is said, three hundred and sixty-five islands in the group, including the tiny ones scattered about in the lagoons and bays of the larger islands. They are of coraline, or shell, formation so far as visible, built by the coral insect, upon the apex of a submarine mountain which rises abruptly from a depth of nearly three miles. Around the islands are coral reefs still in process of construction by their curious artificers. Well defined circles, visible at low water—miniature "atolls"—are to be found at different points. Windy are they—these islands lying out in the Atlantic ocean five hundred miles from the mainland—the red cedar, which is the native tree, growing in exposed positions, telling the story of the prevailing west wind in long branches stretching eastward and the shorter ones, curling in upon themselves on the west. The fragrant oleander grows freely. It is the favorite hedge and wind-break along the roads. The principal fruits are the banana, which flourishes thriftily in protected positions, and the paw-paw, which hangs in clusters at the base of the outspreading branches of its tall tree-stem.

The native population is about 15,000. Sixty per cent. are black. In addition may be reckoned a force of 2,000 British soldiers stationed at the garrisons on the main island. The blacks are of a superior order, polite, fairly well educated and in voice and accent quite English you know. It would be doing the black an injustice to say that he is dissatisfied with his position and condition here. He has equal rights on the islands with his white brother. He has all the school advantages the islands afford, takes great interest in

14

their management and monopolizes the public schools to such
an extent that the white boy and girl are generally sent abroad
for education when the means of the family permit. The black
here, as elsewhere, is not wildly ambitious. He will not,
knowingly, shorten his life by hard labor. He cultivates the
land in little patches; he drives the carriages and does the
necessary laborer's work; he comes into town on a long, springless cart with little wheels and a little donkey between the
heavy shafts—he and his wife and his pickaninnies and his
poultry and his vegetables. The little satisfies him. But if
there are no very wealthy people here, there are also none in
extreme poverty. There are beggars in plenty, but not of
an offensive kind. The young darkies are beggars from the
cradle, but they ask from principle and their gain is spent for
luxuries.

The ground produces abundantly and will yield from three
to four crops in rotation in a year. Irish potatoes are due the
first of February; sweet potatoes follow on the same land—the
latter nearly white and tasting more like the ordinary potato
than the sweet potato of the Carolinas. Then come beets,
turnips, carrots and other roots common to the North. But the
chief of all fruits, the thing above all others on which they base
their hopes of prosperity, is the potent, all-absorbing, ever fragrant onion. Time dates locally from the great onion year, to
which the patriotic Bermudian refers with a pride which the

Fourth of
July can
hardly evoke
from the av-
erage Yankee

15

Easter Lilies.

abroad. Property is reckoned not in bonds or acres but in onions, and prosperity by the crate. Other crops yield handsomely, but nothing can win the native from his first love. An odor as of sanctity hangs about the esculent root which the visitor may mistake for something else but the native—never. With him it is the onion forever. The onion is cultivated in little patches by the roadside; among the trees on the slopes; never in large fields, for the reason, perhaps, that there are few large fields there. What soil there is is found in pockets in the rocks that have been filled, or in places where the rock has weathered and become soil. Flowers grow everywhere. The Easter lily of the Bermudas is noted in both hemispheres.

The roads are the best I have ever seen—hard and smooth— just the kind for cyclists. The ridges are cut through, to make the way practically level, and a single horse easily draws a carriage with four people. The drivers drive like Jehus, and, contrary to the custom of the United States, turn to the left in meeting.

The houses are all of stone, ordinarily one-story in height. The material is dug from within the foundation walls, the cellar furnishing the blocks from which the house is made. It is cut out by means of long single-handled saws—in blocks for the side walls, in slabs for the roof. When first exposed the rock is white as snow, and quite soft. With exposure to light and air it becomes darker and quite hard. The houses are all whitewashed, the rock furnishing admirable lime also. It is said that whitewashing renders the houses much cooler in the warm weather, but the glare is somewhat trying under the bright sun. All the dwellings that I saw looked clean and neat, and many of them had flowers on their walls or in beds about the doors.

There are no wells on the island. Water for drinking is caught when it rains, from roofs or from slopes inclosed and swept clean for that purpose, and kept in cisterns. The inhabitants bury their dead, four deep, in graves cut in the soft rock. They are cemented tight to be opened again when the space is needed.

There are caves here which were submarine grottoes before the coral works rose above the surface. "The Devil's Hole" is an opening of unknown depth full of water, and said to have an underground connection with the ocean. On inquiry we were told that the devil wasn't in but a Sombre Shade in a ragged shawl, which we took to be his wife, showed us around in consideration for an English shilling each. The "hole" was ragged and rocky and swarming with big fish, averaging from two to three feet in length. Out of the green water they poked their noses stretching wide their red mouths to about the size of a pint cup saying plainly as in spoken word, "please feed us"—which we did with bread procured at a little shed near by, and at which they snapped ravenously, their teeth coming together like animated steel traps, while they crowded and jostled and quarreled with each other; in their eager haste, jumping at times a full half-length out of the water to get at the coveted morsel.

At Sea.

"Like Mountains streaked with Snow."

THE LONG RUN.

THE waves that follow us when we sail away from the Windy Islands Saturday evening are like mountains streaked with snow. Sunday, the wind still blows strong and the water is lumpy—waves outrunning the ship and running high—but the day is delightful with mixed sunshine and shower, and a large proportion of the party find their way out on deck. Religious services are held in the morning. In the evening a service of song is held out on deck, and a sacred concert given by the ship's Belgian orchestra in the saloon, during which "After the Ball" is rendered among other gems in good United States style.

The long run of 2,932 miles between the Bermudas and Gibraltar, (which is to occupy eight days), holds promise of dread monotony as looked forward to generally but proves quite the contrary. It gives people a chance to become acquainted with each other, and acquaintanceship sprouting under such favorable conditions buds and blossoms and bears fruit quickly. Here in shadowed corner or on neighboring steamer-chairs where one traveling rug is found ample covering for two; hands touch and soft words are spoken. In the warm sunshine, or out on the windy deck, knots are formed in the web of life, and lines cross and get tangled for better or for worse and the end—ah, who can tell!

To descend to cold statistics. There are, according to the purser's account, about 430 passengers on board, although the revised passenger list shows 444 names. Of this number 34 have the prefix "Rev." (It is whispered that there are about a dozen others of the cloth masquerading as plain "Mr.," and the Wicked Man from the Far West suggests that it would have been better for their congregations if one or two others who had left shop behind had been like considerate.) Further sortings show sixteen "Drs.," eleven "Hons.," three "Cols.," two "Caps.," and one "Gen." There are 196 ladies, old and young, of which 77 have never been married and a considerable contingent who have been but are not—widows and charming of course. (Several cases of desperate flirtation have been detected

"Tangled."

20

"Chums."

already with the have beens in the lead.) There are a number of lively youngsters on deck who have stood the buffeting better than their elders, but it is noticed that the great majority of the passengers wear gray hair and wear it well, for the nature of the cruise has brought together intellectual men and women much above the average.

Thirty-two states are represented. Pennsylvania sends 74, New Jersey has second place with sixty-two to her credit, New York follows with 53, Ohio with 38, Massachusetts 37, Illinois 29, Connecticut 27, Indiana 17, Michigan 10, Kentucky 9, Minnesota 9, District of Columbia 7, Mississippi 6, Nebraska, New Hampshire and Missouri 5 each, Colorado, Maryland and Georgia 4 each, Virginia 3, Vermont, Rhode Island and California 2 each, while West Virginia, Florida, Tennessee, Montana, Kansas and Washington send 1 each. Canada is represented by three. Everybody is getting on famously, learning who every other body is, where they came from, etc. At first many were recognized as in primitive times by notable peculiarities. There were the "Plaid Man," the "Thermometer Man," "The Big Consul," the "Long Dominie," the "Widow's Mite," etc. Congenial spirits soon gravitate to allotted centres. The "Blue and the Gray" shake hands; the "Solid South" and the "Grand Army" are as one family. Clergymen of the many protestant

Getting on His Sea Legs.

21

"The Blue and The Gray."

The Friesland
Band.

denominations and fathers of the Romish Church lie down together and a little child might lead them.

It called for 171 officers and crew to take care of the ship and its passengers. The captain had little intercourse with the passengers, giving his attention, as was perhaps right, very much to the management of his ship. The affable purser made hosts of friends and many a sea-sick mortal was glad to greet his pleasant face in his daily rounds. The steward—man of substance—on him we relied and not in vain, for, to feed us on the trip he laid in at New York upward of 480,000 pounds of eatables and drinkables. There are 31,000 pounds of fresh, and 4,000 pounds of corned beef. 232 beeves yield up their tongues and eighty-four ox-tails get into the soup. There are 4,100 pounds of veal, 11,000 pounds of mutton, 4,100 pounds of fresh pork. Other items are, 190 turkeys, 2,800 fowl, 1,000 ducks, 2,000 pigeons, 2,000 squab, 2,000 quarts of fresh milk, 13,000 dozen eggs, 2,070 pounds of butter, and 2,500 pounds of cheese of various brands—a strong array, and some of it mitey good. There are 500 pounds of tea, 5,000 pounds of coffee, 20 barrels of pilot bread, 12 barrels of Blue Point oysters, 1,200 pounds of grapes, 30 tons of potatoes, and 2,000 pounds of Spanish onions. These last go into almost everything but the ice cream.

Breakfast and lunch are as it happens —first come, first served—but dinner is a fixed festival of august proportions and inflexible flow. It takes from one to one and one-half hours to go

22

The Purser.

through with the programme of ten courses. As the number of passengers is about double the seating capacity of the tables in both saloons, the party is divided into sections, one following the other at meals, each sitting having its compensating advantages, for if the first table becomes over proud its attention is called to the fact that it is obliged to eat at a horribly unfashionable hour, while those who follow can linger at table in the enjoyment of after-dinner amenities as long as ever they like.

Of course there was dissatisfaction on board. In the success of the undertaking was developed its most objectional feature, for every available room and bunk was occupied; would-be passengers gladly taking accommodations which, if not all that heart could desire, were the best that could be had and as such acceptable. This over-crowded condition of the ship made it impossible for the willing but overworked stewards to render such service as the passengers had good reason to expect. Add the distressing experience of the storm and it is not to be wondered at that, under the torture of sea-sickness and inconvenience generally, some kicked—and kicked hard.

"And Clark Smiled."

It was but natural. It did no harm. In these after days when the raw edge of temporary discomfort has become softened by the glow of delightful retrospection one wonders what there was at the time to cause such an ebullition. And through it all the manager, wise beyond his years, saw past the jagged present to the mellow future, and in the face of threatened annihilation just smiled and smiled, and soothed

23

"Chef."

Ring-toss.

with promises to adjust all grievances, and to smooth out every wrinkle in the crumpled rose leaves of the time—in a day or two.

Meantime the ship's company did not waste coal in a vain attempt to make up lost time in the run from continent to continent. Two or three ships were sighted in the passage across but not the promised land of the Azores—those mountain peaks of submerged Atlantis which we so longed to see—for we were due on the other side and still losing. We were moving steadily, however, burning about 112 tons of coal and going on an average 360 miles every day. Every day at noon the ship's clock was set ahead to accord with meridian time, and those who would be correct must turn the hands of their watches around from twenty to twenty-five minutes, according to the distance made. Thus the days passed more rapidly than we had thought possible, bringing many a pleasant thing to be remembered. Pennsylvania day was celebrated with becoming ceremonies. Lectures, concerts, balls, kept young and old, grave and gay, fully engaged. Euchre and whist, back-gammon and chess, in smoking-room and cabin; shuffle-board and ring-toss on the after-deck, letter writing everywhere—the week passes almost before we know it, and with feelings of intense, if subdued, excitement at the thought of stepping on solid land once more, and of the news that may be waiting us, we are watching at the going down of the Sunday's sun for the distant shore. Later we greet with joy the bright lights that mark on either hand the ancient Pillars of Hercules. At midnight we pass through the gates of the wide East that open before us and the misty Land of Childhood's Dreams is ours to go in and possess.

24

Shuffle-board.

GIBRALTAR.

LIKE a crouching lion in black silhouette against a sky luminous with bright stars, rises the great rock of Gibraltar as we look upon it first in the morning while it is yet night. In straight lines along the water front, and tier on tier at intervals against its black bulk higher up, sparkling lights marks the town that lies in terraced lines along its base. With the gray of the slow coming dawn the black shadow separates into masses, the masses into form and outline, and with the coming of the sun, sea-wall and battlement, ancient tower and structure of the later day stand revealed.

And this is Gibraltar! The world's mightiest citadel! The key to the gateway of the Mediterranean! A great mountain peak, or rather a series of peaks, it rises sheer from the sea. East, south and west the water comes up against the cliffs, which are unscalable almost as the sides of an iceberg. At its northern end, which is the head of the crouching lion, vertical cliffs a thousand feet in height overlook a narrow strip of marshy land, connecting it with Spanish soil. Honeycombed with galleries and pierced with port-holes, out of which the mouths of cannons point; with massive sea-

25

The Rock of Gibraltar across the Neutral Ground.

walls, behind which the heaviest of guns lie; its summit a resting place for other guns of mighty mould, that may be sighted by range-finders at the lower level and fired by electricity; garrisoned with a force of such stuff as forms the British soldier and with provisions to last indefinitely—Gibraltar is beyond question the one impregnable fortress of the world. Above the terraced town you get glimpses of cavernous openings into the mountain, masked perhaps but only partially, by young trees and growing bushes. Farther away along in the side of the black rock which faces Spain, lines of openings, indicating the course of tiers of galleries within, ascend gradually as they follow the fluted contour of the mighty cliff. What the rock really contains the public is not allowed to know. Few in authority even know it all. The governor may know, but minor officers have little knowledge of parts except those over which they have command, the other sections being closed to them as to the outside world. Possibly the outside world is encouraged to believe in the existence of grim secrets, of terrible engines of destruction hidden in the bowels of the mountain, and of deadly mines beneath the innocent looking surface—and perhaps these exist mainly in the imagination. But there is evidence to convince anyone that no projectile has yet been invented capable of demolishing it, or earthly power to force an entrance when garrisoned by determined men. The ending of the four years' siege, where the English successfully resisted all the force the Spanish government could bring against them, could have but one natural and to-be-expected ending. Back of British occupancy at intervals through a thousand changing years, Phœnician and Moor, Moor and Spaniard and later Spaniard against Spaniard, struggled for its possession. It was during this later strife, in 1704, that Britain, with true British determination to see fair play, took a hand and, pending the contest, became stake-holder and referee. The question of ownership never *was* settled to the entire satisfaction of the Man in Possession, and he felt obliged finally to declare the mill off and the purse and gate-money confiscated as proper compensation for his services—which seemed an eminently satisfactory solution of the problem. The question of rightful ownership is a question no more. It is held by virtue of British nerve, which knows a good thing when it sees it, and of British bull-dog tenacity, which never loosens its grip while a tooth remains to hold on with. With nine points of law in its favor who shall question the remaining one point? No nation exists to-day which could so well be trusted to combine necessary force with common justice in holding a check over the quarrelsome little nationalities of the East as this same big, sturdy, assertive chap who believes in fair play always and only takes possession of your property when he is fully satisfied that he can administer its affairs better than you can yourself. It would unquestionably be an improvement if he should add still others to his dependencies in the East, where civilization has gone to seed; where it is established policy to spoil the stranger that is within the gates, and where religion makes a virtue of crimes at which true civilization stands aghast.

We had been called in the morning before daylight that we might get the earliest view possible of the famous rock, and also that we might make an early landing for the day on shore. With daylight came a fleet of native boats, scrubby looking craft, with venders of fruit and notions, swarthy of face, picturesque of dress, wildly gesticulating, and clamorous and dis-

cordant of cry as were the noisy gulls which wheeled and
circled around to pounce ravenously on whatever might be cast
overboard. Finally we go ashore
and are duly inspected by officers
in charge at the water gate.

To western eyes the sights are
interesting. There are twenty
thousand inhabitants here it is said.
You would hardly think that the
town could give place for half that
number, but you find that parts are
solidly built, that the streets are
narrow and the dwellings, where
glimpses can be had, are like bee-
hives, swarming with many occupants. The streets are alive with
color of a mixed population bent
on traffic. Here is the Jew with
black robe and skull-cap, Turks
with baggy trowsers and brilliant
fez, Moors with flowing robe and

snow white scarf of many folds wound picturesquely about their
heads, black-browed Spanish and blacker Ethiopian, and English
soldiers everywhere swinging through the streets in twos and
threes, in tight-fitting red coats and shiny boots. The English
soldier gives color and brilliancy to every scene—troops of
cavalry with jingling sabers, companies of artillery, guards
going and coming, or perhaps, off duty and in holiday attire
bound for the cricket-field or in parties to engage in some other
of the many athletic games in which the true Britain takes

delight.   It costs England $5,000,000 annually it is said to run the town and fortress.

Through the market place we go beset by venders of fruit and curios, by would-be guides and noisy cabmen, by traders—Moor and Turk, Jew and Gentile—then we melt away and are distributed about the town, deeply interested in scenes which are all new and strange.   The bazaars and shops along the way are not imposing in size but are rich in color; their owners solicitous, but not apt to make mistakes to their own detriment when making change for the visitor who may not be quite clear as to the relative value of English, French, Spanish and American moneys.   Trades and professions seem oddly mixed.   "Barber and tooth-puller" is a common sign indicating a union of professions not common in the west, and suggesting the necessity of making your wants clearly understood whenever you may have occasion to drop into one of their uncomfortable chairs. A sharp young Turk works up a thriving business by offering "Amereken o-r-r-in-giz-z-z, fresh from Ne-jork," at 2 for 5

cents, and many patriotic Americans buy heavily when common cut-throat natives are offering others just as good at two for a cent.   The last I saw of this Turkish Yankee was at the dock where he was selling "Amereken figs, fresh from Ne-jork." The streets are narrow and crooked but exceptionally clean.   They straggle about in an aimless sort of way, which I afterward found to be common to old Moorish towns; here running along the side of the hill on a line with the roofs of the

30

A Street
in
Gibraltar.

buildings ranged along the street below, now making a dash up some acclivity with a grade like an old fashioned Dutch

roof. Through the residence portion of the town, particularly in the old Moorish quarters, the dwellings present blank walls with narrow door-ways and high windows to the street, or are surrounded by high stone walls, the tops of which are ragged with broken glass set in cement.

The Moorish Castle, built A. D. 711, is a prominent show feature of the town, but the great interest of the visitor centres in the works that are in the great rock itself. Preliminary inspection and registering at the guard-room were necessary before we were permitted to enter, then a heavy gate was unlocked to admit us and made secure after we entered and, convoyed by a sturdy young soldier, we penetrated into the galleries as far as we were permitted to go. What years of convict toil these tunnels represent! They are commonly about eight feet wide and from eight to twelve high, with an ascending grade up or down which horses can be driven and artillery transported when necessary. The way twists about to the right and left, following the contour of the cliff's face, broadening at intervals into considerable chambers in which are heavy cannon and ammunition, and from which port-holes look out on town and frontier and open sea. A closed gate finally barred our way, but from an opening in a projecting angle we marked the tunnel's course in ascending lines of port-holes far above. Downward—we could only guess at the distance—half a thousand feet perhaps, the rock dropped sheer.   On the plain at its base

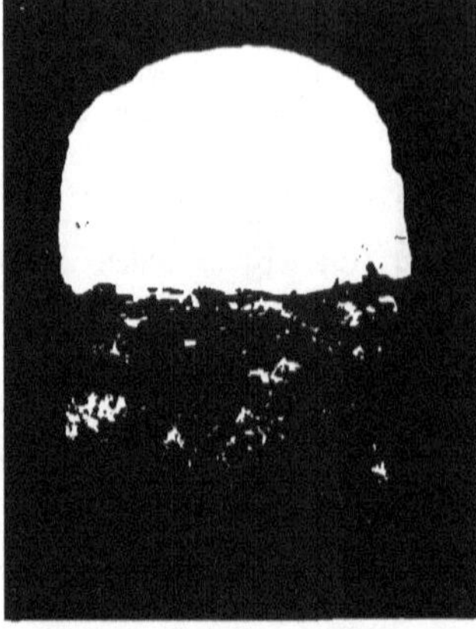

a sham-battle was taking place.   We could see the little puffs of white smoke, then, after quite an interval, hear faintly the rattle of the discharge.   The men were pigmies, the horses capering mites. In another field a game of cricket was in progress; in still another foot-ball, judging from the rush and scramble, and the quick massing and melting of the human atoms.   Splendid fellows physically are these British soldier boys and clean and fresh and manly withal.

Beyond the line of sports and battle ran a line of sentry boxes across the half-mile of land from shore to shore; between which, like clock-work, paced red-coated men.   A half-mile beyond, across the marshy flat which is the neutral ground, in parallel lines is another row of boxes and along back and forth between these paced men of more sombre hue.   England and Spain watch each other here.   Tommies and dons stamp up and down in sight of each other as tommies and dons have done, day and night, for more than a hundred years— the tommies coolly insolent, the dons fiercely threatening.

Threatening Gibraltar! A June-bug hurling fierce defiance at the Sphinx!

Spanishtown is over beyond the line of Spanish sentries. At night when the north gate is closed it is not considered safe to venture out across the flat—you may be mistaken for a smuggler and a shot follow the quick challenge before you have time to explain—but a broad road stretches across from the town to Spanish territory, and in the day time your right to go is not questioned. A motley crowd goes back and forth along the way—carriages and footmen, lines of donkeys bringing huge paniers of vegetables for the town supply or struggling under great bundles of hay for the garrison cattle. The difference between Gibraltar under the English and this border town under Spanish rule is notable and not to the credit of the latter. It is a picture of squalor and decay. Thrift and cleanliness seems unknown. Its buildings are generally of but one story and built of adobe. The streets are lowest in the middle, and the sanitary arrangements of the town seem to consist of throwing the town's refuse into the streets and allowing it to float off—when it rains. It swarms with beggars, but has a bull-ring and Sunday sports for the amusement of its people, who seem hardly able to get their bread to say nothing of butter. In justice to Spain, however, I must say that there were other towns seen later which did not seem so utterly low, and some that would be a credit to any country.

In Spanishtown.

33

Catalina bay has been overlooked. It is on British territory, just around the shoulder of the North cliffs, where the level land ends in a pocket of the mountain. A little circling beach is here, and upward from it, a thousand feet in height, in one unbroken slope, is a bank of white, unstable sand. Thrown upon the shore by the waves, it has been swept upward by the wind to where it now lies against the black rock. Around the bit of beach—in uncertain possession because of threatened avalanche —lies the little fishing village of Catalina. Clumsy boats are on the beach, with nets drying on reels or spread out on the sand. A single street leads along the water front. A little church stands at the head of the only lateral street which is about a hundred feet in length. A gaudily painted image of the Virgin and Child is in a niche over the door; within, lights are burning before shrines; horribly realistic Christs are nailed to painted crosses, and weeping Marys and highly colored cherubs are here resting on highly improbable clouds. Along the streets are chickens and goats and children, and pretty black-eyed Spanish girls and horrible old women.

Back to the ship again, to learn that when the captain on arrival "dropped anchor"—he dropped it literally, and with it a great number of fathoms of chain, valued at about \$2,000, altogether, which it is rumored he must regain in some way if it takes a week to do it. We are in uncertainty as to the carrying out of the programme laid down for the morrow but finally turn in with the understanding that our watchful Paul will call us in time for any event that may need attention. Half dreaming, later we realize that the screw is throbbing and that we are moving through the water once more.

34

Malaga from the Sea.

MALAGA.

Tuesday, February 19, 1895.

ACCORDING to programme we were to be called at 3 A. M., breakfast at will, land at 4, and at 5 start for Granada on a special train chartered for the occasion. We were approaching land when we actually did turn out. The sun was glorifying the Sierras that marked the sky line on the north, and picking out shining points in a city which lay clasped in the embrace of the circling hills, protected from the sea by out-reaching walls of masonry. Beautiful buildings are along the water front; high above them the great cathedral lifts its bulk, and a gray castle stands on the top of the hill which rises sharply out of the city with a double line of massive walls leading up its flank from town to citadel.

Before Rome, Malaga was, according to tradition. It has belonged at different eras to almost every one of the nations that have figured prominently in the history of the Mediterranean. It has been noted for its grapes, its oranges, its almonds and its olives. Its wines equal those of sunny France, according to reports of Friesland crusaders who sampled them in order to be able to testify.

35

"A neat paper box."

We ate our breakfast leisurely; received our "neat paper boxes" containing lunch (two each in fact, for according to the original plan we were not to return until late at night, and although the plan miscarried the lunches held), and getting in line at the gangway—waited. Native boats surrounded us when we anchored, but the boatmen entreated us in vain for we were not permitted to land until certain formalities were gone through with. Officials of various kinds steamed out and then steamed back again. Rumors were rife and various explanations offered. "Native inefficiency," "Lack of system," "National prejudice against Americans," "Must be bought twice—privileges come high with Spanish officials." The man-

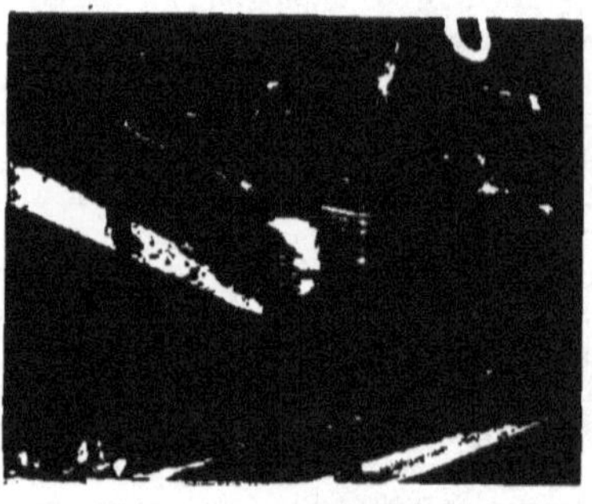

ager went ashore to re-arrange matters, but it was past noon when we finally, one by one, were dropped into barges that had been towed out to receive us; the process reminding one of the cup-and-ball toy, we being the ball and the barges—rearing and plunging on the somewhat boisterous waters—the cup. In the game some of the balls were more bounced than dignified.

At the landing the people of Spain received us with every evidence of being pleased, but the welcome seemed unpleasantly, of the nature that might have been accorded to us had we been a traveling menagerie or a Punch and Judy show. It strikes curiously on one who has some reason to think himself superior in many ways to the people he is visiting, to have the conviction forced upon him that they regard him in the light of a curiosity, possibly expecting him to show up in paint and feathers or beads and a buffalo skin. And when he does arrive in ordinary clothing to persist in believing him a savage masquerading as a civilized being, strikes one as decidedly odd. Such appeared to be the condition here, and every accident of step at landing or the possibly somewhat funny efforts some made to walk a plank, brought forth howls of delight and shouts of boisterous laughter from the rabble that crowded the stone pier where we landed. But there were others there—gentlemen of Spain, who welcomed us courteously, and obliging officials, and a long line of carriages to take us about the principal streets of the city.

There are a number of beautiful parks and some noble structures here. The modern parts of the town show public buildings and stores that might be considered a credit to the finest cities of the world. Doorways along the way were crowded, and hanging balconies filled, with Spanish senoras and senoritas who did not seem averse to the attention they received from the young men and—and must I say it ?—some of the clergymen of the party, who threw kisses to the black-eyed natives. *En passant*, the young girls of Spain are unquestionably the handsomest of all the old world beauties we saw. Pity is it that the sweetest wines turn so quickly to the sourest of vinegar. The Spanish gentleman is handsome also, gracious and courtly of bearing, not great of stature but picturesque with his long cloak falling almost to his feet, with a portion muffled up to cover the lower part of the face if the soft wind turn a bit chilly, and with a fold thrown gracefully

over the left shoulder to reveal its plush, or velvet, lining of brilliant red or yellow.

Some of their customs are not as ours. We were quartered in one of the best hotels where, as is the custom in the East, the dinner comes at night and consists of many courses served in unchangeable order. The guests at table were well dressed, some in evening dress, and evidently ladies and gentlemen. Between courses the men chatted, twirled their mustaches and picked their teeth—not apologetically or covertly behind napkins, but uncovered and open-mouthed. At the close of the meal they light cigarettes and smoke without apology to the ladies present. It may be no news to state that the custom of smoking is not confined to the men alone; the senora puffs her cigarette as complacently as does her wicked *fin de siècle* sister of the New World. The men smoke everywhere except at church, but as church is considered of little account except for women and children the deprivation is not serious. They have a pretty custom of bowing to neighbor at right and left, stranger though he be, at the close of the meal, and saying in Spanish "I hope the dinner may do you good."

The streets of Malaga present interesting features: priests in their long gowns and shovel hats; policemen like soldiers in uniform; peddlers of edibles, cooked and uncooked; of shrimp and white bait, and snapping lobsters.

Beggars are there with ever-extended hand and tears on tap. They come upon you from unexpected corners; they tumble out of dark doorways beseeching at your feet; they struggle to get to you with every appearance of great suffering—they squirm, they wriggle, they swarm. One squad gathered by the roadside, represented in appearance almost every form of misery possible. A dumb man, a blind cripple, an idiot, a young girl carrying a dead baby! I stepped from the carriage with an object and they made for me with one accord. I stopped them with a threatening gesture and held them, astonished and doubting, a moment, while the disguised kodak got in its deadly work. The dumb stretched wide his cavernous and seemingly tongueless mouth, the idiot grinned and slobbered, the blind whined piteously, and the pseudo mother wept wildly, at which the blind, not to be outdone by a woman, gathered breath afresh and howled in very anguish of spirit. In the struggle for the coppers distributed among them the blind man seemed gifted with a wonderful sense of location, and as we drove away the dumb was shrilly berating some one for cause unknown.

Along the roads outside of Malaga are vineyards and olive, and almond, trees. The roadside cabins, poor though

39

Spanish
Beggars.

they be, are often beautiful with rustic trellis and canopy of vines. Queer little donkeys with loads of vegetables, or crates of wine jugs, plod sleepily along. On the steep hillsides are droves of goats, which supply the milk and butter for the people.

A rustic goat-herd comes over the hill singing a queer, monotonous, tuneless song, a flock of goats straggling along after him. When he stops singing they nibble at the grass, when he sings they stop feeding and follow wherever he leads. We climb to the citadel that overhangs the town as the Acropolis hangs over Athens. That is we go as far as we are permitted to and find that we may not enter without authority. Even this old tumbledown Moorish ruin is a Spanish stronghold jealously guarded by lsdoiers stationed there. We descend, and passing through a dwelling built in the ancient city's wall, find ourselves in the old Moorish town. The place is not specially clean. The streets are narrow and crooked, but almost every window has its overhanging balcony and in most of them are potted plants and flowers. A woman fans a fire of charcoal in a brazier standing in front of her door. When freed from gas it will be taken within to temper the chill atmosphere of some room. Few of the houses here have chimneys or means of heating other than of the most primitive kinds.

A Street

in

Malaga.

At night the principal streets present scenes seldom equalled off the mimic stage. Horses and carriages are excluded and the paved roadway swept clean as are the sidewalks. They are brilliantly lighted and filled often from curb to curb with a busy, jostling, good natured crowd, where gallant youth in brave attire go up and down and where dark-eyed senoritas,

40

with deft fingers clasping in graceful folds their flowing man-
tillas, half concealing, reveal tantalizing glimpses of beauty,
and on occasion manage to speak untold volumes by a motion
of the eloquent, ever-present fan.   Here solemn priest and
stiff soldier unbend, bright puppets play on tiny platforms,
and the minstrel with guitar or mandolin gathers his attentive
circle of listeners while beggars creep from dark corners out into
the light, and as if knowing that they have no part in the bright-
ness, ply their doleful calling but half-heartedly.   Wine is one of
the cheaper drinks and flows freely.   You can get it here if you
like, drawn from the original package—the goatskin bottle of
old in bloated duplication of its living shape, with shirred-up
legs and a wooden spigot in its shirred-up neck.   The dance-
halls are in full blast. We ask to be shown the wickedest,
and are shocked to find it very tame indeed.   There are

41

dancing girls in tights of course and their skirts are of the briefest, but they seem more interested in their art than in the men present and the men show them grave and respectful attention while repeatedly, and with but slightly varying form, they dance the "fandango" to the clicking of castanets which they keep time with as they dance. It is not the graceful thing we expected, but rather a question of vigor and endurance, a flinging of arms and legs about in a most mystifying complexity of motion; of snappy kicks and quick recovery and of lightning-like passes; of stamping and posturing that would make the ordinary contortionist turn green with envy. And the one who is able to get herself most inextricably mixed up and come out of it right side up gets the greatest applause. To western eyes it seems neither very naughty nor very nice.

Some return to the ship to sleep, but the greater portion of the party remain on shore to avoid the discomforts of the transfer back and forth in the darkness, and that they may be on hand for the proposed early start for Granada in the morning.

GRANADA AND THE ALHAMBRA.

MILLIONS for pleasure but not one cent for convenience might well be the motto here in Malaga. The public streets had been almost as light as day the night before, now we grope our way to the railroad station and to places in the cars, by the light of smoking torches like twisted grass soaked in pitch, which the trainmen carry about apparently for their own convenience only.

The morning is faintly gray when we pull out of the town, but even at that hour the street crossings show numbers of people who have come out to see us off. With light we get glimpses of the beauty of hillside dotted with orange and lemon trees ; of olive orchards ; of fields cross-hatched with grape vines which have been cut back annually to the parent stalk until they have grown to look like stubs of dwarf trees reversed, their tangled roots spreading out at the top ; of almond trees in bloom, filling the air with fragrant perfume ; of ruined strong-hold or smart villa crowning the hill-tops, or stone hovel built into the steep slopes ; of winding, white road ; of dancing stream and deep ravine. Soon we enter the mountains and climbing upward cross wild gorges; plunge through dark tunnels and wind around the face of dark cliffs, as wild in every respect and as awe-inspiring as are any that echo to the snort of the iron horse in our own wild Rockies, and displaying examples of engineering skill in their construction that might well excite the admiration of Americans even.

Surmounting the Sierras we follow up the broad, high valley which leads to Granada. The wide unfenced fields are marked by irrigating ditches and are evidently very productive. They seem to be held by few proprietors and are worked by laborers in large companies, sometimes a hundred or more in line moving steadily across the field. Farm buildings gather in clusters which are far apart; little villages are along the way and occasionally the larger cathedral town is seen.

Jolly, fun-provoking crowds of natives have gathered at every station, evidently with intent to get a glimpse of the wild "Americanos." They appear to derive a vast amount of sport out of little material, so far as we can discern. They shout and laugh and point out objects of interest to each other—we being the objects—and go into paroxysms of mirth, as might children at sight of some funnily harmless sort of animal which, while affording amusement to them, is itself unconscious of the fact, and supposed to be incapable of understanding, that it is being laughed at. The ladies of our party excite unbounded curiosity from the female beholders because of the fact that some of them wear big hats ornamented with artificial flowers and some have nodding plumes and feathers and even little birds—alive or dead—upon them! Curious fashions are these to a people who incline to clinging drapery and lace as a head covering. Our balloon sleeves are

44

another source of wonderment, and a sealskin sack is soon
marked, some of the women touching it surreptitiously to learn
its real nature. As a whole such a good natured, disrespectful,
unmannerly crowd we saw nowhere else on our travels.

Railroading in Spain does not commend itself to Americans,
if our experience on the trip is a fair example. The first-
class cars do not possess the conveniences even, deemed essential to travel in the United States. They are divided generally
into three cross sections, which are entered by doors at the side.
Each section affords room for four to eight persons, who sit
facing each other on seats running crosswise. They are lux-
uriously upholstered, and quite comfortable, if you can manage
to persuade the guard that the compartment is full when occupied by yourself and friend—and it doesn't require a very large
coin to make the average guard see double or quadruple even if
the train is not overcrowded. Even then you are liable to have
your teeth shaken out unless well gummed in, as there are no
trucks underneath to distribute the jar among a number of
wheels, but instead, the axle turns in boxes fastened to the body
of the car itself. They make short runs and long stops. We
made but an average of about twelve miles an hour in the run
between Malaga and Granada. When about ready to start a

man rings a hand din-
ner-bell. After a little
pause he rings it again
for last call. Then
the guard comes along
and fastens all the
doors on the outside.
Finally the conductor

A Bargain.

whistles, and locomotive whistles back. Pretty soon the train starts. They have a saying that "there's plenty of time to-morrow."

Granada is old and proud and dirty. Some of the streets are well paved; in others through which we drive in the rain, mud is ankle-deep and heaps of semi-liquid mud lie along the way.

" To be carted off ?" I ask.

" Diablo, no!" is the astonished reply. "It belong dere; when dry it spread out 'gen."

In the crypt of the great cathedral rest Ferdinand and Isabella. You may touch reverently the leaden caskets within which repose all that remain of their royal, earthly bodies.

The Alhambra is the object of paramount interest at Granada. "The pride of Gran—" but no, I can not inflict it on the reader even though everybody else has from Moses down. It is within a seemingly impregnable fortress on a hill overlooking the city—a palace within a citadel. It was the crowning glory of Moorish days, the perfection of Moorish architecture and the model of all that is beautiful and perfect in the Arabesque. Carriages take us through narrow streets and up steep ways to

the great gate of the outer wall and through the park, zig-zagging upward until the entrance to the inner court is reached and we find ourselves confronted by suggestions of the ancient grandeur of the vanished Moor and the modern penny-grabbing devices of his noble conquerors. Within the walls are towers and dungeons, barrack and stable, storehouses for food and water, amphitheatre and shrine —in short a fortified city capable of accommodating

46

*A
Spanish
Gypsy.*

40,000 people and provided with all that was necessary to their comfort in continued occupancy.

The palace of the Alhambra—the " Red Castle "—occupies a comparatively small part of all, and, after the manner of its Moslem founders, hides the Oriental splendors of its interior behind rude outer walls, its beauties dawning gradually on you as you penetrate to its inner courts.

The architecture of the Alhambra is like cobweb on the solid rock—a blending of solid forms borrowed from an earlier people, with the dainty tracery of the Arabian—exhausting all conceivable designs in its arrangement of graceful and complex lines. As a whole it is a combination of slender columns and Moorish arches, supporting great, overhanging masses; of vaulted ceiling reduplicated many times within itself in diminished form, and with pendants like stalactites, rich in color; of arch and architrave, cornice and wall covered with the purest of arabesque, in woven lines of intricate pattern and infinite variety of design, all in relief and picked out in strongly contrasting colors, which in the original have stood the test of seven centuries, remaining as bright to-day, and as harmonious as the brilliant, closely woven colors of a Persian shawl.

Here, in the zenith of its glory, dwelt the last of the Moorish kings. From it went out Boabdel and with him the vanishing glory of his race. The Spaniard came but not to stay. He added fresh splendors according to his light, but the hand of the Christian, seeking to obliterate all traces of the Infidel religion, made fearful havoc with a refinement which he could not appreciate, and later judgment finds in the act but inexcusable vandalism. Workmen set to deface the walls—so the story goes—found it easier to fill with soft plaster than to chip off by repeated blows the beautiful carving in relief. Thus bits were left in obscure places, or their destruction only partial. The sections thus preserved furnished a key to the whole by which the major portion has been "restored" in stucco. It is beautiful but disappointing in that so little of the distinctively Moorish handiwork remains.

We are shown through tower and dungeon, court and hall. In spite of its beauty it strikes me unpleasantly as of some beautiful thing dead ; a dainty captive dishonored. "Like sweet bells jangled—"

> " O'er all there hung a shadow and a fear,
> A sense of mystery the spirit daunted
> And said as plain as whisper in the ear,
> The place is haunted."

Perhaps that is why the royal Spaniard finally abandoned it to his professional brigands and they, to their non-professional, though expert, brothers who infest the place to-day.

Before other monuments of the noble past—be it cathedral, catacomb, or mouldering ruin—you feel the atmosphere of becoming reverence. Here the glory is of a conquered people pointed out by alien finger as a curiosity simply. They trot you about as in the Greatest Show on Earth and fill you up with pre-

The Alhambra.

posterous showman's yarns. Incidentally you learn that the Spanish government expends from $6,000 to $20,000 annually in taking care of the ruins and in "restorations" which are being constantly made. You wonder at it, for the Spanish government is not noted for doing something for nothing, but perhaps as the railroads which bring people here belong to the

"Court of the Lions."

state, and in view of the crowds that come and the prices charged for transportation, the government is not so much behind the Yankee showman after all.

The principal courts are The Court of Alberca, paved with marble and with an oblong water-filled basin filling centrally the greater portion of the area, and Court of the Lions, the most celebrated of all, in the centre of which stands the fountain made famous in song and story and over which sentimentalists rave. "The alabaster basins still shed their diamond drops, and the twelve lions which support them cast forth their crystal streams as in the days of Boabdel." Pretty ; but—what had the vanished Moor to do with carven lions ? As soon look among his works for the symbolic cross. His religion utterly forbade the making of any graven image or the likeness of any creature having life. No outline of living thing is seen in all the hundreds of feet of surface shown. The only hypothesis reconcilable with fact is that these "lions" did not resemble any thing living on the earth or in the waters beneath the earth closely enough to shock the sensibilities of the most devout of Mussulmen, but I hazard the opinion that the alleged "lions" did not come in until after the Moor went out.

In the splendid " Hall of Embassadors " Ferdinand and Isabella gave audience to Columbus when he approached them for help to come over and discover us—not so entirely helpless either as to be unable to drive a pretty shrewd bargain with the royal pair, insisting as he did on certain honors to be his, in case of success, and a percentage on all "finds" in the new country—even making a feint of going away until, fortunately for us, they wilted. Otherwise we might have remained undiscovered unto this day. Now the guide points out the window from which Isabella called Christopher back after he had left them, she having determined that he should have his ship if it took every jewel in her casket. You are also shown the place where the Great Admiral discomfitted his envious co-navigators by making the egg stand on its head after they had ignominiously failed. (Most unfortunately the egg itself

The Alhambra.

has been mislaid, entailing an irreparable loss on the veracious guide of to-day, for without it there remains no absolute proof of the truth of the story.) Here also is the chapel used in the days of Columbus, and in it a balcony gilded with gold leaf beaten from the gold which he brought back from the New World. This chapel was a mosque in the days of the Moorish kings. In a niche facing toward Mecca the Koran then rested. On the wall in graceful tracery are quotations from the Moslem's sacred book. They tell that when King Boabdel surrendered he begged as a last favor that the entrance to this holy place be forever closed, that it might not be profaned by the foot of the Christian. His conqueror gave his kingly word and stopped the door with solid masonry. As it was then it remains unto this day. No Christian foot has since crossed that threshold— they simply knocked a hole through the side-wall and went in and out that way.

And Boabdel, the last of the Moorish kings, went southward over the snow-clad Sierras, and as from the highest point he turned to take a last look at the kingdom he had lost, he heaved a Vast Historic Sigh which, echoing down the Ages, is reproduced with much effect by the gifted guide. He also wept bitter tears. Then he slid down the other side, his great heart broken, and crossing over to the shores of Africa went into the piratical business—he and the noble Moors who were with him. Boabdel himself is now dead but his followers survive. They soon found that ordinary piracy was too tame to satisfy their great natures and abandoned it for a more exciting and profitable calling. They are now the guides and hack-drivers of Algiers.

Algiers.   Facing the Quay.

ALGIERS.

Friday, February 22d.

AFRICA has always been associated in my mind with burning sands, dark jungles and impenetrable, serpent-haunted swamps. Instead, the shores that border on the Mediterranean are rocky and bold, rising at times through all the varying scale of climate from tropic base to snowy summit. The morning of Washington's birthday finds us at Algiers. Behind us, outreaching arms of solid masonry have clasped a portion of the sea ; at the front lies the city in bright sunshine. From either end of the long quay the roadways, built on gradually rising stone arches in duplicate lines, zig-zag back and forth up to a higher level, where magnificent buildings bound a broad esplanade facing the sea. Back from this, other splendid buildings rise in terraced lines, with less noble ones continued east and west along the harbor, all suggestive, however, of Paris rather than a town in Africa. And indeed very like Paris it is, for all the modern parts have been built under French occupancy, and largely through French enterprise. Higher up against the steep hillside rests the old Moorish town, appearing from the distance more like some deserted stone-quarry where blocks of rock had been only partially removed, than human habitations.

We are set ashore in flat-boats and given over into the hands of pirates who, with much shouting and loud snapping of whips, drive us up and down the city and round about its corners. Through the modern part with its broad streets and fine public and private buildings we go, and up the hill-roads outside the walls, to park and summer garden, wondering and interested in the many odd things seen by the way. We follow along splendid stone roads; we note rude dwellings, like caves, cut out of the hillside and tombs in the cliffs, with sculptured fronts, and gigantic figures of men and animals cut from the living rock, guarding their portals. We see orange and lemon, almond and fig trees, and the red clustered pepper, with graceful date-palms and other tropical growth in numbers and in species unknown. The steep hills are terraced, vertical walls displaying more surface than the level bit of soil they hold in place. Vineyards claim most of the ground. The vines are set in rows from two to three feet apart, and stand about a foot high, slim or stocky according to age. Every spring the fresh growth is cut back to leave only two or three buds on a shoot, and this constant pruning results in a big knob of rootlike branches at the top, in fruitage suggestive of an open umbrella with clusters of grapes hanging on its radiating ribs. Algiers is a noted winter resort for people from northern cities and has many elegant private residences and parks. Moorish houses are here also, with closed doors and barred windows or surrounded by high, blank walls. No glimpse

56

could be had of their interiors, but we were told that within were beautiful courts with dainty fountains and tropical trees and plants and flowers.

Returning we leave the carriages where the ancient and modern parts of the city are dovetailed together and in a moment almost, step backwards nine hundred years. It is a stone city we enter, honeycombed with labyrinthian passages and tortuous tunnels that run in ziz-zag ways without order or apparent object, now climbing abrupt acclivities, now coiling in sinuous lines like a snake's trail about some irregular mass of buildings, like a great worm-eaten rock, throbbing with life and reeking with fetid odor. There seems to have been no order in building except that of concentration around some central point for mutual protection or warmth, as dogs gather closely of a cold night, each successive new-comer building as closely as can be, and still leave a means of ingress and egress, to the central pile. Some of these streets are scarcely three feet wide, some six, some expanding into broader spaces from which others radiate. Carriages cannot pass through; the only means of transportation, other than human, are the patient, overloaded little donkeys—stupid little beasts of burden—which creep sleepily along through the tunnels, climb the steep hillsides or go sliding down the slippery alleys without questioning the will of their drivers. These streets, which may be five or six feet wide at the bottom, are narrowed above by the projecting second stories, supported by rough timbers slanting outward from the walls below. At times but a narrow ribbon of sky shows over head, at others none at all. One might go all over this part

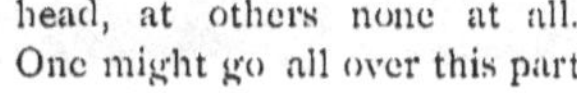

57

A Street in Old Algiers.

of the city from roof to roof, except where high walls bar the way.   The roofs are flat and are the lounging places where the people who live down below sometimes come for light and air. The pavements of irregular stone, slope to the centre where not infrequently runs a stream of liquid filth.   Where the grade is too steep for easy ascent over the slippery rock there are stone stairs, the steps high at the ends, in the centre worn to nothing almost by generations of passing feet.

The common trades are represented in little holes in the wall, and overflow into the street.   The coppersmith, the locksmith and the wood-worker have their benches against the wall.   The tailor sits tailor-wise and nurses his oriental goose in a little niche, and the cobbler, half buried under piles of dilapidated slippers, works, appropriately enough perhaps, directly under foot.   Here on the pavement sits a kingly Moor who hardly deigns to give you a passing look as you, perforce, step over or turn aside, that you may not do injury to the half-dozen little heaps of oranges, lemons or figs which constitute his entire stock in trade.   Here is a dealer in meats which, cut in little chunks, or long, thin strips, hang within easy reach on a lattice frame, through the centre of which he peers watchfully.   Here is a recess in the wall six feet high and as many wide and deep. In it the owner eats and sleeps and wakes to display at the front his wares of complex nature and unknown purpose.

And through these channels flow a steady stream of pictur-esque humanity—Jew, Turk, Moor, Arab, Nubian, Berber, the Wild Man from the Congo and the Curious Man from far away, each in the distinctive costume of his country or religion— the high caste wearers of silk and their brothers who go about in the material of which coffee-sacks are made—a motley crowd

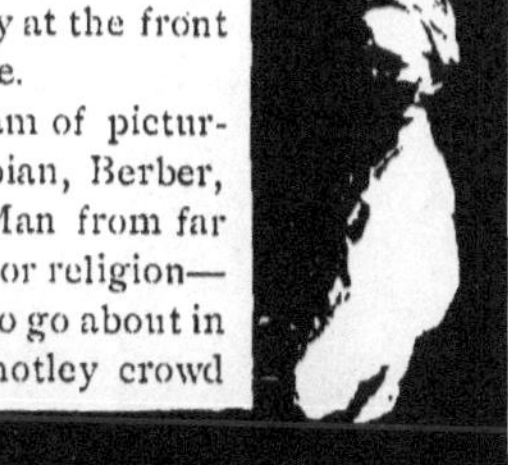

of men, women and children, some with much clothing, some with little, and some with scarcely any at all.   Here is an object somewhat resembling an animated feather bed superimposed on a pair of inflated pillow-cases which are joined at uncertain, varying and alarmingly insecure points.   Low slippers cover what appear to be human feet, and through a slit near the top of the pile peers a pair of eyes.   It may have a head.   It doesn't much matter what sort of a head; there isn't much in it anyway, and if there was it wouldn't count—woman isn't wanted for her head here.   And this object is a respectable middle-class woman of Algiers.   The women belonging to the higher class of men (I use the word belonging advisedly, a man can have as many wives as he can pay for here as the article is cultivated extensively for home consumption) are not often seen walking on the streets.   They are at home behind bars, or if taking the air, are in carriages and generally under guard.   In quarters not very select and with women of a like nature, the face is not always covered, but the dress is practically the same.   In the off-color sections (the distinction is not so obvious to the ordinary beholder until the matter is explained) you will meet women bold of eye and gaudy of wrap and with faces painted to rival the rose—the Jacqueminot species—old women frightful to look upon, groveling mendi-

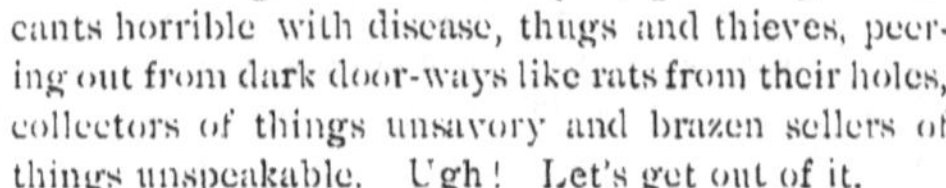

cants horrible with disease, thugs and thieves, peering out from dark door-ways like rats from their holes, collectors of things unsavory and brazen sellers of things unspeakable.   Ugh!   Let's get out of it.

Through the Moorish quarters, we come out into the sunshine once more and find our pirates who have driven around to meet us here, lying in wait for us. Confidingly we trust our precious selves to their care and are driven off over the west side of the city and along shore, get nowhere in particular, and finally return to the city. It develops later that the manager, desirous of giving us an excursion about town to show its most interesting features, arranged with a local guide for a two-hours' drive, and he—one of the pirates in disguise—in collusion with the rest of the gang, kept us in grasp as long as possible, then demanded of individuals the extra compensation for the extra hours. Some little time was saved, however, in which to visit the principal bazaars and mosques.

Of mosques and marabouts, tombs and sanctuaries of the saints, there are upwards of a hundred in the city. One mosque may be accepted as the type of all. A crowd of beggars hang about its doors. Surrounded by a cloud of buzzing flies others lie sleeping in the sunshine. From the hood of one looks out a startlingly handsome Medusa face. The interior is dark and gloomy, rich though its decorations may be. Its floors are covered with rugs. In the porch is a great basin with running water. About it, turbanned men are gathered, washing their feet, for their religion demands that they shall be clean—so far as the feet are concerned. Here are men reciting portions of the Koran in a monotone, seemingly oblivious to the presence of the infidel visitors. On the rugs, kneeling, are other men facing east toward Mecca, bending at intervals to lay their foreheads to the floor, then advancing on their knees to bow to the floor again, and forward again until the end is reached. At the entrance you slip your feet, shoes and all, into a pair of slippers which are furnished you for that purpose, for to the Moslem the place whereon you stand is holy ground, but you need not

Medusa.

remove your hat, for it is not a mark of respect to uncover the head in their presence.

The streets are swarming with beggars and hucksters and sellers of trifles who crowd about you clamoring, thrusting their wares on you and importuning you to buy. Some trifling article offered, you ask the price.

" Four franc."

" No."

" Three franc."

" Don't want it."

" How much you give ? "

" One franc."

" No, no ; two franc."

" *No.*"

"*Take !*"

And you take it at your price. No one pays what is asked even at the better stores. At one of these a merchant, who presumably does not know " English as she is writ," exhibits with great pride, an endorsement from an American. It reads: "*This man's goods are very nice; offer him a fourth of what he charges—never pay more than a third.*"

We sail away from Algiers with the going down of the sun and paint the ship a patriotic red because of the day.

*The wearers of the
Coffee Sack.*

HISTORY OF FOUR DAYS.

(Extract from note book.)

Saturday, February 23, 1895.

GOT up. Ate breakfast. Sat in steamer chair. Looked at sky and water. Lunched. Sat in steamer chair some more. Looked at more sky and more water. Dined. Meditated. Turned in.

Sunday, February 24th.

Early in the morning the island of Malta is passed. Religious services are held in both saloons, bringing out some bits of local history. It appears that many years ago a preacher named Paul went sailing hereabouts with a lot of Roman soldiers. Their experience must have been something such as we had the second day out, but their ship was evidently not as seaworthy as the old Friesland, so they ran her aground and "they all escaped safe to the land." The account goes on to say:

"And when we were escaped, then we knew that the island was called Melita. And the barbarians shewed us no common kindness; for they kindled a fire, and received us all, because of the present rain, and because of the cold. But when Paul had gathered a bundle of sticks, and laid them on the fire, a viper came out by reason of the heat, and fastened on his hand. And when the barbarians saw the beast hanging from his hand, they said one to another, no doubt this man is a murderer, whom, though he hath escaped from the sea, yet Justice hath not suffered to live. Howbeit he shook off the beast into the fire, and took no harm."

63

Monday, February 25.

This is New Jersey day, and celebrated by the People of that Nation in the picturesque garb of the women of Algiers—im-

provised for the occasion from sheets and table cloths.

Tuesday, February 26th.

In the middle of the afternoon we enter the harbor of Alexandria. The island of Pharos, lying just outside the city beach, re-enforced with lines of masonry, affords protected anchorage for vessels. On Pharos was erected the famous tower where fires were built at night as a guide and warning to mariners. This early light-house was said to have been nearly five hundred feet high, and was considered one of the wonders of the world. Where the ancient Pharos once blazed are now modern lights, while modern ships mingle with the picturesque though modern, Egyptian.

At night, some of the pilgrims land and proceed by special train to Cairo; others remain to inspect the Town by the Sea first and will follow later.

THE NILE DELTA.

LEXANDRIA, we learn from history, was founded by
Alexander the Great, 332 years B. C. It is built on a
strip of sand, which, cast up by the restless Mediterranean, outlines as a silver binding the northern border of the
delta. Like a great open fan with ribs a hundred miles long
and with a sweep of a hundred and fifty miles around its northern edge, is this great triangle of matter brought from more
than 1,800 miles away. At Cairo, the axis of the fan, the
many-mouthed river breaks, and radiating, flows through the
spreading land like the raveled strands of a great rope.

Alexandria was once a city of half a million souls. It now
numbers about two hundred thousand, one quarter of which
are Europeans. In early days it was the seat of almost everything. Poetry, art, music and the sciences were every-day matters. Here Eratosthenes exploited his geography and Sosibius
pushed his grammar to the front. Here Archimedes shrieked
" Eureka " and made his historic bluff of lifting the earth and
here Euclid sprung his forty-second problem on a long-suffering
world. Here, also, one Cleopatra came and encouraged the attention of certain foreigners, by name respectively Cæsar and
Antony, to such an extent as to attract public attention even in

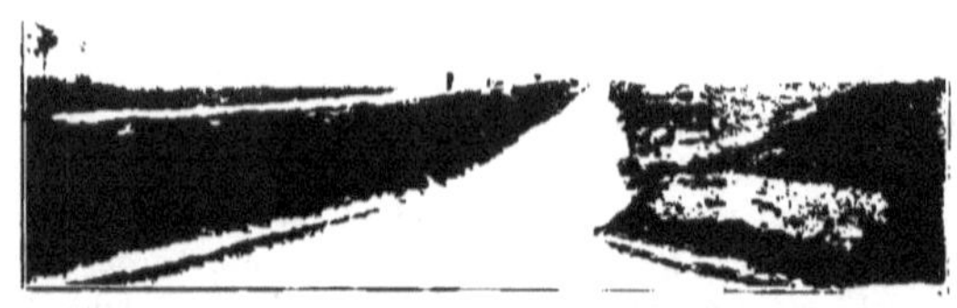

An Irrigating Canal.

those days.   Later it became the centre of the Christian faith, where Christian and pagan alike by turns cut each other up in a bloody see-saw, with little thought of the golden rule.

But little of the ancient is noticeable about Alexandria now, except Pompey's Column, which is a single shaft of red granite, 67 feet in height, exclusive of base and capital. Cleopatra's Needle, which had stood at Ramleh, a suburb of Alexandria, for over eighteen hundred years, was, in 1880, taken down and now adorns Central Park, while its mate, which had lain for ages in the sand at its side, stands on the Thames embankment in the city of London.

From Alexandria to Cairo is 130 miles.   Express trains make the distance in about four hours.   The road leads past shallow lakes and over long stretches of land just rising out of the water by the added atoms of Nile mud deposited at each annual overflow, as all of the great delta has been lifted from the sea in ages past. Occasionally broad canals are paralleled or crossed, and small ones, out from which extend lateral lines of irrigating ditches, are frequent.   Embankments divide and sub-divide the surface into squares, or connect distant mounds of solid

earth which rise above the level of the water. On these mounds are the villages of the people, some of them considerable towns, with mosques and towers, some merely mud huts, huddled together without form or comeliness. Some are flat roofed or cane-thatched, affording a place where goats and fowls and children lie about in the hot sun. A better condition shows instead of flat roof, small domes over the square walls as the simplest manner of constructing a self-supporting roof. Around these little villages are mud embankments to keep

out the flood when the water rises around them in the annual inundations.

Gangs of laborers are at work along the way. They carry the mud in baskets on their heads, taking it from the bottom of the ditch and dumping it at the top of the embankments. The water carries it down again at the next inundation to be sure, but it can be brought up again as before. And up, and down, and up, it goes in a never-ending round, for the digger of ditches is not very expensive in Egypt. He gets for his labor from fifteen to twenty cents per day, out of which he feeds and clothes himself. He is not particular as to food; as for clothing—it not uncommonly consists of a thick coat of mud and some wraps about the head and neck.

Egypt is no longer entirely covered during the annual inundation. Dikes shut the water out from places where it is not

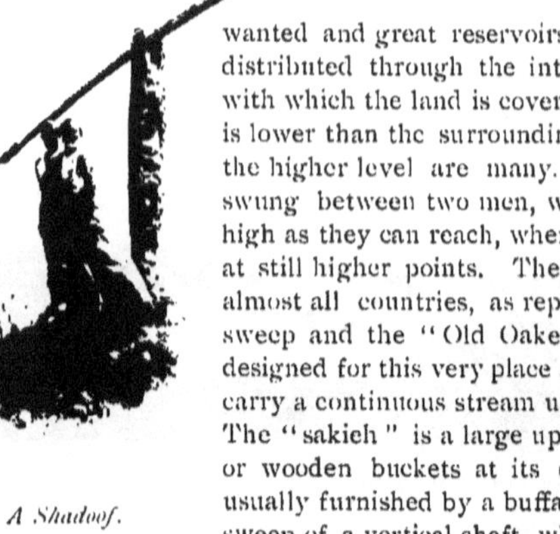

A *Shadoof.*

wanted and great reservoirs are filled and hold it until finally distributed through the intricate system of irrigating canals with which the land is covered. When the water in the canals is lower than the surrounding fields the means of getting it to the higher level are many. Sometimes it is a heavy bucket, swung between two men, who dip and empty into a pocket as high as they can reach, where other men dip and hoist to others at still higher points. The "shadoof" is a common sight in almost all countries, as represented by the old-fashioned well sweep and the "Old Oaken Bucket." Archimedes' screws— designed for this very place and purpose by its great inventor— carry a continuous stream up the slopes of high embankments. The "sakieh" is a large upright wheel with a row of earthen or wooden buckets at its outer rim. The motive power is usually furnished by a buffalo, often a cow, hitched to the long sweep of a vertical shaft, which is in turn geared to the shaft of the water-wheel. The beast is often blindfolded, whether to prevent its getting too much enjoyment out of the scenery, or to encourage it with the idea that it will reach its journey's end sooner by hurrying in its endless round, is a question, but as it goes round and round the big wheel turns over and over, and its buckets dip water from the lower level and empty it at the highest point into troughs, through which it runs off to the fields.

A *Sakieh.*

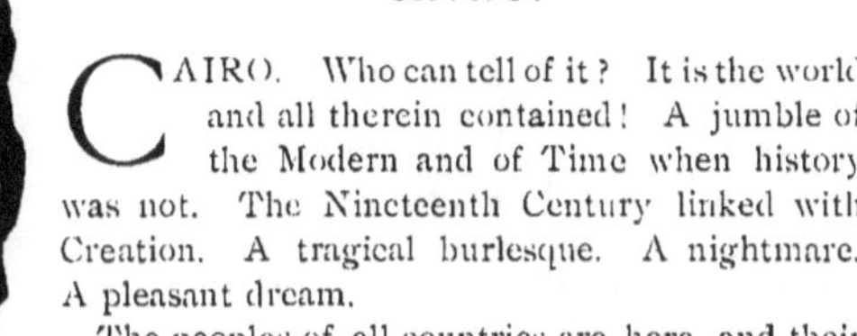

CAIRO.

CAIRO. Who can tell of it? It is the world and all therein contained! A jumble of the Modern and of Time when history was not. The Nineteenth Century linked with Creation. A tragical burlesque. A nightmare. A pleasant dream.

The peoples of all countries are here, and their country with them. The burning Tropics and the frozen Poles are represented, to get or to give. The stranger wonders at what he finds. The native wonders what there is to wonder at but does not let it interfere with his business of taking the stranger in. He is not in business for his health. The Oriental cannot understand what there is in travel to interest people. He reasons that those who come so far just to *see* things must be either weak-minded or insane, and treats them accordingly. The visitor is experimented on, craftily, as a creature who, whatever his mental condition generally, may have occasional glimmerings of sense, and perchance insist on certain absurd rights he may think his regarding the money he brings. He must therefore be wheedled or frightened, according as tests in these directions result in little or much bakshish.

*Obelisk
of
Heliopolis.*

The leavened mass is Oriental and the Oriental does not have a very high opinion of the European, or of his offshoot. In his opinion the European does everything wrong end first—back handed—as he writes, from left to right, instead of from right to left ; he wears his shoes in the sanctuary and uncovers his head, and stares about in holy places.

Through many classes the shades are sharply drawn, and, like a rich oriental shawl, the threads which harmonize as a whole are distinctly marked as individuals. The Fellâhîn form the bulk of the population. He may be seen just outside the city, or coming and going, loaded with the products of the earth. He is the tiller of the soil, the common laborer, the typical Egyptian. He is strongly built and heavy of movement; frugal as to food and dress. He generally eats a coarse bread made from maize, sometimes having an admixture of bean-flour, and—during their season—enormous quantities of pumpkins and cucumbers, which are very cheap. For special meals and occasions he dips his bread in a highly salted sauce of onions

and linseed oil. He wears a white head-covering and a flowing, sometime white or indigo blue, cotton shirt, or gown, reaching nearly to the ground. (The women of this class wear a shawl or handkerchief twisted about the head, and, apparently, a single garment of black cotton, hanging from the shoulder to near the feet, flowing, and often gaping wide, the matter of fastening seeming to depend rather on the temperature than on any sense of propriety.) The fellah lives in a hut made of Nile mud, which hardens almost to stone. Windowless?

What need has he for windows? His house is simply a place in which to stow small articles and to sleep in during the cold season. In the warm, he sleeps under the stars. He never changes. He is the same Egyptian to-day that he was in the days of the Pharaohs. He never rises above his class. He has an idea that he is not justly treated but does not go far enough to decide who is responsible. He is a Mussulman by tradition and is sustained by the blessed hope that in the next world the other fellow will be damned and all good things come his way. He is a good natured beast generally, as is his brother, the domesticated buffalo. He labors patiently to get necessary food to satisfy his hunger. When that is assured he lies down in the sun and the flies come and feed on him. It would not be proper to say of an Egyptian "there are no flies on him"—because it would not be the truth. Flies cover the native as nimbi surround the heads of the saints. In the times of Moses they were a plague, now they are an unqualified blessing, for they are the scavengers of a people that know not cleanliness—a people prone to all the diseases that filth can bring.

The Copts are also Egyptians but of another class and religion. They are nominally Christians, believing in the Holy Trinity, the Holy Mother and all the saints. They are more intellectual than their brothers of the soil. They are the skilled artisans of the town, the smiths, the workers in precious metals and, to a considerable extent, the bankers and money-lenders.

The Berbers come from Nubia. The name is said to mean non-Egyptian. There is no love lost between the Berber and the native Egyptian. The native has a poor opinion of the Berbers, considering them an inferior people. The Berbers

*One of
the Army
of
Occupation.*

have a like opinion of the Egyptians. They are probably both right. The balance, if any, is in favor of the Berber, for he has peculiar ideas of honesty, which with a native Egyptian would be considered a weakness. He is the porter of the town; the door-tender and watchman, the coachman, the house servant, the cook. He does not marry the Egyptian woman. He looks forward to a return to his native land when he has gathered sufficient from the foreigner to carry him back with credit.

The Negro is of the very lowest class here and performs the most menial of services. Slavery practically exists in Egypt, although the law permits the slave to become free if he wishes. He generally doesn't. The old condition suits him best, for it relieves him of all anxiety as to food and a place to sleep.

The brains of Egypt are imported. They are found in the Turk, the Levantine, the Armenian, the Jew, and in all the people who come from all the countries of Europe. The government machinery is Turkish. The fuel is supplied by the Greek and Jew. The balance-wheel is in the English Army of Occupation.

The most picturesque figure in Egypt's land is the Bedouin—the free lance of the desert; the wild rider; the proud Arabian. Of mixed blood and fire, he will rob you or make you welcome to his tent and half of his last crust, as the spirit takes him. Occasionally one sweeps down along the edge of civilization and is recognized as a man. Wild as in nature's

A Porter.

form perhaps, but a noble specimen withal. His less noble brother may be found on the edge of the desert, where he has pitched his tent, and about him his camels and his flock. You will find him at Gîzeh, among the palms at old Memphes, and along the borders of the Nile. Sometimes he curbs his nomadic impulse and is found about the city as dragoman, as outrunner before the great man's carriage, as the wild donkey-boy, as guide and puller-up of winded humanity at the pyramids.

Wherever met with you will at times see flashes of his fiery nature breaking out, of Pride in rags, with the carriage of a King.

The streets of old Cairo are like a kaleidoscope, a wonderful combination of changing form and color, of writhing lines of picturesque humanity; condensing and dissolving, swelling and melting, crowding and jostling; a babel of noises; of strifes that mean nothing; of fierce threatenings that are harmless; of quarrels that seldom come to blows. Everything is continually getting out of the way of something else at a sacrifice of

73

A Sheik.

A Street in Cairo.

all dignity. The right of way is readily accorded to might.
The universal law seems to be—not care to prevent running
over the weaker but alertness on the part of the weaker to
prevent being run over. Where the Englishman would resist
an imposition the Egyptian dodges and takes it out of his
smaller brother next time. The footman gets out of the way
of the man on the donkey, the donkey slips from under the feet
of the horse, while horse and carriage, and everything else,
give way to the loaded camel, who swerves not a hair's breadth
to right or left, though the King himself come that way.

All the trades are on the streets and indiscriminately mixed.
The metal worker, the tailor, the shoemaker are on benches
or little shelves, in alcoves, or on platforms, narrowing still more
the already narrow way. The hatmaker is there and will iron
your fez while you wait, also the dealer in toys and curios and
in strange gods and in bogus antiquities. Here the devout
Mussulman kneels in prayer and the crowd step over or around
him. Here a number of gray-beards are reciting passages of the
Koran. One sits on a shelf-seat against the wall meditating,
without seeming thought or interest in the busy life around him.

Porters carry things of enormous bulk by
means of a rope or strap across the forehead.
The streets are watered by men with skins of
goats, spraying the surface where necessary by
loosening their clasp on what was once the
throat of the animal to which the skin originally belonged. Native women are sometimes
seen barefaced on the street, but they are a
low class indeed who do not follow the Eastern
fashion of covering the face with a veil. Here

75

Meditation.

it is held in place by the "ko-ró-za" (I spell it phonetically), a brass tube with saw-like rings around and supported by means of a cord passing through it and over the head. This instrument of torture, which is almost universally worn by women in Egypt, seems to place them on a par with other savages who wear as ornaments metal bars thrust through their under lip, or rings in their noses—and ears.

In the city you do not feel that you have an indolent people to deal with. The bare-footed boot-black of Cairo is fully as importunate in soliciting your patronage as his soiled brother of the West—and about a hundred times as noisy.

The Arabian donkey-boy is a distinctive feature of the East. While in your employ he is a staunch supporter, often guide, philosopher and friend. He is indispensable in visiting some of the narrower streets, which are usually dirty in ratio as they become interesting. The cost for a donkey and attendant is from fifteen to twenty cents an hour. If you are fortunate in getting a good donkey the sensation of riding is rather pleasant and restful than otherwise. He glides along under you with his little mincing trot, giving you a succession of shocks like the throbbing of an intermittent electrical current, while the attendant runs behind and encourages the little beast by the use of choice Arabic and a cudgel, both of which he applies freely.

Hotels are sufficient. Many of them are palatial and above reproach, according to Oriental standards. But some of us *did* long for just one square United States meal. We heard of a place where meals were served on the European plan, but we found the things themselves Egyptian. Our dragoman convoyed us to a place where he said we could get English dishes served. The proprietor named the English dishes with much pride. They were— "spuds and meat."

A common sight in Cairo is of the be-turbaned schoolmaster, seated in some open court surrounded by boys who are writing on their metal slates or reciting verses of the Koran with much swaying of the body. Education in these schools consists generally of the commitment of portions of the Koran to memory. It is not necessary that it shall be understood, but to be able, parrot-like, to repeat the written law is an accomplishment not uncommon.

Overhanging latticed balconies are almost universal along the

second stories of houses on the better streets, affording members of the family a chance to see without being seen. In every view is certain to appear one or more of the many mosques of the city, and at certain hours, away up on

77

A Dining Pavilion.

Teaching Young Ideas to Shoot.

the slender minarets may be seen the "muez-zin," whose voice comes down calling the faithful to prayer.

The beautiful mosque of Sultan Hassan is said to be the finest specimen of Byzantine-Arabian architecture existing. Within the Citadel is the "Alabaster Mosque," which is the tomb of Mohammed Ali. Here also we see the place where occurred the massacre of the Mamelukes in 1811, and a portion of the wall is pointed out where the only survivor escaped by forcing his horse to leap to the broken ground below. We descend into Jacob's well, a black shaft sunk from the heights straight down to the level of the Nile, and around which, in a sharp spiral, winds an incline by means of which water can be raised to supply the garrison in time of siege.

The tombs of the Caliphs are among the exhibits of the city. Each tomb is a mosque, dedicated to some one of the early sultans. They once had troops of paid attendants but now are more or less in ruins and infested with beggars.

The dancing dervishes gave an exhibition of religious gym-

"The Alabaster Mosque."

nastics, which we attended. They postured and wheeled and whipped the floor with their long hair and worked themselves up into a high state of ecstatic frenzy and—took up a collection. With them insanity is a desirable condition. Their belief is that the soul of the insane person has been taken to heaven as specially favored of God. They profess to be above earthly considerations, but I noted that when a visitor failed to drop anything into the box, the deacon—or whatever the collector may be called—made remarks which no one could mistake for blessings.

But Cairo is not all old, or poor, or dirty. It has magnificent boulevards, beautiful parks and stately public buildings. With all its noise there seems to be perfect system in all things with which the public has to do. The

Tombs of the Caliphs.

police supervision is admirable. We had occasion to note on several occasions that any uncommon gathering quickly brought an officer to the ground. Perhaps the provoking way the inspector of police (who is an Englishman and an ex-army officer) has of appearing at unexpected points and moments, has some effect in keeping the native police alert. Individually the native policeman seems quite Eastern and human.

81

A Moslem Cemetery.

Market Place,
On the Way to the Pyramids.

We chanced to pick up in our wanderings a very intelligent young Arab, Mohamed Mohmoud by name, whom we called "Charley" for short. Charley knew good English ; he knew the city, and he knew many things which the average dragoman did not know, but unfortunately he had not a license as dragoman, and the regulars made a row when they saw him riding about with us. Our second attempt to take him brought a mob of violently protesting dragomen, who assured us on their honors that Charley was a thief and a liar and would probably rob us if we persisted in carrying him around. A policeman was summoned, who yanked the boy about after the manner of policemen generally, and proposed to make an example of him for attempting to lie without a license. Mingled with the officer's volcanic sense of duty was an occasional softening which led me to think he was open to reason. I could not speak his tongue nor he mine, but there is a universal language, more potent than Volapuk, current in the East. His hand lingered in mine a moment, then we carried Charley off triumphantly, leaving Cairo's finest to explain the niceties of the law to a crowd of scowling fellow natives—and it only cost a dollar. After that it mattered not which way we drove we needed to go but a little distance to find Charley running at our wheel.

The Oriental does not understand a joke—our jokes at least— and I presume we do not understand his. As soon think to tickle the Sphinx with a straw as to get a Western witticism into an Eastern head. He takes everything in dead earnest. He can never see the point of the most bare-faced attempt. You must explain everything, and then it produces only a sickly smile, forced because he thinks you expect it. Certain ones of

83

"Charley."

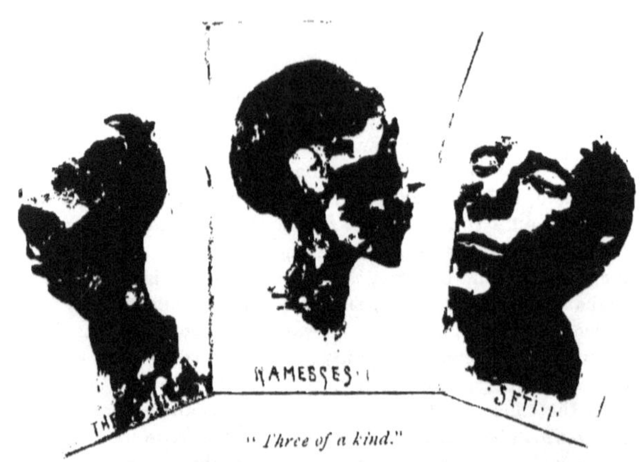

"Three of a kind."

the party wanted—*a la Talmadge*—to see the seamy side of Cairo, and a particularly intelligent guide was engaged for the occasion. It was explained to him, in somewhat veiled phrases perhaps, that the party wished to visit the most interesting parts of Cairo by night—in fact they wanted, after the American fashion, to "see the elephant"—the point punctuated with a wink. The guide winked back knowingly, to show that he understood—and took them to a zoölogical garden.

The Museum must not be forgotten. In it you are face to face with the Ages. Here are great statues and works of ancient Egyptian art ; jewels and ornaments of gold and silver taken from tombs where they have been hidden for thousands of years ; priceless records, that have clothed what was once considered myth in the garb of unquestioned history. Here is royalty that existed before the Exodus ; faces that laughed at the cry of the oppressed ; brown lips that sneered at the messages of the Most High ; bodies that throbbed with life and passion more than three thousand years ago, now only poor, dried, blackened shreds of flesh, of bleached bone and matted hair—a dust-covered exhibit for the curious to look upon. Here is old King Tothmes, here Great Setí, and his greater son, Rameses, the Pharaoh of the Oppression, who played see-saw with Moses in promises made but to be broken, and who persecuted the poor Israelite until one can almost approve of the command which made the chosen people thieves and robbers when they finally went out: for "they spoiled the Egyptians" according to command—and acquired a lasting habit in so doing.

A Snake Charmer.

A Camel
Loaded with Alfalfa.

THE PYRAMIDS OF GÍZEH.

THE WAY from Cairo leads across the Nile bridge, where the great stone lions keep watch, past the busy market place, and along a broad road over which the quick-growing acacia has thrown a canopy of green. Here in seemingly unending line come the sleepy camels, bringing great backloads of alfalfa or cases of goods from across the desert; the slow buffalo, drawing long, springless wagons, on which sit the native Egyptian and his family; and numberless stupid little donkeys pattering past, sometimes almost hidden by their overhanging burdens.

You have seen the Pyramids almost from the start—dimly at first, if, perchance, the west wind has filled the air with sand—and they are disappointing, seeming so much smaller than

The Pyramids.

Cheops the Great.

you had thought. Gradually, however, they begin to weigh on the senses but yet you can not estimate their value in the scene for want of some unit of measurement. At last you understand! You note that objects of recognized dimensions with which to compare them, are invisible, simply because of the distance, which was not at first realized. Forms of men and of animals on the green flats at your feet, diminish into atoms long before the white sand is reached. The sand itself shows but waves, as the surface of the sea. They stand in a line gradually diminishing, the nearest "Cheops," the second "Chefren," the third "Menkaura," with lesser ones on their eastern flank. Now they are drawn together and "Cheops the Great" covers all.

At the end of the avenue of trees the carriages are left and, on foot or on donkey-back, we ascend to the base of the great pile. A cloud of white-robed, wind-blown Bedouins swoop down on us as we reach the upper level, their frantic efforts to secure patrons not limited to voice alone—although pandemonium would seem quiet beside—for they snatch at their victims as dogs might at a bone. They capture first and persuade afterward. They hunt in pairs with a watchful third to assist. The man who hesitates here is lost, so far as control of events is concerned, for almost before he knows it two muscular Arabs will have him out and on the way to the top, and if he is not determined in rejecting him, a "booster" comes tumbling after. Friends are separated after one brief moment of time, in which they may be vouchsafed opportunity to breathe a promise to meet above, and then they are off.

I selected two—or perhaps, more properly speaking, two selected me—and waiting only long enough to be satisfied that their English was understandable, started for the top. At the

second tier I looked back and saw a mixed mass of black
and white, the white struggling fiercely for possession of the
black, pulling and hauling in counter ways, and not infrequently coming to blows before the question was settled. From
the fifth tier I saw that the mass had separated into detached
sections, and each black was flanked by a pair of whites, with
sometimes a third bringing up the rear. The climb up the
stairway, where every step is three or more feet in height, requires considerable attention, even with a lithe, sinewy Arab
pulling at either hand. They climb as easily as cats. Their
bare feet reach up and take hold of a high shelf with a sweep
which gives one the impression that they could easily step on
their own shoulders if necessary. My men gave me to understand that their everlasting honor depended on my safety—I
need have no fear. They pumped me to learn my name, residence, and object in coming, and gave me theirs, with considerable family history. My chief was named Assin Mahomed and
rejoiced in the honorary title of "The Doctor." The other was
Mark Twain. Mark was the first to discover signs of weariness
in me and to insist on dusting off a soft section of rock with his
night-gown, and in doing it managed to convey in a most reverential manner his great admiration for me and a longing to give
me something by which I might remember him. It ended in
my paying him a franc, for a two-cent scarabie. A little later
the Doctor became very solicitous for my condition, and *he* insisted on dusting out a soft corner and bracing me up in it,
while, from unsuspected quarters in his robe, he produced a little
green god which he pressed on me as a keep-sake from him.
It pained him to accept anything for it, but it was the only
thing he had worthy of me, and if I insisted on giving him any-

thing in return it would cost about two francs to satisfy the person to whom it belonged. This was all right too. But when I saw, a little later, symptoms of a desire to find other soft places to fit me into I called a halt and said:

"See here, now, Doctor and Mark Twain, I have taken a most remarkable liking to you. You are both great men, only it hasn't got around yet. I am going to make you both rich and famous, for I shall send friends over as soon as I get home and they will have nothing to do with these other common fellows. We are friends. I want you to *give* me something to remember you by."

I prize very highly the damaged bug and the bogus Roman coin received from them, with repeated pledges of their eternal friendship. It seemed the only way to head them off. After that it was only occasionally that I was obliged to check their absent minded efforts to get additional bakshish by counter requests for additional tokens of remembrance.

We were twelve minutes getting to the top of Cheops, 551 feet above the base. Revenge is sweet. I got my breath and kodaked my helpless friends on their arrival. This greatest of all pyramids covers an area of nearly thirteen acres. The stone is from a range of hills across on the east side of the Nile. It is built on a rock foundation, which undoubtedly at one time defined the outline of the valley. About 500 yards distant in an air line is the top of the second pyramid. One of the Bedouins engages, for a consideration, to go from the top of the one where we stand to the top of the other in ten minutes. Like a fluttering white moth, rapidly diminishing in size, he goes down. In two minutes he is seen moving across t h e sand; in another he h a s d i s a p p e a r e d around the base of Chefren; in s e v e n more he is waving his arms on its summit! The space has now been encroached on by the desert, so that the pyramids are surrounded by sand

and with a considerable bank piled above the edge of the green flats below. Toward the east is the green valley-land through which, straight as an arrow flies, runs the acacia-shaded road to Cairo. Stretching north and south as far as can be seen is the border of sand, pressing in eternal warfare against the line of green, its way at the south punctuated with pyramids, to distant Memphis and beyond. The Libyan desert spreads westward. Its sand, whitish yellow, mixed with shell-like bits

"Ships of the Desert."

of rock, lies in wind-rows or along the hollows of the rock-surface as new fallen snow sometimes spreads in spots on the hard frozen, wind-swept crust of a former deposit. Its surface is rolling, like great waves, and verdureless to the horizon's edge.

The ancient Egyptian believed that the immortality of the soul depended on the preservation of the body, hence the embalming of the body, the tombs cut deep into the rock, and the great pyramids, which are but tombs, each designed to protect for all time the body of its builder. The three great pyramids of Gîzeh date from about three thousand years B. C., and mark the successive dynasties of Cheops, Chefren and Menkaura, in the order of their size. The entrance to Cheops is on the north side, about fifty feet above its base, the passage descending at a sharp angle to a chamber far below the original surface and directly underneath its centre. Sixty feet from the entrance the way branches, one sloping upward to the King's Chamber, which is almost in the exact centre of the entire mass. The tunnel is 3½ feet high and 4 feet wide the greater portion of the way, so that you must crouch low, or on hands and feet like an ape. Cross notches, into which you step, are gouged in the stone along

93

Entrance to Cheops.

The King's Chamber.

the slopes, but even then great care must be taken to prevent slipping, for it is worn smooth as glass and as slippery as soap-stone. The general temperature is 79° Fahrenheit. The air is dry and the way dusty, but I did not find it so insufferable as I had been led to expect. To be sure it lacked the freshness of air that blows over the mountain top, but it had no unpleasant odor, and, except that it was somewhat "stuffy," seemed pure and wholesome as the air ordinarily found in dry limestone caves. Indeed, while the exertion of making progress in un-comfortable postures, necessitated by the low tunnel, made me uncomfortably warm, I do not think I suffered more than I would under the same conditions in the open air. The King's Chamber is 34½ feet long, 17 wide and 19 high and lined with enormous slabs of granite. At one end rests the great granite sarcophagus which was undoubtedly intended to hold the body of its builder until the sleeping soul should be called to take possession again. The body? No one knows. Tradition has it that Cheops was so hated by the people because of his op-pressions that after death his body was not allowed to occupy the costly house he had builded for it.

When on the return we reached the bottom of the long shaft, up which we must climb to the outer world, the north pole star was shining into it. Is there any significance in the fact that this single, seemingly immovable sun of the north should alone light the heart of the pyramid as it has done in the ages past, and as it will while the pile endures?

Danger in trusting the Arab? Travelers had told me blood-curdling stories of adventures with the Bedouins in these subterranean ways. It was said you took your life in your hand to venture in unless well armed and in parties of twos or threes. Indeed one of our party was, according to his own account, subjected to the most outrageous treatment by the ruffianly dragomen who accompanied him, until he was finally obliged to take one of them by the throat and brace him up against the rock to teach him proper respect! But my experience was different. The day was nearly done and visitors were leaving when I entered. I was alone except for the three Arabs who accompanied me to carry my apparatus and show the way. We visited the King's Chamber and the Queen's Chamber and made photographs of the interior. My conductors did, individually and collectively, on several occasions in the heart of the tomb, press me for extra backshish for imagined extra services and gave me to understand that it was the invariable custom, by an unwritten law, to give certain amounts when certain points were passed. I even suspected that, toward the last, they assumed tones and attitudes intended to appear threatening—simply for its moral effect, as there seems to be no law in Egypt against frightening people—but when I laughed at them they invariably became somewhat silly, and when we finally got out in the starlight they accepted with a profusion of thanks what I gave to each, one even making change for me without attempting to retain more than he was entitled to. If they were inclined to take advantage of visitors they never could have had a better chance than was then offered, for I was practically alone with them and unarmed. It may not sound well to admit it, but I have a suspicion that it is more horribly uninterestingly safe with these big, overgrown children of the desert than the average traveler thinks.

THE VISITOR should not be satisfied with a single visit to Gizeh. The pyramids grow on one with every look. Familiarity but adds to respect. The Sphinx utterly refuses to become common. When I reached the carriage at the base of the hill the night of my visit to the interior of Cheops I found my friends awaiting me somewhat impatiently, and the bejeweled conductor in a high state of outraged dignity, which it required some little bakshish to soothe. I went a second day. At the base of Cheops the camel-driver and the donkey-boy lay in wait for us.

"Will 'Merica-man ride 'Rabian camel?"

Is there anything that anybody else has ever done that the Man from America will not do just to see how it feels? The Merica-man *will* ride 'Rabian camel. And the man from Seattle, the Judge from the Provinces, the Honorables and the Colonels, the M. D.'s and the D. D.'s, the stately matrons, the charming widows and the dainty girls—all take a mount. It is a proud day indeed. And when Æsculapius—the traveler of many

97

Old Glory at the Pyramids.

climes—climbs to the apex of one of the biggest and flaunts Old Glory over the African continent, the enthusiasm knows no bounds.

When you are ready to go aboard the "Ship of the Desert" the captain proceeds to make him lie down. He protests at the proposed indignity, cries plaintively, blows off steam, and finally doubles his many-jointed legs under him and comes to anchor on his keel. You climb up onto the roof, and make yourself as secure as possible on the ridge-pole in a sort of saw-buck lashed to his belvedere, grasping the storm stays and stanchions which stick up fore and aft as a further security. You think the beast is asleep but he isn't. He is simply smiling. There is a tradition that he gets up on his hind legs first, but don't you believe it. He always gets up first with the end you are thinking will be last, and his gentlest motion in doing it is like the swish of a catapult. You can not play the foolish virgin on him—you never know when the upheaval is going to occur, or what direction the disturbance will take when started. It may run from fore to aft, or contrarywise, or, starting diagonally, change midway at right angles, and end in a spiral snap which dislocates your neck. When the convulsion terminates he takes a nap, or, if you still remain aboard, gets under way and makes you sea-sick. It is said that the ideal camel has a gait so easy that one may drink a cup of coffee going at full speed without spilling a drop, but with the one that got me nothing short of a hot-water bag and a rubber hose would have answered. When he walked, the motion seemed something between a ship in a chop-sea and a cork-screw. When he dropped into a trot it was a cross between a bucking broncho and a pile-driver.

The Sphinx stands east of the pyramids staring out toward the Nile—a lion with the head of a god. From the dawn of creation it was there for it is a part of the living, eternal rock, but no man knoweth of the day when some ancient sculptor cut away the surrounding mass and set it free. In that early time, undoubtedly, the sands of the desert were at its back, beyond the pyramids, and its solemn eyes looked out over the green valley at its feet, greeting the rising suns of centuries untold. There came a time when the sands overwhelmed it and for hundreds of years it was as though it had never existed. Then it saw the second resurrection. Now it rests in a hollow scooped out around it—like some great, strange creature in its shallow nest—but even in its low estate, mutilated and dishonored, it stands immutable, the grandest figure of unassailable majesty that the world knows! Well might the ancient Egyptian revere it. To him it was the Emblem of coming Light; the God of Plenty ; the Conqueror of Death ; the promise of a resurrection and of immortality.

Near by, also below the common level of the sand, is the Temple of the Sphinx, discovered in 1853. It is of immense blocks of granite and slabs of alabaster. Through it a system of rock-tombs are entered. Now, the temple is a show place which you pay for entering. In it you find the omnipresent Arab, with what is not so common but which proves quite acceptable—coffee, piping hot; yours for bakshish.

Entrance to Temple of The Sphinx.

99

Temple of The Sphinx.

THE SHADOW OF THE SPHINX.

February 27, 1895.

In the shadow of the Sphinx
I am sitting, and the links
Of the Ages pass along in solemn file,
Where the desert's shifting sands
Ever press the border lands
That are watered by the overflowing Nile.
Where great Cheops lifts its head,
And the long forgotten dead
Rest unnumbered, by the everlasting pile,
Come the ghosts of ancient days—
Egypt's radiant noon ablaze
With the glories that have vanished from the Nile.

And when, in Egypt's early morn, did first thy solemn eyes
Look on her swarming millions, born beneath the cloudless skies?

Tell me—didst thou know the fame
Of The Dreamer ere he came—
How the sun and moon and stars should bow the while?
Didst thou see the maidens stray
By the river-side, that day
When the little ark lay rocking on the Nile?
Didst thou glory in the flood
Of the waters, turned to blood?
Is it sweet when plague and pestilence defile?
Was thy hard heart in accord,
When the Angel of the Lord
Smote the first born of the valley of the Nile?

The blood of beasts; the hearts that yearn; the anguished soul that cries!
Unheeded all; as suns that burn through Egypt's glowing skies.

101

Didst thou wonder at the light
When the stars sang in the night
With glad tidings of a Life that knew not guile ?
Didst thou see that Perfect One—
Great Jehovah's gentle Son—
When his young feet trod the borders of the Nile ?
Didst thou mark the Queen whose sway
Made men puppets in her play ?
Or the Light which failed on Saint Helena's Isle ?
Thou a wonderous tale can tell
If thou wilt but break the spell
Of thy silence—thou grim Watchman of the Nile.

Men come and go, and love and hate, and nations fall and rise,
While changeless stares that Thing of Fate from out the sunset skies.

Art thou heathen in thy birth ?
Did the gods send thee to earth ?
Did fair Hathor, Queen of Love, thy youth beguile ?
Art thou Horus, throned in light ?
Or Anubis, dog of night ?
Art a god—or demon, gloating o'er the Nile ?
Speak out, thou battered thing,
If one saving grace you bring,
Half man, half beast, and altogether vile !
Have done thy satyr's grin,
Thou embodiment of sin !
Thou hideous, baleful monster of the Nile !

As one who ponders mighty things the great unfathomed eyes
Change not: And Egypt's midnight brings new glories to her skies.

THE NILE was, to the ancient Egyptian, a deity. To it they looked for all good. Its rising and falling marked time to the foolish, as the heavens, to the wise. It brought blessings from its unknown source. It made the land, which without it was as a stone, leap with life and laugh with plenty. It was a god to be feared also and appeased. Its anger meant disaster, its withholding, famine. For ages the Egyptians were content to believe that its annual inundation was a mystery which it was not good for man to attempt to penetrate. It is now known that it is more than 3,000 miles in length, and that for half that distance (from the junction of the White and Blue Nile) it traverses an absolutely barren country, receiving only one tributary stream in all that distance, and loses by evaporation and by absorption in the thirsty soil along its course about one third its total volume. The annual floods come from the Blue (or muddy) Nile, as the result of the periodical rains which fall among the Abyssinian mountains. The river begins to swell about the first of June. In October it attains its highest level. In April and May it is at its lowest. The average rise and fall at Cairo is about 25 feet. A couple of feet more would bring disaster to vast fields of cotton on the delta. If much

Nile Boats.

less than usual it is equally damaging, because of the shortened supply of water on fields and crops requiring much. The depth of the deposit at Cairo is about 50 feet.

Rain is a rare phenomenon in Upper Egypt. Winter storms sometimes blow in from the Mediterranean and up beyond Cairo, but they amount to little, for the desert winds with their immense absorbing power soon gather the moisture and hold it. To one who has always in his mind associated only scorching and deadly winds with the sandy desert, it is curious to learn that instead, the wind is generally pleasantly cool and of delicious purity, impregnated with saline particles and possessed of remarkable health giving qualities. It is the regulator of climate over all Egypt. Without it the territory of the delta would be a malaria-breeding waste, uninhabitable because of its stagnant water and rank vegetation. The mean temperature of the delta is 58° Fahrenheit in winter and 83° in summer.

At the Nile bridge a forest of slender spars, like gigantic reeds, fringe the river's edge, and on them like creeping insects or white fluttering moths go the sailors. Here we go aboard the "Karnak," a steamboat with modern machinery, Turkish of decoration and furnishing, thoroughly Egyptian in management.

A Dahabeah.

A Sakieh. Our way lies up the river for about fifteen miles. The day is delightful. A strong wind blows down on us from the south and with it come many craft with picturesque lateen sails wide spread, some with unknown merchandise, some to the water's edge with masses of alfalfa, quite commonly two, lashed side by side. Here is a " dahabeah " flying the stars and stripes, doubtless chartered by some wealthy American for the cruise up the Nile. The " dahabeah " will accommodate a party of ten people and requires about an equal number, including cooks and sailors to manage it. It may be rented at a total cost of $800 to $1,000, covering all expenses, for the season and is the delightful way of doing Upper Egypt.

Here the current runs three miles an hour although the river falls but about seven inches to the mile. Shoals and low lying islands are along the way. The banks are low in places, over which the river flows, changing at will. At other places, high banks come close to the river's channel and hold it. The " shadoof " and the " sakieh " are common. The fellahin operating the first move like clockwork, the buffalo carries the sweep in endless rounds. At intervals the banks are broken by heavy gates that hold the water back, or allow it to escape as desired. Villages with square-built blocks of Nile mud among the groves of feathery palms are the homes of the fellahin.

" The Devil lives there " said the captain of the Karnak, pointing to a deserted looking pile of buildings on an island.

He was an intelligent man, sufficiently so at least to be captain of a Nile steamer, and although not above taking bakshish for little favors, was no doubt qualified for his position. I

A Water Gate.

looked enquiringly at him, thinking I had at last discovered an Oriental joke.

"The Devil lives there," he repeated, and I finally got his explanation, soberly given, that the owner of the place had died a number of years ago and the devil had moved in, as he always did on such occasions. I

A Mud Village of the Nile.

had wondered at the number of deserted buildings, and deserted parts of buildings of which other portions appeared in a prosperous condition, to be seen throughout the city. The explanation was given me later by an English resident. The Egyptian believes that when a death occurs in a family an evil spirit comes in and remains, and the family moves out if it is possible for them to do so, forsaking all.

We came to land against the west bank and were received with much enthusiasm by a delegation of natives and donkeys

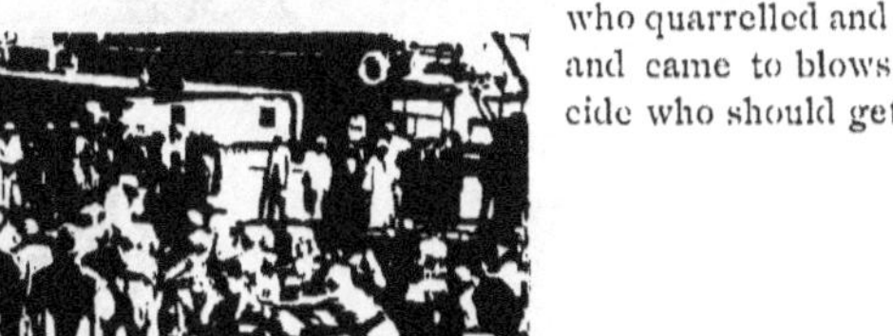

who quarrelled and brayed and came to blows to decide who should get us.

MEMPHIS AND SAKKÂRA.

ORDINARILY the man on the donkey has about as much to say in the management of the beast as might a bag of meal in a like position. There are bridle reins, sometimes a mere string, which you can hold, but the donkey never understands what you want him to do unless you hit him with a club—and the boy hangs on to that. There are magical words, also, which seem to affect him somewhat but you never get the combination. He either goes his own way or is thumped to the right or left by the runner who shouts continually. There is a saddle, round, and easy to sit on as a log, and stirrups also attached to the ends of a single strap which see-saws through a slot in the saddle, which same are a delusion and a snare, for when you bear down with one foot the other goes up and helps you off. I was fortunate. The party who got me was young and bright and a good runner, and the donkey was fast—an uncommon combination. I was glad to learn that the beast I bestrode was named "Yankee Doodle." It gave me a

feeling of security, of pride of country. I felt that I was once more under the protection of the starry flag.

"What is his name when the Englishman comes, oh Rameses?" I asked.

"Him Johney Bull then," said my man, soberly.

I do not think he saw anything funny in the situation. It was simply a matter of business with him.

Along the bank we skim with Rameses thumping Yankee Doodle; across the railroad, which seems so out of keeping with the scene, and over a broad irrigating canal to the village of Bedrashên, where Egyptian women are going with great stone water-jars filled and upright on their heads. The buildings are of sun-baked bricks, made of Nile mud and straw, undoubtedly such as the Children of Israel made in the days of Moses, hunting their own straw when it was found they were having too easy a time. Great, feathery date-palms stand among the buildings, and a high mud wall encloses the greater portion of the town, although what any one in his right senses could expect to find within worth stealing was beyond my comprehension. On the walls in many places hang flat, raft-like boats which are probably there for use in case of extreme high water. Natives in varying shades of dress and nudity watch us as we pass. They evidently have the instinct of the ostrich which pokes his head under a stone and believes he is out of sight.

109

Al Bedrashên.

More than one garment seems superfluity. One young creature is wreathed in smiles and a handkerchief. All are dirty. All want bakshish, men and tottering old women, children in arms—the babes stick out their little hand and say "'seh, 'seh."

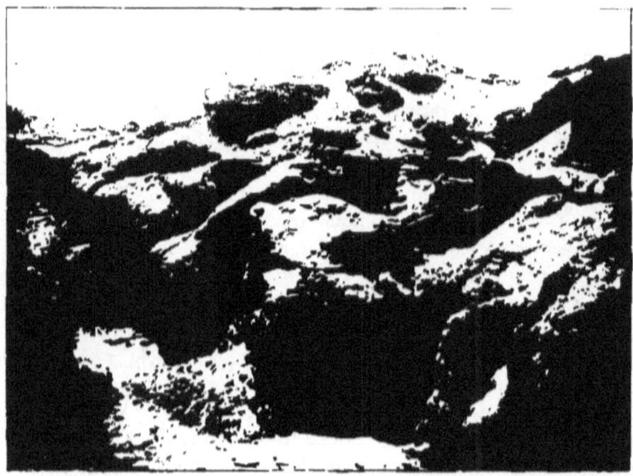

Ruins of Memphis.

Some of the houses are little better than mud kennels. They are indiscriminately packed with lounging men and women, fat-tailed sheep, insolent goats, children, befogged with swarming flies, and dogs kicking and scratching where the wicked flea pursueth. I could not help pitying the dogs.

Past Bedrashên we follow an embankment to a bit of rising ground which is the site of ancient Memphis. Memphis dates from the first Egyptian dynasty. Its glory was the wonder of all the world. Its destruction made its plunderers rich. From its ruins came the stones of mighty cities of a later date. Now no part remains to suggest its former magnificence save scattered fragments of marble and granite, mounds of broken pottery and earth and masses of buildings in lines and blocks of mud bricks, which were universally employed by the Egyptians in the construction of ordinary buildings and which in that rainless region are practically indestructible. The ancient boundaries are unknown. This island formed but a part. Menes, its founder, turned the Nile aside it is said to make room for the city. At the west the great necropolis of Sakkâra suggests the vastness of this old city of the living. Two colossal statues of Rameses II., which at one time stood in front of the great temple, are here still. They were not available for building purposes to the ancient plunderers and are too heavy to be stolen by the modern. Now a forest of palms covers the broken surface. Here the Arab spreads his tent

Statue of Rameses II.

through which the young goats charge in play, and here his black-robed women watch stolidly through the rift in their veils. The Arab's tent isn't much to brag of. It is of a kind that he can fold expeditiously and silently steal away. Stealing seems natural to him.

Beyond Memphis our way leads through broad flats which are under water from September to November. Here the plowman goes forth with the same kind of plow in use five thousand years ago. It is simply a long, heavy pole with a cross-piece of wood, shod with iron. It is usually drawn by oxen, while a fellah struggles with the heavy handle to keep it down. The Egyptian has been held up before a progressive

A Bedouin Encampment.

public as an example of dense ignorance because he has not adopted the Yankee plow. Just why he should adopt it I am in doubt. The old kind has stood the test of time. It breaks up the hard baked surface ; what more could a heavy Yankee plow do ? After the ground is broken they go along and smash the chunks with a club, or a sort of grubbing hoe, pulverizing enough to give the seed a fighting chance, then turn on the water and soon the place blossoms like the 17th day of March. The land is rich enough to stand reducing for some crops. I saw where sand had been brought from the desert and mixed with the broken soil in trenches in nursery ground where maize and beans, and what I took for lentels, were growing.

Egyptian Plowman.

Sakkâra is a mud town at the edge of the valley and not particularly attractive. The buildings are substantial enough but

At Sakkâra.

the odors which come out from them are not what I had been led to expect of the famed odors of Arabic —or perhaps it was a different breed of Arabs. Dignified lords of the soil stalk majestically past followed by women carrying loads on their heads. The owner of a well sits with his family beside his walled in preserve, dispensing, for

Her Lord and Master.

a minute consideration, the water to women who come and go

113

An Autocrat.

with earthen jars. In a grove of palms beyond, Bedouins are encamped. Climbing a hill of sand we are again on the edge of

Camel and Young.

the desert. All about are ruins, masses of broken pottery and sand. At the east, through the level valley, run embankments and irrigating ditches; west is a boundless, rolling sea of sand, unbroken save by crumbling pyramids, the greatest of which is the Step Pyramid, the oldest monument of antiquity known, dating from the third Dynasty.

This great necropolis has been

114

Step Pyramid.

for hundreds of years a mine from which priceless treasures of

Ruins at Sakkâra.

antiquity have been drawn. Here Marriette discovered the

tombs of the Apis, with their immense granite sarcophagi which once contained the remains of the sacred bulls. Here also is the mastaba of Ti, with its illustrations of the days of the fifth Dynasty, its paintings still fresh and bright. From lately discovered tombs come the rare jewelry of royalty. There are thousands of unnamed

Entrance to Mastaba of Ti.

tombs and not the least interesting is the burial place of the sacred cats. My last recollection in looking back over the great, silent city of the dead was of the one visible bit of life—a crippled beggar creeping across the sunlit sands.

Our exodus from Egypt did not present the difficulties which attended the going out of the Israelites. Some of the party returned to the ship at Alexandria; some, who desired to spend a longer time at Cairo, came later cross country  to Port Said, where the ship was to touch after landing its first contingent at Jaffa, and where, when it finally did return for them and started on its way out, it grounded on the muddy banks of the Suez Canal and remained fixed solidly until native stevedores lightened it by removal of a large part of its coal. Fortunately no harm was done except a trial of patience in those who were anxiously longing for the mecca of the pilgrimage—the shores of the Holy Land.

Latent Energy.

JOPPA.

Sunday, March 3d, '95.

MY first view of Palestine is of misty mountain ranges under the morning sun and a gleaming line of white marking the edge of the blue Mediterranean. As we near the shore, Jaffa—the Joppa of old—appears as a flattened dome, covered solidly with buildings, square sided and generally flat roofed. North and south as far as the eye can see stretch the bordering lines of sand, unbroken save for this hill on which the city stands. There is no harbor here save such as is afforded by a broken line of rocks, which stick up out of the water at intervals, like a row of ragged teeth, through which the waters charge and suck angrily. In the days when the gods and goddesses of mythology made earth their playground, Andromeda was chained to one of those rocks and left to be devoured by a great sea monster with a weakness for goddesses, but it so happened that Perseus, who had been out on a head-hunting expedition, came flying by and, just in the nick of time, descending, killed the monster and married the maid. It was from this port that Jonah took ship, and later was cast overboard to find harbor in the cabin of the whale where, according to general belief, he proved himself as unwelcome a

117

passenger as on shipboard, and after a somewhat tumultuous voyage was cast on land again near the spot from which he set out. To this port Hiram, King of Tyre, sent wood of the cedars of Lebanon in floats to be carried thence up to Jerusalem for the building of the temple.

When the sea runs high it is impossible to land. When comparatively quiet the native boat makes landing possible, the charge varying from one to five dollars, according as the native boatmen may be able to impress their victims with belief in the actual danger, or by threats of personal violence after they have started. The danger at times, however, is real, and Joppa has the unenviable fame of more lives lost in landing, or in going out to vessels, than at any other port in the world.

We anchored in the offing some little distance from shore and waited. The " Fürst Bismarck " (a sister voyager with a party who were making a somewhat similar trip as our own), which lay closer in shore than the place we had chosen, hoisted anchor and circled around us, plunging through the great waves like a mighty dolphin, to come to anchor again at a point much nearer shore than before. This broke the monotony of the long delay, which we understood was due to the high sea running at the time. Well on into the day boats put out from behind the line of rocks and, after a long time, are under our sides. We see as they approach that they are huge, clumsy looking craft, managed by muscular, dark skinned, barefooted men in Turkish jackets, or loose shirts and baggy bloomers. A noisy set they are, gesticulating wildly, shouting fiercely, apparently quarreling as to who shall first get the gang-way,

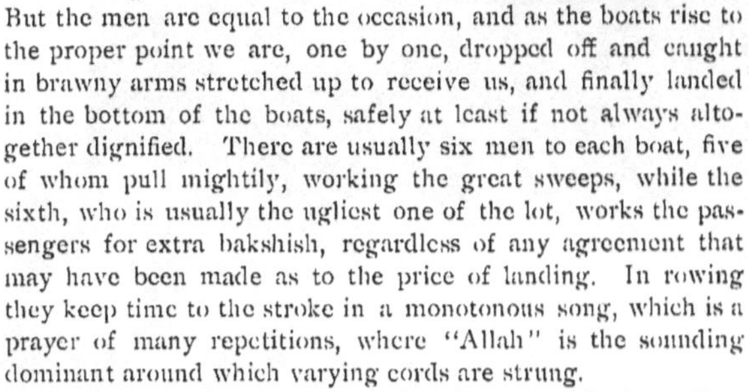

and threatening each other in a manner which seems to portend certain death to at least half the number. The heavy boats rise and fall on the waves that go sweeping past, at times far below, at others rising and threatening to brush away, as the flimsiest of straws, the stairs which hang on the ship's side. But the men are equal to the occasion, and as the boats rise to the proper point we are, one by one, dropped off and caught in brawny arms stretched up to receive us, and finally landed in the bottom of the boats, safely at least if not always altogether dignified. There are usually six men to each boat, five of whom pull mightily, working the great sweeps, while the sixth, who is usually the ugliest one of the lot, works the passengers for extra bakshish, regardless of any agreement that may have been made as to the price of landing. In rowing they keep time to the stroke in a monotonous song, which is a prayer of many repetitions, where "Allah" is the sounding dominant around which varying cords are strung.

Approaching the shore we take chances with the rollers which are breaking over the debatable ground between the deep sea and the beach, and where it is not uncommon for a boat to be caught on the crest of some breaking wave or, overtaken by a racing comber, have its crest come tumbling over inside, often thoroughly drenching its occupants and sometimes

The Sea at Jaffa.

filling and swamping the boat itself, so that loss of life is not uncommon. Our boatman made the most of the situation with varying success. In one the natives struck for bakshish and threatened to abandon the boat to the waves unless their demands were complied with. Arguments were in vain until a valiant knight from Pittsburg presented one in the form of a club, in such a convincing manner that the chief mutineer, after picking himself up from among the rubbish at the bottom of the boat, proceeded meekly—he and his followers—to pull for the shore. One boat caught the crest of a big roller on the turn, and came to land bringing about a ton of water in addition to a number of thoroughly drenched passengers. Most of the party, however, passed around the jutting rocks and landed in good form on a substantial stone quay, thankful to feel their feet once more on solid ground.

And the ground on which we stand!

What though the surroundings are not particularly pleasant to sight or smell? It is the "Holy Land," and that name means much, and much can be forgiven for what it has been. The narrow streets through which we go are filthy in the extreme, our way beset by aggressive natives suggestive of watchful jackalls besieging a straggling caravan, our welcome, nil; yet through all and over all is an abiding feeling of pitiful respect which one may entertain for genius in ruins ; a reverence for the land even though its sacred places are degraded and its temples become as dens of thieves, for even in its low estate we can not forget that here was enacted the great Drama of Earth, that it was the cradle of the purest religion the world has ever known and the home of that Perfect One whose coming changed the old dispensation, which was one of blood, to the newer one of love, and gave again with peculiar sweetness that perfect rule which is the foundation of all religions and may well be termed the "golden."

Jaffa was anciently a Phœnician colony in the land of the Philistines. It is scarce a third of a mile its longest way yet contains a population of over 23,000 people. The Hebrews called it "The Beautiful," but it is anything but beautiful at the present time, except from a distance. It has some good hotels, although the accommodations were not sufficient for all our party—particularly on the way out—which overflowed into various hospices and convents and stables and goat houses, where the conditions were anything but enjoyable, according to accounts given when the victims compared notes later on. Myself and friends were fortunate in securing rooms at the Grand Hotel Oriental, outside the city walls, which proved to be the best we had found anywhere in Palestine and altogether all that any reasonable person could ask.

The public with all its varying atoms is seen to best advantage in the market place of a morning, when it is filled with its jostling, noisy crowd to sell and to buy of the meats and poultry and eggs and vegetables and the fruit with which the surrounding country abounds.

The house of Simon, the tanner, is the one object of special traditionary interest in Jaffa. At the end of one of the zig-zag ways, which is characteristic of eastern towns, you are shown a low stone house, or rather a section of an irregular pile, as the

Market Place at Jaffa.

house where Simon lived. Through its cheerless, tomb-like hall, or main room, you go to an inner court, where is an ancient well and a great stone trough, said to be the tan-vat of old, under the spreading branches of a noble fig tree. From this court, stone stairs lead up to the roof where Peter slept and saw that vision of the sheet let down from heaven, by which he was given to understand that salvation was not for the Jew alone but for all peoples. The walls of the old house have the appearance of great age and may have been standing in the days of Peter. The fact that all buildings in Palestine look old after a few years is not to be held against claims of antiquity generally; and although the town was practically wiped out of existence in the 12th century, there is no positive evidence to show that it was *not* the house of Simon the tanner.

Here, and everywhere else in Palestine, you must not be too exacting or scan too closely the evidence offered. More evidence can be furnished or concentrated if required. There seems to be much valuable evidence going to waste, for there are few important events of bible history that have not occurred in at least two or three well established places, while sacred

relics have multiplied to an extent that the widow's cruse of oil appears a very common affair indeed. And why should *I* seek to know whether the crude, angular facts must of necessity fit accurately into

The House of Simon the Tanner.

the artistically rounded creation which points a beautiful story, or question things whose chief office is to illustrate great truths? The thing itself is but the visible figure in an object lesson and for the one who questions, hundreds accept and are made better thereby. It is true the food may be served at times by unclean hands and the vessels may not be the sacred things they are claimed to be, but the food satisfies the hungry and the most skeptical can but believe that in the fifteen thousand pilgrims who annually pass this way there are very few who are not profited when by sight and touch they have been made to feel the reality of what before was but belief in things unseen. Of course you are at liberty to rip up your toy balloon to see how the wind looks if you want to, because it is yours, but do not insist that others shall do likewise. I must confess there were times when I wished they would let up a little; when faith in things religious stood sadly in need of a holiday. Possibly an interrogation point may at times slip into chapters that follow, but as a rule I shall tell of things as I found them and leave you to settle the questions of belief. It is the easier way. It is not the lack of evidence but the multiplicity of it that troubles one. I *did* have some doubts about that story of Jonah, but seeing is believing, and when you are shown the very bones of the whale that was associated with the prophet in the transaction what more can you ask? The evidence is as complete and as convincing as ever went with any fish story ever told.

Around Jaffa are orange groves where the trees stand thickly shoulder to shoulder and the golden fruit hangs heavy in the shade. Around the groves run walls of stone, or impenetrable hedges of giant cacti, or rows of lemon trees with interlacing thorn. Sweet lemons are common and the oranges which the natives brought to us were the most delicious I ever tasted. You may get them almost at your own price, the common charge being two piastres (8 cents) a dozen, including the basket of plaited reeds in which they are carried.

Inland from the coast stretches a wide plain covered with vineyards and fields of grain. It is under a high state of cultivation and very productive, suggestive of the valley of the Nile. There are no fences, but stones are set at intervals to mark boundaries. Irrigating ditches run through it, cutting it into narrow sections and lines.

"All aboard for Jerusalem." That isn't what they said— those numerous semi-conductors at Jaffa, as darkness came on, but—that's what it amounted to.

A railroad to Jerusalem! A locomotive screeching under the walls of the Sacred City! The country did not feel the need of a railroad! The people did not want it. It disturbed established customs, and the East does not like to be disturbed, but it has come at last. One hardly knows whether to be pleased or sorry. The coaches are hardly equal to third class in England or France, but we make the best of it all as a diversion, and after we have been packed closely into the narrow, uncomfortable seats and investigated and counted a number of times by various officials, we are finally allowed to get under way.

And thus we move out across the plain, between the terraced hills, and up the mountains—singing as we go the worshipful songs of Zion, familiar wherever the English tongue is known—to Jerusalem, the city of the Great King, toward which all christendom turns with reverential heart.

125

The Transfiguration.
Raffaelle's Masterpiece, now in the Vatican

JERUSALEM.

JERUSALEM! Holy city of Zion! Witness of the incon-
ceivable glory of the coming of the Son of Man and of
the heavens opened—to thee the great heart of Christendom turns.

Though the beautiful fountain be broken and thy great truths
buried deep under the rubbish of formalism, yet out of thee
came Earth's supremest good, and because of thy great past a
worshipful world will ever yield thee reverence.

As I expected to find it?

Yes—externally. When its frowning battlements first appeared under the star-bright skies, I knew it at once. When
the morning sun revealed its towers and domes it seemed like
coming back to well-remembered places. I had looked upon
its gray walls and massive gateways many times before through
the medium of paintings and engravings and in pictures printed
by the sun on the sensitive film, multiplied until every outline
was as familiar as the forms about my own home. But there
is something lacking. The atmosphere is intensely religious
yet does not impress you as such. You have—perhaps, unconsciously—associated in your mind the golden streets and a
new Jerusalem. Here you find all the perceptive senses of-

fended by that which you see in the streets of this earthly Jerusalem. It is unlovely in its decay; out of harmony where attempts are being made to restore or shore up ancient works with smart surroundings, or ridiculous in arrogant piles erected to cover insignificant objects of doubtful authenticity.

On every side are names familiar in bible history, and figures commemorating events of transcendent importance in the great plan of human salvation, about which you have ever thought with only reverence, yet here presented flippantly, or with ostentatious display as the case may be, but always so obviously for a price, that but very little reverence remains. Your ideal is so shattered before this, which they tell you is the real, that if you are not already disgusted with the spiritual shams it becomes at times simply amusing. There is so much rubbish; traditions materialized to supply a want; sacred relics reduplicated and multiplied to meet the needs of rival factions, and events which you had always supposed occurred at widely separated points grouped, often under a single roof for convenience of display, that at times it comes to you with a started sense of wonder that *these* are the things which of old you dreamed about under the same name but pictured so differently. You feel the hollow mockery of the display made for your benefit as of a bait to catch gudgeons. It is religion gone to seed. It is, literally, a "Holy Show." The empty husks are flaunted furiously in your face, and whether you believe or not, is a matter which seems to interest the performers not at all so long as you pay liberally for the entertainment.

And yet in all this mass of husks are kernels of precious grain. Through the tawdry tinsel of the stage settings are suggestions of the mighty tragedy. We may not say, *here* is

the spot where He rested; *here* He healed the sick; *here* He
gave sight to the blind; but we believe that somewhere among
these Judean hills all these wonderful things did happen.   The
mountains round about saw the glory of the transfiguration,
and from some one of them He ascended unto the Father.   If,
in passing, I may seem lacking in reverence, believe that it is
not for the sacred thing commemorated but for the rubbish under which it is buried.   Those who are charged with the duty
of exemplifying the great truth here, too often give good reason
for the contempt with which the name of Christian is regarded
by Jew and Mohammedan alike.   But then Jew and Mohammedan alike, while possessed of certain notable virtues peculiar
to each, are themselves open to charges which seem to average
them up—or down, whichever is the better term—to the average of the Christian faith as displayed here.   Each claim virtues
of which they make the most, and the virtue of one class is
sometimes held as sin with another, while the unclassified little
peccadilloes of each don't count at all.   The truth seems to be
that religions, like individuals, are not altogether good or absolutely bad.   The proof that saving virtue is in all is in the fact
that they exist.   The impression given by the surface against
which we rub is not the exact truth.

The dry leaves rattle noisily in the wind, the fruit ripens
silently.   We see what we call evil, and judge the actors un-
sparingly, wondering at their blindness.   And the most astound-
ing part of it after all is, that when we explain to them where-
in they are wrong they simply laugh at us—even Us—when
anyone with average common sense can see that we are always
right.

That you lose all reverence for the alleged sacred places is

129

to be expected. You go about as you might in a museum, your feeling that of curiosity mostly, wondering in a tired sort of way what new surprise the keepers are preparing to spring upon you; and such is your adaptability to environment that even this becomes wearisome in time and gives place to that stronger one relating to animal comfort and personal interest —the ignoble one as to what you shall eat and drink. On my return, a friend, filled with ideals of the Great Story, asked with upturned eyes and reverential thoughts, concerning the sentiments that filled my soul when I walked about the sacred streets.

"Can you," she asked, "recall the great, absorbing sensation of the hour?" And I answered—

"Hunger!"

It was the literal truth, but I shall never forget the look of shocked incredulity when I broke the hushed, expectant silence to reply.

The stars were gleaming frostily when the train came to a stop at the station that Sabbath night when we came up from Joppa to the City. Over beyond the valley of Hinnom rise the walls of Jerusalem. The open space outside the station door is filled with cranky vehicles, shifty horses, and howling madmen. Bedlam let loose would seem a restful silence compared with the din of the mob that assaulted us in a senseless rush and struggle for our bodies, even though every carriage was filled almost before it could be brought into position and many were obliged to wait for their return. It is the way of the country. Without noise nothing is done there that is done—publicly.

The members of the party were parcelled out among the

various hotels and hospices in and about the city; a large contingent being assigned to the "Sisters of the Rose." The name was delightfully suggestive of sweet and fragrant comforts but it developed that the blooming Sisters had little to do with it, so far as we were concerned; they furnished the quarters (a new convent building outside the city walls) while we became subjects of the contract system, in which an enterprising Syrian Yankee leased the plant and put us up for so much per head.

And what a cheerless place it was! The chill of the tomb was about its halls and great rooms when we reached them. There were no fires, and no visible provision for such, outside the kitchen. A glimmer of joy touched us, however, when it was announced on our arrival that dinner would be served in the refectory. Dinner at midnight in a Convent! Visions of jolly old monks; of mighty roasts; of toothsome dainties; of great steaming bowls of fragrant brew; of frothing tankards; (N. B.—the frothing tankards don't cut the least figure with the writer, but it sounds mediæval and appropriate) rose before our imagination. Then we gathered, sixty strong, at the table in a long, narrow, whitewashed dungeon where wildly excited Arabs spattered thin soup over us and shouted, and jostled each other in haste to serve with things we did not want, or united in burying us under duplicate dishes when one of them happened by chance to hit upon what we *did* want. But it was all done with such an eager, transparent effort to gain recognition which should eventually lead to bakshish that we could not help taking kindly to them and life became bearable at last.

A big room with concrete floor, stone walls, whitewashed and with vaulted stone ceiling, windows iron-grated, with

white curtains but guiltless of blinds, sections partitioned off
by curtains strung on wires a little higher than your head—such
are our sleeping apartments. Within each curtained area is
an iron bedstead (suggestive of a steel trap that may shut up
on you at any unexpected moment and nip off projecting portions of your anatomy in its sharp jaws), with coarse mattress
and coarse sheets, and quilts with a habit of sliding off over the
side like a stiff cascade, or of creeping up over your head, leaving
your feet exposed. There is a small section of rug on which
you are supposed to place your feet when you dismount (but
which usually isn't where you suppose it to be, and you find
your feet on the cold floor), a chair, and a tin, or iron basin
and pitcher on a wabbly wire stand (which shows a tendency to
creep around spider-like on its springy legs in a most unac-
countable manner) is the sum total of furniture. Anything in
shape of a mirror is too frivolous to be thought of for a moment. If soap is considered a necessity you must provide it
for yourself. Your candle is charged extra in the bill. This
is a fair inventory of the comforts of the ordinary hospice.
Clean? Spotlessly so—to an agonizing extent; the whitewash
comes off on your clothes if you look at it. The virtue of
cleanliness is suggestive of that early puritanism which warned
you to distrust anything that seemed pleasant. You do sometimes long for a little comfort, even if a moderate amount of
healthy dirt comes with it. The hospice is a semi-religious
institution usually connected with a convent or monastery, and
established originally by the various orders for the entertainment of pilgrims of their own faith, but now generally open .to
any who may care to ask their hospitality. They make no attempt to gain patronage—offer no special inducements. You

are made welcome if you ask. Nominally it is all free. On leaving, however, you are expected to contribute according to your means, usually at about the rate of five francs per day. The hotels are more pretentious and are run for revenue only, charging at the rate of from eight to twenty francs per day. The best are cold and comfortless compared with European or American houses. There is a fortune awaiting some enterprising Yankee who shall first establish a first-class hotel at Jerusalem and run it on American or English lines.

Custom has decreed that breakfast shall be what the name is in two syllables, and is taken as it may be caught, with little regard for time or forms. It consists usually of coffee and rolls. The coffee is brought on in a tin pot, with a long handle and a long spout coming from its sides at right angles with each other. A similar pot containing hot goat's milk is brought in at the same time, and out of each in turn the servant pours coffee and milk into your cup in proportion to your liking—usually with an arm over each of your shoulders. The roll of the East is suggestive of an ostrich egg. If you succeed in breaking the shell you will usually find a sweet and palatable kernel within. Butter is made from the milk of the goat—"black sheep" they will tell you—and although not regularly served at breakfast, can be had if wanted. It comes to the table in shape like the rolled shaving that curls from the joiner's plane. It is served fresh daily, and is fresh in that other sense, that it contains no salt. I was quite happy in its use until I saw one day a woman sitting on a door-sill, rocking the distended skin of a goat backward and forward on her knee, while some liquid contained within could be heard slopping and chucking about. When I was told that this was the native churn my longing for native butter vanished and came not back for three days. Eggs may be had on order for breakfast, but are usually charged as extras. Luncheon at noon is breakfast with the addition of cold meats, fruit and eggs. Dinner, which occurs at the close of the day, is a very serious function. Its rules are as fixed as the laws of the Medes and Persians—whatever they may have been. At hotel, hospice, or in the desert where the tent of the princely dragoman is spread but for a night, the forms of serving are conscientiously observed, and rules are broken by guests at the risk of losing caste even among those who serve. Dinner invariably begins with a soup, followed by some kind of a stew, which is the soup grown thicker, and this in turn by the roast, in which is revealed the parent stock from which soup and stew in common sprang. It is usually mutton. Vegetables of the kind that grow above ground are sufficient;

A Goat-Skin Churn.

those which grow below not so common. A pudding of some unknown nature appears toward the close of the repast, and stewed prunes, figs, dates, raisins, etc., followed by oranges, nuts, and coffee *ad lib*. They also have something which they serve under the name of tea, but—

The houses of Jerusalem are universally of stone, with low domes, or flat roofs supported by an inner arch. Flowerpots and troughs are built into the roofs for the reception of flowers and plants, and even quite large trees are sometimes grown on these upper gardens. Frost and snow are not uncommon, yet but few dwellings have chimneys and little provision is made for heating other than by means of charcoal braziers, which are carried into the houses, the smoke escaping through doors and windows. The average temperature is sixty-three Fahrenheit,

rising to about seventy-six in August and falling to forty-eight
in January. There are no living springs on this high land.
The water which falls on roofs and open spaces is preserved in
private cisterns on the ground or in the larger ones of the city.

The native people of Jerusalem are picturesque in their varying dress, which preserves its individuality among the different
classes. From the wealthy Syrian in his silken robes to the
Fellah with his single, coarse, bag-like garment which he hangs
over his shoulders or wraps about him, the fashion is believed
to be practically the same as in the time of Christ. Here comes
a stately Arab with patrician face and garments of the coarsest
material, but worn with the air of royalty; here a son of Ham
with raiment no more coarse perhaps, but his air is of the dregs.
Here is a camel driver from over the desert perhaps, with naked
legs, but thickly swathed head and coat of sheepskin worn with
the wool inside, equally efficacious in keeping out the frost that
nips or the sun that burns. Here beside the Bedouin's tent are
black-gowned women, half-clothed children, meditative camels
and impertinent goats. Here a group which may be one family
or a half dozen, where old and young, content with the goods
vouchsafed to them so long as they are not over hungry or uncomfortably cold, lie or sit sleeping in the hot sun. Clothing is

not essential to their happiness; it seems
to be considered purely in its utilitarian
sense, for the youth of the native species
burrow in the hot sand, or flit about in the
sunshine as innocent of covering as that
first pair before they had tasted of the for-
bidden fruit. Here come a number of
Moslem women, gorgeous in silks out-

135

*Moslem Women
in Street Costume.*

wardly, with faces covered by veils of some gauzy material through which run sprays of overwork effectually hiding the features that are underneath. Here is a Syrian woman all in white except her low slippers and variegated veil, her costume suggestive of her coming temporarily out of bed and neglecting to leave the bed clothes behind. The sheets are held by two pins. I *may* be mistaken about the number of pins but the sheets are a visible certainty. Here is a woman undoubtedly in the lower walks, for the single garment she wears is more substantial than elegant, and on her back, supported by a rope which passes over her head, she brings a goatskin of water from some distant pool. Girls may be seen carrying water jars balanced on

*A
Syrian
Woman
and
Child.*

their heads along the country ways, as comely, no doubt, as were the maidens in the days when that early green-goods operator unloaded his passé daughter on Jacob, who had worked seven years for the blooming Rachel, only to find that he must give another seven if he got the prize. But then Jacob got even with the old man in the variegated cattle trade later on, and honors were easy.

*A
Goat-Skin
Water Bottle.*

Here comes a dignitary of some kind, clothed in purple and fine linen and riding on an ass. The supercilious air with which he favors us makes it quite necessary that he should be preserved as one of the picturesque features of the land; later I find that my kodak holds the Greek Patriarch of Jerusa-

136

lem, who is a very important personage indeed, with authority

extending over the larger part of Palestine. And I have him attended by his kavass, who trots meekly along behind, carrying his master's official staff of office. Over the dusty roads to the city come herdsmen with their flocks. By the wayside are the blind beggars, their sightless eyes lifted to the sun, beseeching pitifully for alms; their plaintive cry as the stranger approaches is "bakshish, bakshish, oh Howadji, bakshish!"

The lepers sit in the blazing sun at Gethsemane, their faces like the dead or horrible with the red ravages of the disease. They hold out twisted and fingerless hands and misshapen stumps of legs, or display festering sores, to excite commiseration, until, in very horror of it, you drop your money into their pails and get away from the sight of such hopeless misery. Not the least of the sickening feeling you have is in the belief that they take pride in the

137

Blind Beggars.

Lepers at Gethsemane.

ghastly distinction of their repulsiveness, which is their stock in trade, and are working you for all there is in it. There are about fifty lepers about Jerusalem. The lepers' hospital is open to them, but some prefer the freedom of this beggar's life. It is claimed here that, contrary to general belief, the disease is not infectious, but hereditary only. It does not show itself in early life, and children are born to them doomed from the beginning to this loathsome disease. There seems to be no law restraining or denying them the privileges of the road. It is even possible that the powers that be do not look with ill-favor on their presence in certain quarters, because they are characteristic features of the country, and the stranger who spends his money in traveling about the country to see its features would be disappointed if he failed to find the leper sitting by the Garden of Gethsemane.

Jerusalem is on the heights of the mountain ridge which extends nearly north and south through Judea, inland from the Mediterranean a little more than thirty miles, and about 2,500 feet above its surface. The distance by rail from Jaffa is given as fifty-four miles; the time about three and one-half hours. The fare is 70 piastres "medjidie," first class (about $3.00 of United States money); second class, 25 piastres.

The walls of the city enclose an area of a little more than half a square mile, varying in height, externally, from twenty-five to seventy or more feet. There are seven gates, the most important of which are the Jaffa Gate on the west, the Damascus Gate on the north and St. Stephen's Gate on the east. The Jaffa Gate is the most important gate of the city. Around it, outside and in, is carried on the principal commercial business of the city. At the east and north are the principal hotels,

JERUSALEM FROM

*1. Armenian quarters, S. E. corner of city wall.   2. Tower of David and Damascus Gate.   3.
7. St. Stephen's Gate.   8. New Golgotha.*

MOUNT OF OLIVES.

Omar.   4. Golden Gate.   5. Church of the Holy Sepulchre.   6. Northwest corner of city wall.
torks' Tower at Northeast corner of city wall.

Jaffa Gate.

consulates, and hospitals, this newer city covering more ground than the older one within the walls. Many of the buildings are modern and of considerable importance although not generally of much beauty of architecture. They are mostly of the creamy white, or gray, limestone taken from the foundation on which they are erected.

For figures given thanks are due to "*Baedcker*," which is almost indispensable to the tourist, and good reading also for the student who may not feel able to absorb the whole ocean of literature with which the Holy Land is flooded. You may feel that in attempting to be impartial the book leans somewhat obliquely toward the Man in Possession, but that is a matter of opinion. From it we learn that Jerusalem has a population of 42,000 to 43,000. About three-quarters (30,000) are Jews, 7,500 Mohammedans, 4,000 Orthodox Greeks, 2,000 Latins, 500 Armenians, 300 Protestants, 100 Copts, and a few Ethiopians and Syrians. The Jews are steadily increasing in number and all are imbued with the belief that time shall again see their race established in its glory in the Holy City. Many are self-supporting. Others, who have been subject to persecutions elsewhere, undoubtedly come that they may be subjects of the benefactions of wealthy Israelites who have done so much for the chosen people, of whom Baron Rothschilds is the most notable example.

The various elements do not blend.   The city is separated by its principal streets severally into the Jewish, Moslem, Christian and Armenian quarters, and each section is occupied almost exclusively by the followers of the faiths named.

The principal streets run to the cardinal points of the compass, sub-dividing the whole into irregular blocks, which are penetrated by narrow ways twisting and turning deviously and ending usually in blind alleys.   These principal streets are but narrow alleys, arched over in many places to form tunnels, the steeper slopes laid with stone steps, often undergoing repairs which never seem completed, miserably paved, and dirty in the extreme.   Through these streets go throngs of men, numerous little donkeys carrying burdens, occasionally camels and women, never a wheeled vehicle.

Native stores are niches in the walls, the stock in trade often seeming not to warrant even the small space devoted to it. Here is a dealer in tobacco, with bladders of snuff hung temptingly in festoons along the front.   The seller of snails sits on the pavement with his basket of slimy goods audibly protesting. The dealer in cuttlefish is there, his hands black as the inky dainties he is weighing out.   Dried octopus—the devil-fish of romance—with his parrot beak, staring eyes, and long suckercovered tenticles bound in a bunch, is displayed, as are various other unrecognizable things, smoked, dried and pickled.   There are plenty of fruits, but vegetables do not look tempting. Fresh meat is mostly limited to mutton of the fat-tailed variety, with possibly a goat, or section of a camel for a change.   Beef is hardly known; eggs are plentiful and a staple food.

Ordinarily you are expected to make your own change with dealers for small articles you may desire to purchase.   To supply this demand the money-changer exists. You will find him seated in the market-place, in the busy streets, in the court of the temple, with his case containing various coins before him, protected from the quick, ever-ready hand of the passing native by a wire screen, ready to change your gold or silver into the smaller coins of the realm, for a percentage. With you the exchange is a matter of faith. Your native guide is apt to take a hand, and somehow you have a well-grounded suspicion that between your man and the money-changer exists a good understanding as to a division of spoils.

The question of money values in Syria is one that daunts the bravest soul. Few are able to master its mysteries. The French franc, with its established value of twenty cents, is the only piece where you and the native agree, the only firm ground on which—as an American citizen neatly put it, the tottering intellect of the victim can rest the sole of its fut—when you try to grasp the financial problem involved in negotiations for an olive wood knife or a string of beads. The prices of small articles are given generally in piastres; still smaller things in "paras"; the larger in francs, in piastres "medjidie," and in piastres plain. The commercial value of a para is about the tenth part of a cent; forty paras are equal to a piastre, which is four cents. They tell you a thing is worth so many piastres, and if you don't look startled they will say "medjidie," and this means about ten per cent. more than if they had not added that little word which strikes you as a meaningless ejaculation. The government has one rate of exchange, trade another. A

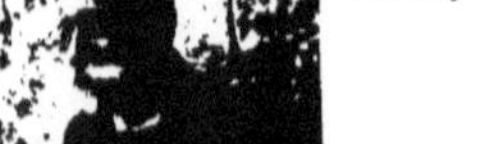

piastre "sagh" is about 2 *d.*; a piastre "shuruk" is 1¾ *d.* English and French money goes; American, "nit." Local

144

*The
Money
Changer.*

coins have variable values in different parts of Syria. A current coin of some cities will not be accepted at any price in other cities. Some of the younger members of the party claimed that they had mastered the problem of Syrian coin (after they were outside the borders of Syria), and glibly rattled off various aspirates and arrested gutterals having a somewhat familiar sound, but it was noticed that they invariably became thoughtful when they had done and were objects of regretful regard among their relations for some time thereafter.

From St. Stephen's Gate westward through the city leads the Via Dolorosa, "the Street of Pain," commemorating the journey of the Saviour from Pilate's judgment hall to Calvary. It is a crooked way, leading under arches and through dark tunnels. Along it at intervals, and at its end, are the fourteen stations commemorative of events of that woeful journey. The Ecce Homo Arch, thrown like a flying buttress across the street, marks its beginning where Pilate said "*Behold the man.*" Tablets set into the walls mark the stations of the journey, and indicate points of interest. We pass the place of the poor man Lazarus, and later, the house of Dives. The fact that Jerusalem has been several times destroyed since Dives went to his reward is not allowed to seriously interfere with the dwelling. These things all seem to have the rejuvenating characteristic of Truth crushed to earth and Banquo's ghost combined. The fifth station marks the spot where Simon of Cyrene took upon himself the cross. A little farther along is a stone let in the wall, showing a depression in its surface, where, it is said, the hand of Christ rested. Now, it is

145

*House
of
Dives.*

Church of the Holy Sepulchre.

worn smooth by the lips of countless pilgrims who have gone that way. At the seventh station He passed through the wall of the old town out to Golgotha, now covered by the church of the Holy Sepulchre, within which are found the last five stations.

The Church of the Holy Sepulchre dates from the days of the Crusaders, although changed in some respects at various times since, to suit the ideas of its custodians. It is owned and occupied in varying degrees of harmony by the Greeks, Latins, Armenians and Copts, but is under the general guardianship of Turkish soldiers who, as disinterested parties, are stationed there to preserve order between the Christians. Among the religious branches the Greeks are the most powerful and are most in evidence.

The quadrangle outside the entrance is often lined with dealers in curios and sacred relics and pictures of a religious character, with carvings of the Holy Family, of Marys, and of Christs on the cross, and with rosaries of olive stones, and olive wood, and ebony, and porcelain, and mother of pearl.

Within, you find an awe-inspiring gloom, a confused massing of objects, gathered without seeming order or unity of design. Here are chapels of the various creeds; jewel-decked altars with lights burning and censers swinging, with priests intoning, acolytes chanting, and worshipers kneeling devoutly telling their beads. Lines of hushed pilgrims move softly past, bearing wax tapers in their hands to light their way; now disappearing into some cavernous recess, now like apparitions coming from out the dusky void, while at intervals voices of singers roll through the echoing dome and die away into a silence which seems almost painful. It is a weird picture of mystery, changeful as a dream and not soon forgotten. Under this one

The Angel's Chapel and Entrance to the Sepulchre.

roof are grouped the symbols of that mightiest of tragedies! The mind can not grasp the wonder of it at first! Here, within the sound of a human whisper, you behold the Creation and the consummation of the Divine plan of salvation. It is Alpha and Omega. It is The Tragedy itself.

Here is shown the traditional prison of Christ; here the place where He was nailed to the cross; here where it bore Him on its cruel arms, and here, the cleft in the rock, split asunder in the darkness of that terrible day. Here stood the Roman soldier who thrust his spear into the Saviour's side; here is the place where they cast lots for His garments and here the stone on which His body was anointed for the tomb—and around it, gather pilgrims, kneeling and weeping.

The Holy Sepulchre is within a marble pavilion, rich with sculpture, under the great dome. The entrance is through the Angel's Chapel, in the centre of which stands a great square urn containing a section of the stone which was rolled away from the mouth of the tomb on the morning of the resurrection. The opening is narrow and you must stoop to enter. The space within is six and a half feet long and six feet wide, but a portion of this width is taken up by the stone on which the body lay, now covered over with marble. From the high ceiling are suspended 43 lamps, kept constantly burning, except on Easter, when they are extinguished, to be lighted again by fire miraculously sent down from above. Thirteen each of these lamps belong to the Greeks, the Latins, and the Armenians, respectively, and four to the Copts.

The authority on which rests the most convincing knowledge of this sacred spot is Helena, mother of Constantine, who, prompted by a divine vision, made a pilgrimage here, and in

response to prayer was miraculously shown the place of the tomb and a portion of the true cross. Coming down to later days, I was permitted to examine the cross and spurs of the great crusader, Godfrey de Bouillon, and to hold in my hand, for a consideration, the great two-handed sword with which he wrought such knightly havoc. I have not even named all objects of interest. It may be worth mentioning, incidentally, that here was originally the garden of Eden. The tomb of the elder Adam is also shown, and a plate let into the floor indicates the centre of the earth and the spot from which the Creator took of the dust of the earth out of which he created man in his own image.

In past days riots have occurred here among the fanatics, jealous of their faith and burning with a zeal hardly in keeping with their professions. On Easter nights, when the miraculous fire descends into the chapel of the Sepulchre and is passed out through small openings by the attendant priests, the waiting multitude fills the edifice almost to suffocation. Large sums have been paid to the church for the first fire that issues, and a mad rush is made to get it when it appears. The most disastrous event in the history of these riots occurred in 1834, when the Turkish guard fired on the struggling mass. In the panic which ensued three hundred people were either killed outright, or were suffocated, or trampled to death. Even now mistaken zeal often leads to scenes at which all the good of all the churches protest. And there is no doubt also that the wily Mussulman welcomes such as a diversion in which he shines by comparison, and makes much of the occasion when opportunity offers.

The Mosque of Omar stands on ground of absorbing interest to distinct classes of people. To the Mussulman it is second to no spot on earth short of Mecca, as having witnessed some of the most marvelous events in the life of the mighty Prophet. To the Jew the glory of the Great King was here displayed in the wonderful Temple, and here dwelt that Supreme Presence whose name even it was sacrilege to speak, and here in coming time the Chosen People shall be called again to great power, where, until that day, no Israelite may go, lest peradventure he step with unsanctified foot upon the Holy of Holies. To members of the Mystic Brotherhood, Mount Moriah and the Temple are associated with the Great Tragedy which to them pictures the earthly life, and teaches its lessons in beautiful symbolic ceremonies. Within the grounds you must submit to the leadership of some one of the Moslem custodians, however competent your own guide may be. You usually see a Turkish officer or two, and the courte-

sies shown you depend somewhat on the manner in which you see him.

The Mosque of Omar is eight sided. From the guide we learn that each of the eight sides is 66 feet 7 inches in length, and that the dome rises 99 feet above the floor. The date of its construction can not be known. It seems to have been a growth, commemorating that greater Temple of old, and assuming something of its present form somewhere about the tenth century. It did not impress me as perhaps I ought to have been impressed. The appearance of decay and general bracing up; its naturally handsome features constantly in need of repair, and a general air of half thorough restoration going on all the time, detracted from its beauty and dignity. Its eight walls are covered with marble to the height of the window sills. Between the windows and above and around the great drum are porcelain tiles, through

the general blue of which run bands of Koranic inscriptions.
The dome is covered with lead. The interior is indescribable.
The roof and dome are supported by concentric lines of beautiful columns, surrounding the sacred rock which is in the centre.
The walls and ceilings are covered with mosaics, in which
flowers form a large part. The floors are of mosaic. There
are marble, and bronze, and copper, and silver, and gold, and
with all its magnificence it is dark and gloomy.

The portion of the sacred rock that is exposed measures
about 50x60 feet. It is not improbable that the great sacri-
ficial altar stood here. A channel in the surface, believed to
have been made for carrying off the blood of the victims, is
shown. According to tradition this is the spot where Abraham
prepared to offer up his son Isaac, an act which is presented as
illustrative of great and beautiful faith, but I sometimes wonder if the old man would have been so ready to obey had the
command been for him to stick the knife into himself instead
of his helpless boy! In these times he would have been put
into a straight jacket, or set to breaking stones for the state—
but then they did things differently in those days.

Underneath the rock is a cavern where David, Solomon,
Abraham, and Elijah, prayed. Mohammed said that one prayer
here was better than a thousand elsewhere. From this cavern
he started heavenward, possibly forgetful of the rock which
formed the roof. When he struck the rock, it started to go
with him, but its course was arrested by the angel Gabriel, who
placed his hand upon it, and you are shown a deep indentation
in the under surface where the prophet's head came in contact
with the stone, which, unable to accompany him, opened and let
him through. It now, according to the Moslem belief, hangs

The Dome of the Rock.

miraculously suspended in mid-air where the angel stopped its
upward course, although to ordinary eyes it seems anchored
firmly enough on a substantial wall. Underneath this cavern
is the "Well of Souls," where all the dead come twice a week
to pray. You are not permitted to intrude on their privacy,
but the attendant raps on the floor, which gives forth a hollow
sound, and satisfies you that it is there all right enough.

We are permitted to see the slab of jasper in which Mahomet
drove nineteen golden nails, one of which was to fall out at the
end of each succeeding epoch, and when the last falls out the
day of judgment will come. One day the devil succeeded in
stealing all but three and a half of the nails, but was detected
and sent about his business by the angel Gabriel, who again,
fortunately, turned up just in the nick of time. It has now

been discovered that contributions by visitors has a tendency to fix the nails more firmly in place, and also that the contributor has years added to his own life according to the amount of his donation. We each of us secured a few. We saw the place where Solomon stretched a chain, which a truthful witness could grasp without producing any effect but which, when touched by an untruthful witness, would lose a link. It had evidently been touched too often. To keep a chain like that in repair under the present management would make an ordinary blacksmith very tired. Not the least interesting of many curious things, as showing human desire to know futurity, are the two columns standing quite close to each other in the Mosque El Aksa, which has the miraculous quality of separating, so that those who have gained a right to paradise may pass through between, and of squeezing those who attempt it, who have not yet earned that right. In proof that a great many are to be blessed are the inner surfaces of the two columns, worn away to an extent by the passage of unnumbered bodies that threatened their total destruction, and it was found necessary to stop further attempts with iron bars.

In the city wall east of the Mosque of Omar is the Golden Gate—the "Gate Beautiful,"—where, according to tradition, the lame man was healed, and through which Christ came on his triumphant entry into the city. It is now closed with solid masonry, to be opened again only when He shall come again in His glory. Near the Golden Gate a round column, laid horizontally across near the top of the wall and projecting outward something like six feet, indicates the spot from which in the day of judgment a wire will be stretched across to the Mount of Olives, over which all the dead must pass, while Mohammed sits on the mountain and Christ on the wall, to judge them. The righteous will pass over without difficulty, the wicked will fall and perish.

The wailing place of the Jews is against the great enclosing wall, cityward from the Mosque of Omar. Within the temple area the faithful do not go, lest  they tread on the holy place, but here, against the great blocks which they believe once formed a part of the ancient Temple wall, they come lamenting. The men are not models of the latest fashions, the women not free from suggestion of uncleanness, but there is every appearance of earnest study of books reverentially held, while women are sobbing and moaning as if their very hearts would break for the glory which has departed from Israel. At times the leader standing in their midst with solemn voice recites the burdens under which the people are cast down, and for each sorrow expressed all the people join in the hopeless response—

> " For the palace that lies desolate."
> > " *We sit in solitude and mourn.*"
> " For the walls that are overthrown,"
> > " *We sit in solitude and mourn.*"
> " For our great men who lie dead,"
> > " *We sit in solitude and mourn.*"
> " For the priests who have stumbled,"
> > " *We sit in solitude and mourn.*"

ROUND ABOUT JERUSALEM.

A LITTLE north of the Damascus Gate the surface of the rock, which originally rose into a considerable ridge, is cut down on a line with the outside of the city wall which passes over it. Under the arching strata is a narrow doorway, shored up with blocks of stone in a solid wall. Provided with necessary authority and guides, we enter. The way descends sharply, broadening out finally into a great cavern, the roof supported by piers of solid rock. The Moslems call it the Cotton Grotto for some unknown reason. By others it is known as King Solomon's Quarries, with like satisfactory authority. Concerning it, ancient history is silent. All knowledge of its existence had been lost when it was re-discovered in 1842. Guides pretend not to know its extent even, and warn visitors not to wander beyond the reach of their voices—possibly to heighten the effect of a mystery which would be snuffed out by a Yankee in short order. In it are many chambers and branching tunnels leading to unknown points. Water is found here, but whether welling up from below or the result of surface drainage is unknown. The air is fresh and wholesome, and at times a breeze is felt, seeming to indicate other openings than the one where we entered.

157

*Entrance
to
King
Solomon's
Quarries.*

St. Stephen's Gate.

Great blocks of stone lie about; some as they were taken from the walls, others with sides smooth, as prepared for the building. Vertical slots, cut deep into the rock by some sharp instrument, possibly like a laborer's pick-ax, indicate the means by which the great cubes were separated from the parent mass; for in these clefts, blocks of wood were driven, on which water was poured, causing them to expand with an irresistible force and split the rock asunder.

There is a tradition among Masons that in these caverns, so deep under the earth that there could not come from them the sound of ax, hammer or other metal tools, the stones of the Beautiful Temple were cut, squared and numbered, and conveyed thence through some passage now lost to knowledge, direct to the Temple area to be placed in position under the supervision of the widow's son. Also that here Freemasonry began, and the first rites of the mystic brotherhood were enacted in one of these vaulted chambers when operative Masons alone—and of such only those who had passed through the great ordeal with becoming fortitude—joined in solemn commemoration of the tragedy in which they had themselves taken a part, and which, with its lessons and symbols, was to be enacted in after times in every land, and in almost every tongue on the face of the earth. Here the Masons of the Friesland, who from the far West had traveled East to the birth-place of the order, under flaring lights and with the dark approaches duly tiled, joined with their Eastern brethren in the mystic ceremonies of the Mother Lodge. What transpired there is no secret—to those who are entitled to the knowledge.

Across the road in a rocky hill is the Grotto of Jeremiah. Here, it is said, the patriarch wrote his Lamentations, and you are impressed with the conviction that if it were as dismal and unwholesome in the days of Jeremiah as now—and particularly if the same octopus was in charge to work his extortionate demands on the prophet that he attempts on visitors to-day—you do not wonder that the old gentleman's writings were of the lamentation order.

This low rocky hill, which attracts but little attention from the mass of pilgrims, is called the " New Golgotha," and among Protestants who have any opinions at all on the subject, is accepted as answering generally the understood requirements of the place of the crucifixion. From certain positions it has something the appearance of a flattened skull. As corroborative evidence, the Jew pays his involuntary testimony to the belief that here Christ suffered and was buried, by casting stones at it as he passes, and cursing it because of Him who brought dishonor to the race. Here is the chamber in the rock which answers to the description of the tomb of Joseph of Aramathea, in which

no man had laid until they placed there the body of the Crucified. Within, has been found ancient characters, indicating

159

The New Golgotha.

"And, behold, there was a great earthquake: for the angel of the Lord descended from Heaven, and came and rolled back the stone from the door, and sat upon it."

Christian belief in the sacred nature of the place. At the entrance is the usual receptical for the stone which closes the portal of the rock tomb. At the Tombs of the Kings, with its noble vestibule, its columns and carven cornice, I first saw and understood the nature of the "stone which was rolled away." My ideas, formed I know not how, were perhaps the ideas of others. I had pictured the stone as a great round boulder, which, by mighty force, could be rolled against the opening, like a cannon ball against a rat-hole. Quite recently I saw in a religious paper a picture of the sealing of the tomb by the chief priests and pharisees, "lest his disciples come by night and steal him away;" and the sealing was by means of long ropes passed over and around the stone and attached with neat seals at various points against the face of the rock! Instead I saw here a rock like a thin mill-stone, standing on edge in a slot cut to receive it, and this stone could be rolled as a wheel in front of the opening or "rolled away" at will.

On the opposite side of the city, outside Zion's Gate, we visited an imposing pile in possession of the Moslems where, "in a large upper room," is shown the place of the Last Supper. My attempts to photograph the room with my disguised kodak, is betrayed by our guide and brings a howl of protest from the half dozen Moslems who have joined us in the round. We present

161

Vestibule at the Tombs of the Kings.

the usual arguments but not with the usual results ; we succeed in overcoming the scruples of all except one, who may be more faithful, or possibly waiting for a higher price, but finally fail. In going out I again come near precipitating a riot and secure a picture of the court where Peter denied his Master, and the place where the cock stood when he crew, to remind the volcanic disciple of his shame. (In a rival establishment over in the city they show the imprint of the cock's feet, where they rested on the stone, but here you must accept the fact without the incontrovertible proof of an impression in hard rock.)

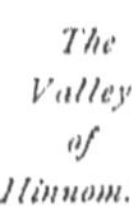

The Valley of Hinnom.

South you look over into the valley of Hinnom, the horrible place so detested by the Jews, where children were sacrificed to Moloch, the Gehenna of the New Testament, which came to signify "the place of fire" of the Old. Now it is as delightful a section to look at as can be found anywhere about Jerusalem.

From the southeast corner of the city wall we look down on the valley of the Kedron and see on the far side a typical Syrian village, with solid, block-like houses of stone, which might be a part of the native rock or an uneven section of some quarry, so much a part of the hill is it. In this native village of Silwan we may behold the "Siloam" of old, but few would associate its shadeless cliffs and dry valley bed with "cool Siloam's shady rills." The pool of Siloam is itself but a cistern; its waters, when there, but the

162

Silwan.

overflow of other pools higher up or such as may fall on the hillside round about.

Along by the walls toward the north and on the slope, are innumerable Moslem graves and monuments. On the opposite slope is the Jewish burying ground, thickly covered over with white tombs and surface graves. Near the bottom of the valley are tombs and monuments cut out of the living rock, among which Absalom's tomb is the most notable. It is

<table>
<tr><td>*Tomb of Absalom.*</td><td>*Pyramid of Zacharias.*</td></tr>
</table>

nearly fifty feet from base to top. Tradition has it that Absalom, having no sons to perpetuate his name, determined to erect a tomb which should ever keep his memory green. He succeeded! The Jews have never forgotten him, nor forgiven his disobedience to his father. They pelt the monument with stones in passing and a hole broken into its face is good evidence of their marksmanship. In the rock back of this

Garden of Gethsemane and Mount of Olives.

tomb is the tomb of Jehoshaphat. Farther to the east the grotto
of St. James, marked by openings guarded by columns, is cut
out of the rock.   Beyond that is the pyramid of Zacharias, also
cut out of the rock, and about thirty feet in height.   Around
on every side rest the bodies of the waiting dead.   Beyond, the
land rises into the Mount of Olives.

The Mount of Olives is east of Jerusalem, rising two hundred
or more feet higher than the city.   On it are a few scattered
olive and fig trees, and a number of chapels and religious institutions owned by various denominations and celebrated for
their sacred traditions and associations.   Through the valley of
Jehoshaphat (or Kedron) the waterless bed of the Kedron
runs, crossed by white roads leading toward Bethany and Jericho and up the hillside.   On the left of the road across the
valley, just before it divides to run over the hill, is an enclosure
within which lies the traditional "Grotto of the Agony," its
entrance showing as a tunnel at the extreme left.

The Garden of Gethsemane is on the right of the road, surrounded by a high stone wall.   Within are cypress and olive
trees.   The entrance is through a doorway on the far side,
where you must bend low to pass.   The garden is about 70

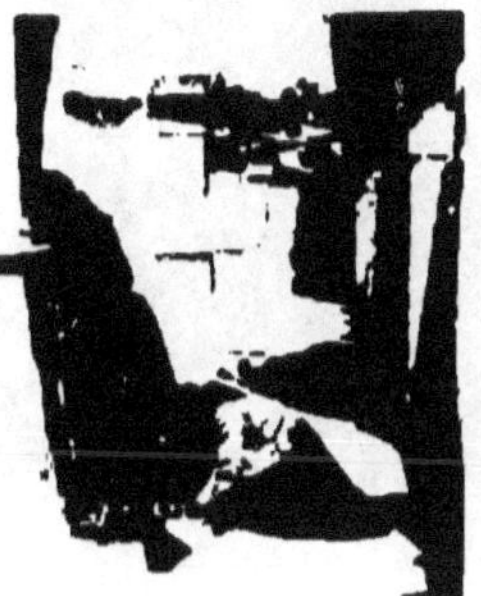

paces in length its longest way. In
the northeast corner is a building
occupied by the custodian, an old
Franciscan monk.   At intervals on
the inner sides of the walls are the
fourteen stations of the church, where
pilgrims kneel and kiss the ground
in their devotions.   An inner fence
of pickets encloses the central part,

where are the cypress and olive trees, with flowers of coarse varieties and brilliant hues. Of the latter the attendant offers you some, fresh picked, and adds a blessing for your contribution. Olive oil from the trees of Gethsemane brings a high price, and rosaries made from its olive stones are considered specially sacred and valuable. Some of these trees are very old. One is said to have been living in the time of the Saviour. At present it is but the shell of a big trunk, split and knobby, with a fringe of thin green branches. I desired a picture of this most venerable one, with the monkish gardener, and showed him in pantomime that I would like him seated on the mass of earth which the spreading roots had gathered in a cone around the base. When he understood, he started back as if the suggestion, even, was sacrilege, and falling on his knees instead, bowed before the tree as if in penitence for some sin committed. It suited me just as well.

*Ancient Olive Tree
in Garden of Gethsemane.*

Just outside the entrance they show the rocks where the disciples slept, "for their eyes were heavy," while the Master

withdrew from them to pray. "And he was withdrawn from them about a stone's cast and kneeled down and prayed." The place of the Agony is located in a little grotto which is now a chapel belonging to the Latins.

A small court with a high wall on three sides is believed to be the spot where Judas said " 'Master, Master,' and kissed him." The wall where the traitor kiss was given is defaced and broken by stones that had been thrown against it by pilgrims, testifying in this way their horror of the act.

The Tomb of the Virgin is near the "Grotto of the Agony." It is a cavern in which are the tombs of Mary and Joseph and of Mary's parents. Here also are altars belonging to the Greeks, the Armenians, and the Abyssinians and a prayer recess of the Moslems.

Well up toward the summit of Olivet are the Tombs of the Prophets. At the surface is seen an uninteresting opening in the rocks. Through this opening you descend into the vestibule, and through this still deeper into a circular chamber from which radiate passages like the spokes of a wheel, and like the rim of a wheel with projecting cogs is the outer circle, each cog being a tomb-niche. Near the summit of the mountain is an underground chapel where the apostles are said to

167

Entrance to the tombs of the Prophets.

have drawn up the creed. A little higher is the beautiful "Church of the Lord's Prayer," where, according to tradition, Christ taught his disciples to say "Our Father which art in Heaven." In the walls of the cloisters which surround a court of shrubbery and flowers are thirty-two stone tablets, on which

Church of the Lord's Prayer.

the Lord's Prayer is inscribed in as many different languages.

On the summit of the mountain is the Chapel of the Ascension. It is owned by the Moslems and a Moslem stands guard at the door of the court. In the centre of the court is an octagonal chapel, within which is shown the imprint of a foot in the rock's surface where, it is said, the Saviour last touched earth. There are times when one cannot believe all that is told, but this struck me as being a genuine foot-print, hand-made and well finished.

Near by is a tower which affords a commanding view of the surrounding country. Over beyond the mountains at the east the gray valley of the Jordan is seen with a varying line of green marking the course of the river, and the blue of the Dead Sea apparently near, although in fact distant seven to eight hours' journey. The usual way of computing distances in Syria is by hours rather than miles.

168

Place of the Ascension.

Bethany is over on the east slope of the Mount of Olives. The village is but little better than ruins and the homes of its dwellers are pictures of abject poverty. Here we are shown the foundation walls where, we are told, stood the house of

Mary and Martha. Within, were sturdy, uncompromising, unlovely bushes and frail white flowers, perhaps not unfitly emblematical of the sisters who here served the Saviour, each in her own peculiar way. Near by were the tomb of Lazarus and the ruins of the house of Simon the Leper.

We pass the tomb of Rachel on the way to Bethlehem. A comparatively modern "wely" covers the spot where it is generally believed Rachel, the beloved of Jacob, died in giving birth to Benjamin, "and was buried in the way of Ephrath which is Bethlehem." The tomb is revered by Moslem, Jew and Christian alike.

Bethlehem of Judea is surrounded by terraced hillsides, planted thick with olive trees. It lies at about the same level as Jerusalem and is solidly built with stone, after the fashion of the towns of that region. It contains about 8,000 inhabitants and is notoriously dirty. It is also specially noted for its carvings in olive wood and mother of pearl, but of main interest as the place of the nativity. The church of the Nativity is owned conjointly by Greeks, Latins and Armenians,

and covers the grotto to which tradition points as the place where the Saviour was born. The principal entrance is low and mean looking, suggestive of the back door rather than the entrance to a great church. Enter and the most noticeable objects are the double lines of columns of reddish limestone, each a monolith nearly twenty feet in height, and a general air of rusty magnificence in altar forms and trappings. The grotto, about forty feet long, a dozen wide and ten feet high, is paved and lined with marble. At one end is a recess where lamps are ever burning, belonging to Greeks, Armenians and Latins. In the centre of the recess a silver star let into the pavement indicates the place of the nativity. At one side is the chapel of the Manger in which the child was laid. A wax doll represents the infant Saviour. The genuine manger, which according to tradition was discovered by the irrepressible Helena, was carried to Rome. It is not impossible that in this cavern the Saviour was born. Just such caverns are found in many places and not uncommonly used for stables to-day as, presumably, they were in the older times. Caves in the rocks about Jerusalem are not the damp, unhealthy places one might expect to find, but every bit as dry as houses built of stone on the surface. They are cooler in summer and in winter warmer with the warmth of mother earth and unquestionably more comfortable to the people who make no provision for artificial heat.

David Jammel, Dragoman.

FROM JERUSALEM TO JERICHO.

IN short trips about Jerusalem a carriage or donkey is most
convenient ; for extended journeys through the Holy Land
you must go on horseback. There are horses *and* horses in
Palestine. An Arab whom you might consider an object of
charity from general appearance, often rides a horse which cost
him a hundred pounds, and which could not be bought at any
price. He will sell anything else in his possession, including his
wife, for a very moderate sum, but his horse is a part of himself.
Some of the beasts furnished for travelers do not look as though
they were worth twenty-five cents, yet even the most miserable
looking beast is somehow capable of wonderful endurance.
They are sure-footed generally, and with all their cranky ways
seem intuitively to know their rider's wishes. To one accustomed to the Mexican saddle the slippery thing provided here
is rather unsatisfactory, and it is some time before you can feel
even fairly secure in your position. The bridle is not to be
depended on in any way as a support, being simply a means of
punishment in shape of that instrument of torture known as
the "gag" bit, which with a leverage of its long arm when the
rein is drawn taut, presses the iron up into the roof of the
horse's mouth and makes him frantic. After a little, however,

you come to an understanding with your beast and simply indicate your wishes, leaving him his own way of securing the end.
You let the reins lie loosely across his neck, pressing them
gently against it to the left or right, as you may wish him to
turn, or giving the direction by motion of the hand, which he
readily obeys.

David Jammel, dragoman and contractor, was charged with
the duty of conducting our party to the Jordan. Jammel is a
Syrian of commanding presence and with gifts which belong
to the successful general. He has guided many notable parties
in his day and shows interesting testimonials of service. He
is royally eastern and a striking figure when decked out in
tunic and trousers of purple silk, with streaming silken head
covering of solferino and silver; with black and russet leather
trappings, silver trimmed and edged with heavy fringe; with
mighty sabre and arsenal of small arms, and mounted on a
beautiful Arabian charger. If you want to go anywhere in
Syria, where it is possible to go under any circumstances, all
you need do is to write to David Jammel, Jerusalem, stating
your wishes and mentioning the number of the party. He will
provide horses, carriages, tents, attendants and everything
necessary for your comfort or convenience, according to Syrian
standards.

In addition to the helpers necessary to provide for your needs
the party must be accompanied by some member of the tribe
through whose territory you may be obliged to pass, not for
anything he may do, but to see that the tribute which is
exacted by the sheik of the tribe over whose territory you go
is duly paid. His presence is a guaranty to bands of his tribe
that such right has been secured. Without such presence there

might be some little danger. With us went two fierce looking Arabs from the land about Jordan and the Dead Sea, armed with murderous weapons. They were threatening looking creatures at the start but near the end of the journey developed into anxious seekers after bakshish worthy of their importance, which was of course in addition to the tribute paid by the conductor.

"A certain man went down from Jerusalem to Jericho and fell among thieves." *We* landed plump into the midst of the gang at the very outset. Theoretically the chief dragoman is paid in a lump and secures you from all the rest. Practically no such beatific conditions can be hoped for under the system. The fundamental principles on which society in Syria rests is the exacting of tribute—by force if in power, by threat if possible, by abject beggary the other two failing, and the last as a legitimate right which carries with it no sense of obligation. Even Jammel could not rise above existing conditions or protect the innocents from the horde of pirates he had let loose on them under the guise of servitors. I am not sure that he tried to. I do not know that he saw in it anything that was not to be expected—it is the way of the land—the average Syrian considers you an oyster, from which it is his duty as well as pleasure to extract the pearl.

The persecutions began as soon as we mounted. Horses were slyly goaded into frenzy, and when in proper condition the men would seize them by the heads with much show of bravery and apparently exert every power possible to restrain them. Demands were made for payment for services rendered or imagined ; for doing necessary things, for doing unnecessary things, and for not doing things that are covertly threatened. " Bakshish " is demanded with a fierce insistence worthy of a better cause. To give once was to invite more violent demands at the next opportunity, which was not long in coming. You gained only temporary relief by paying for the questionable guardianship and personal attendance of the native who had marked you for his special prey. To be sure he fought the others off but *that* immediately created opportunities for additional demands, so that at times you suspected it was a good-natured farce in which benefits were shared. One member of the party admitted to having disposed of small coin to the amount of over $5.00 to one special attendant on the trip—and it was still some distance back to Jerusalem. Such a barefaced levying of black-mail I never saw equalled anywhere else in my life.

My opportunities were presumably the opportunities of others. Results varied according to disposition. My first mount, (brought after a friend had rashly intimated that I knew how to ride), was a tall fellow who seemed hung on wires, with a disposition to start before I was fairly seated. I tried to restrain him with the reins—not noticing that they were attached to the extreme ends of the levers of a curb bit—and he went backward. I encouraged him with the riding whip and he bounced up and down, while my camera, which I carried by a strap over my shoulder, thumped me in tender places. He was finally quieted, but I was easily persuaded that this was not the sort of beast to go photographing on however satisfactory his mastery might become under other circumstances.

Number Two put his ears back and showed his teeth, but that is a habit many of them get there, and I started. Before I was out of the crowd he began to act funny, and immediately a burly son of Belial in a fiery fez and a night-gown had him by the head and was demanding bakshish for some unexplained service, which I found to be no service at all, but a proposition to become my special attendant and I his special prey whether I would or no. I tried to throw more savagery into my expression and to yell louder than he, but it didn't work. Ordinary conversation there is filled with gore and dynamite, and nothing short of a club will convince them that you mean what you say. After a while I satisfied this one that he was wasting his time, and he transferred his attention to another member of the party who was just then emerging from the depths, and succeeded in putting so many kinds of cussedness into the head of the beast he rode as to render it unmanageable, so that its rider finally, in a somewhat sulphurous cloud, threw up his hand and went back for a fresh deal. Later I worked the confiding, idiotic, don't-understand-what-you-mean smile on the bakshish plunderers and found it generally effective. My Number Two had peculiarities, and did not enter heartily into my scheme of photographing from the saddle. He would not agree with me as to the best points of view, objected to being put into desirable positions and developed a tendency to jump whenever I snapped a picture. Descending into the valley of the Kedron a view of much interest presented itself to me, and dropping the reins as usual, I made the exposure. My horse, as usual bolted, but not in the usual way. He added a circular motion and before I knew what was going to happen I found myself flat on the ground among a lot of donkeys and the beast I had been riding, on the opposite side of the road with a turned saddle. Possibly I dropped onto some of the donkeys. I don't know. They seemed to be all right when I found time to look

at them and made room for me as for one of their own kind.
Anyway I saved my precious camera and no harm was done
except some slight damage to my dignity and the clothes I
wore. My first thought, naturally, was a wonder if any of my
friends were in sight. One was. And he my dearest! Would
he tell? His two hands were clutching firmly at the rim of his
saddle; his teeth closed in a deathless grip; his two eyes looked
out straight ahead with a far-away expression, like unto that of
the Sphinx, and I knew that he was making the supreme effort
of his life. Would he see me or might I hope to remain un-
noticed among the other donkeys? It all depended on whether
or not the beast on which he rode should, in its turnings, head so
as to bring me into line. It was a moment of extreme suspense!
then, like the priest and the Levite of old he also passed by on
the other side and gave no sign. He has since told me that he
saw me, but— ! Possibly we have always done an injustice to
the memory of the priest and Levite. The real reason why
they did not succor the one who fell among thieves may have
been a well grounded fear that they might tumble off if they
so much as looked even. A wild Arab came swooping down
toward me, mounted on a splendid beast. It was his opportunity—and mine. He caught my horse and at once demanded
"bakshish." It ended in a compromise, he taking my horse
and I his for the time being.

Number Three was really a beautiful creature. He did not
object to my photographing from his back, and a number of
opportunities were improved, where the blind beggars sat by
the roadside and the lepers had gathered about Gethsemane.
By the time I had finished in the valley of the Kedron the
last of our party had long since vanished over the hill and, with

stories of outrages perpetrated on defenseless stragglers fresh in mind, I felt that it was time an effort was made to overtake them. My attendant offered to relieve me of the camera, which was promptly transferred to his shoulder, and we started. Then my Number Two, on which he was mounted, promptly ran away with him. He saved himself by clinging to the beast's neck, but the camera went down into the dust of the road, and when I finally picked it up the lens was broken from the box and other damage done, the extent of which could not be known until further investigated. After a time the crestfallen horseman returned, but I decided to carry the camera myself thereafter. While getting into shape for another start a number of Bedouins swept by like a whirlwind and my beast pricked up his ears as though he would like to join them. I had tried him at a gentle trot and had been glad to get him back into a walk; I thought now to see if he had not a better gait. I held the reins loosely and flung my hands upwards as I had seen the others do, with a rising motion in the saddle, which he seemed quickly to understand, and we were off at a pretty sharp clip. Soon we came up with the procession! we sweep past pilgrims on horseback and in carriages! past my friend with firm shut teeth and heroic expression; we are up with the vanguard where ride the young men; we are up with the ambitious leaders! we lead all at last except one Arab, with whom we go neck and neck for a time, to finally fall behind as we climb the slope where stands the Good Samaritan Inn. It was a good race. Here I tinker my camera into serviceable condition at last, and lunch, but when I go for my peerless Arabian I find him changed into a frowzy, tufted, little sorrel skeleton with a variable gait and a habit of going to sleep immediately you ceased to urge him on, and the most transcendent failure as a horse that it was my privilege to ride on the journey, excepting Number Five, which I drew for one of the later stages, when I happened to be late and was forced to take what was left.

The Good Samaritan Inn, so called, is simply an inclosure in which is a well (two piasters to the pirate in charge, for a pail of water for your horse), its entrance an arched porch through which we ride and where, on rugs spread over the floor, we sit, Turk-like, and eat our lunch of potted meats, boiled eggs, bread and coffee.

Our party is not alone in possession of the "Inn," but a small army of Russian pilgrims are here preparing, or eating, their frugal lunch before continuing on their way. We have seen them all along the road in twos, in threes, in dozens, and in long processions, and will continue to see them all the afternoon and the next day. It is estimated that there are over five hundred on the road between Jerusalem and the Jordan, and on Easter there will be at least five thousand in and about the Holy City. They are a stolid people, heavy of form and motion. The weather is extremely hot and the lightest of summer clothing seems at times a burden, yet these people seem dressed for the coldest of seasons. The men wear heavy cloaks, often lined with sheepskin, wool side in; fur caps and leather boots reaching to the knees. The women have on padded sacks, thick shawls about their

180

Trilby.

heads and necks, legs swathed in many wraps and wound with
tape or cord.   On their feet are traveling shoes of plaited reeds
or rope, while their dress-shoes are carried usually strung about
their necks.   They carry bundles of blankets for bedding and
bags of food, with tin or copper dishes for cooking purposes,
and tin teapots.   Almost every one has a bottle in which, when

they return, they will bring water from the holy river.   They
have come from far away homes in Russia.   They were landed
at Joppa and are making this pilgrimage to holy places, which
must include a visit to the ford of the Jordan where the Saviour
was baptized.   Each one brings a white garment in which he or
she will bathe in the Jordan, and which at death will be their
burial robe.   To make this pilgrimage is the great life object of
many of the Orthodox faith, and is held to give a certain distin-
guishing holiness as does a pilgrimage to Mecca to the Moslem.
Peculiar credit comes to those who make the toilsome journey on
foot.   In the ranks are the old and feeble, some seemingly
scarce able to drag their weary feet—unlovely atoms of humanity, yet beautiful in their devotion—toiling painfully along the
sun-lit road or stretched in a wavering line over the barren
Judean hills.

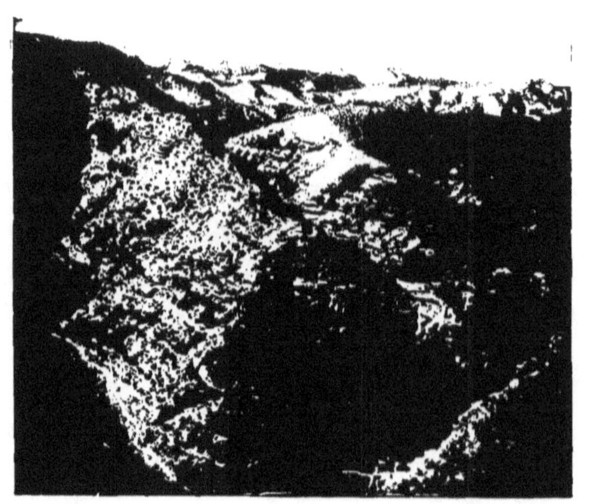

Brook Cherrith.

And more barren grow the hills as we advance. Up around Jerusalem the dreary waste is relieved by groves of olive trees covering the hillsides and spots of springing wheat wherever a pocket in the rock may give place for a handful of soil, and the roadside glowing red with masses of wild poppies, but here is only the chalky road and scanty grass, thin and dry, growing in tufts upon the hillside along which run innumerable sheep paths, with here and there a flock, guarded by watchful shepherds.

The road must at one time have been a fine specimen of Roman work, broad and level, cutting through rocks, and bridging chasms with substantial arches. Now, however, it is gullied by water, portions washed away and the surface covered with loose stone which the easy going horseman goes around or over rather than take the trouble to throw it out of the way. The way is continually downward. On one hand are the spotted cliffs and steep water-worn hillside, on the other deep gulches or "wadys" as the smaller valleys are called here. Away down at the bottom of the one at our side a tiny streamlet begins its course. They tell you that it is Brook Cherrith, where the ravens brought food to the prophet Elijah of old. Up the winding path to where we pass, devotees have toiled with full jars of water to stand by the roadside and offer those who come—free to the poor pilgrim, at a price to those who seem able to pay and who venture to touch the not overclean vessel in which it is offered.

At last through a notch in the rifted hills we look over into a spreading valley. From where we stand the white road runs zig-zag down until lost in the gullies of the broken bottom land. The whole slope is a succession of water-lined terraces

The Valley of the Jordan.

and deep gorges. A little way out is an irregular patch of green, within which a cluster of white buildings forms modern Jericho. Farther away a second line of green indicates the course of the Jordan. Centrally, among the mountains on the far side, somewhere, we must look for Nebo, from which Moses looked over into this, the Promised Land, which he was not permitted to enter. At the right, seemingly but a short distance although in fact eight miles away, are the blue waters of the Dead Sea. At the left rises a low square-topped mountain from which Satan showed the Saviour "all the kingdoms of the world." At its foot is a gray terrace where, according to tradition, stood ancient Jericho, whose dwellers no doubt laughed to see the crowd of Israelites marching round and round about her walls, with priests blowing on the rams' horns in such an absurd manner! But when on the seventh day the priests blew, and the people shouted, and the walls fell, the laughing was on the other side, for all were destroyed by the sword save she and hers, from whose window hung the scarlet thread. To-day nothing remains but formless ruins and earth and mixed fragments of crumbling stone and brick.

The cause of the oasis in which stands modern Jericho is revealed in a reservoir near old Jericho, which they call Elisha's Fountain, where it is said the prophet "cast salt into the waters and healed them."

The people who call the legitimate results of monkeying around the heels of a mule "a Dispensation of Providence," and see in a fit of indigestion a divine chastening because of original sin, will tell you this land was cursed and rendered barren because of the wickedness of its people! By the exercise of just a little bit of common sense the most casual observer will see that all the land needs is water, and, that the blessing would surely follow is demonstrated by the condition of sections where water is applied. When the Israelites complained to Elisha saying "the water is naught and the land miscarrieth" they undoubtedly had reference to quantity rather than quality of water, having in mind its effect on the rich lands of Egypt about which their fathers had undoubtedly told them while in the wilderness. Here was a section not unlike the valley of the Nile in its wonderful fertility and they saw that where the water was permitted to soften and moisten it, it responded mightily, producing abundantly of every green thing good for man. As in those days, it is now. This whole valley could with proper irrigation be made one great productive garden spot. The abundant flow of the river Jordan would afford a never failing supply of water. Its rapid descent makes it possible to draw its waters from it at any level needed and carrying them through canals along the valley's sides distribute them over its upper terraces, or flood the bed of the valley at will, until the entire section down to the borders of the Dead Sea laughs with plenty. The reason why this condition does not exist to-day may be looked for in the oppression of the Turkish government which exacts from the tiller of the soil a tenth part of all the ground produces, and, to make sure of its share, provides that the crops must not be removed from the fields until passed upon by the official measurer. This agent is supposed to be paid for his services by the government, but he is generally so overworked that unless a most liberal bakshish is forthcoming from the producer, the grain spoils on the ground before he is able to give it attention! As a result it does not pay to cultivate the ground except perhaps close about the cities, or in sections beyond the reach of the rate collector by the tribes which, while nominally under the Turkish government are practically independent and yield obedience only to their respective sheiks.   And this is why this section lies fallow and the long lines of grain-laden camels from "beyond Jordan" are seen crossing its fords and going up to Jerusalem or to the seaport towns of the Mediterranean.

Modern Jericho is a collection of miserable mud huts occupied by a degenerate set of Arabs—and when you strike a degenerate Arab you are getting pretty well down.   The houses are usually of mud bricks and roofed with the same or with brush plastered over with mud. The bricks are mud mixed with straw and dried in the sun and are probably the same as the Israelites made down in Egypt. Here I saw "women grinding at the mill." The mill is usually a flat stone with a shallow depression in it in which the grain is crushed and ground by means of another stone or pestle moved round and round over it by hand.   At one of the huts a woman was baking bread on a flat stone laid across other stones and under which a fire was burning.   The bread, in shape of a large pancake, was about the color of chocolate and of the consistency of moderately tender sole-leather.   Three or four healthy looking savages stood restfully around watching the woman and the bread and incidentally trying to negotiate privileges with me.

Brick making.

187

A house in Jericho.

The general depravity of the place is relieved by the presence there of a Greek monastery and hospice where, in the general room, we saw numbers of the Russian pilgrims wrapped in their blankets, lying like lines of sardines along the floor. It has also a couple of alleged modern hotels where some of our

party were so unfortunate as to obtain rooms, and brought away with them visible evidence that they were not the only occupants of the beds provided. The major portion, however, in whom dwelt no fear of native wild beasts, found delightful quarters in the luxurious double-cloth tents which had been brought down from Jerusalem and set up for our use, each tent containing three or more iron bedsteads with fresh, clean clothes, and each superbly carpeted with the green plush which nature had there spread out over the ground.

At the close of the day we gathered in the big tent for dinner and while we balanced gently on the edges of our respective seats, feasted and exchanged stories of hazardous adventures, and hairbreadth 'scapes, and struggles with wild steeds—in which we were of course victorious, for none of us would willingly dampen the general ardor or seek to depress our hearers with unimportant details as to the times we had fallen off. And the concensus of opinion crystalized into an axiom then and there may be accepted without question, to the effect that a ride from Jerusalem down to Jericho of a hot day on a Jerusalem horse gets one so accustomed to the delights of the saddle that one doesn't want to sit down on anything else for some time thereafter.

Dinner over, we gladly seek our couches and are lulled to sleep by the music of screaming jackalls, barking dogs and braying donkeys.

In the morning we rise up early and prepare for Jordan and the Dead Sea. It is the early clergyman that catches the best horse—at least some who got away first were on better beasts than they had the day before. It seemed odd that some who at home would wrestle on their knees all day long, with only slight intermission for meals, to save your soul, actually could not tell the beast they rode the day before from the best one of the pack. I admit that horses are not mentioned in the ten commandments, or if they are included they don't really belong to the fellow who chances to get a good one, so we can't hold them there—first come, first pick was the rule observed, and some of our preachers developed into as good judges of horse-flesh as a deacon. I don't wish to be personal—it would be too sweeping—perhaps it was in the air. And if the air had such an effect on clergymen what could you expect when it tackled a layman? I actually saw a man: good; of unlimited means and undoubted probity, one who delights in addressing inno-cent little children in Sabbath schools—swipe a spoon! It wasn't much of a spoon either—just a little brass affair. And the act seemed all right when he explained later that he was making a collection of souvenirs. I know also where the mate to that spoon went. Possibly it was in the land—you see, it was a low down place anyway—nearly thirteen hundred feet below

Jericho Camp.

the level of the ocean, and must have been always thus. Even the Chosen People became thugs and cut-throats, according to sacred history, as soon as they struck the country—but to return to the horses. We who were late felt that it did not show a brotherly spirit in those who got up early in the morning and made off with the best ones. It certainly was not dignified.

Approaching the Dead Sea.

A better way is to leave the matter with your special Arab, who is a thief naturally, and who if properly impressed in advance may be depended on to lead one of the best from some sequestered spot when you appear, and you may mount leisurely and follow the company without the risk of having some envious person intimate that you got up early to steal your friend's horse while he slept. I wish I had thought of this earlier. When I found what sort of a beast remained for me that morning I almost resolved to become an early riser.

South, over the gullied land we go, its surface becoming more and more sterile as we advance. Even the coarse tufted grass and wirey bushes are left behind at last, and we stand on the shores of the Dead Sea. The scene is one of utter desolation· but the morning is so beautiful that we are more impressed with a sense of peace and restfulness, than with any thought that this is a land of death. The water, clear as air almost, breaks in gently lapping wavelets on the crescent beach which, circling to the mountains east and west, slopes gently down to the water's edge. The worn stones and variegated pebbles run through all the shades of red and yellow to brown and black, their dull splendor under the hot sun changed to a soft flickering radiance where they are covered by the highly refracting water, until finally lost to sight far out in its sapphire depths. On either side, beyond the blue water, rise the gray hills growing fainter and fainter, and finally vanish in a soft haze miles away. Between them stretches the sea, rising with the rotundity of the earth's surface heavy and dark against the luminous southern sky. Back from the beach is clay and salt and gypsum, soft with water or hard-baked like stone, but barren of life. They tell of the apples of Sodom growing here, which turn to ashes in the mouth, but we looked for them in vain. It has been said that birds who attempt to fly over the water fall down dead, but the natives had the grace to deny this. It is asserted

191

The Dead Sea.

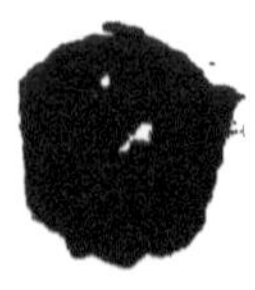

that no living thing can exist in the Dead Sea, but this also I am prepared to dispute. I, myself, saw several living creatures—among them a Doctor of Divinity—sporting in its crystal shallows.

Curiously enough, with all its traditions, facts and figures were not forthcoming until Americans took the matter in hand with the result that a government expedition was sent out by the United States in 1848. This is the lowest habitable spot known on the globe. The surface of the Dead Sea is 1293 feet lower than the level of the Mediterranean! It is 9½ miles wide at its widest point, and is 47 miles long. Soundings have been made to a depth of 1310 feet. It is estimated that 6,000,000 tons of water are poured into it daily yet it has no outlet. The burning atmosphere as of a furnace which at times surrounded us must drink up this enormous amount of water by absorption daily. The human body floats easily. Over 7% of the bulk of the water is salt in solution, besides which it contains large quantities of the chlorides of magnesium and calcium and large masses of asphalt. The mountains round about often show frost and snow, but neither frost nor snow reach this depression. Its climate is ordinarily such as may be found well down toward the equator.

Northeasterly from the head of the Dead Sea we go to Jordan, striking it at the ford, where it is believed, the Children of Israel crossed when they came to take possession of the land.

"And as they that bear the ark were come unto Jordan, and the feet of the priests that bear the ark were dipped in the brim of the water (for Jordan overfloweth all his banks all the time of harvest),"

" That the waters which came down from above stood *and* rose up upon a heap very far from the city of Adam, that *is* beside Zaretan ; and those that came down toward the sea of the plain, *even* the salt sea, failed, *and* were cut off : and the people passed over right against Jericho."

"And the priests that bear the ark of the covenant of the LORD stood firm on dry ground in the midst of Jordan, and all the Israelites passed over on dry ground, until all the people were passed clean over Jordan."

* * * * *

"And it came to pass, when the priests that bear the ark of the covenant of the LORD were come up out of the midst of Jordan, *and* the soles of the priests' feet were lifted up unto the dry land, that the waters of Jordan returned unto their place, and flowed over all his banks, *as they* did before."

At this spot, according to tradition, Christ was baptized of John when the heavens were opened and the form of a dove was seen descending "and lo a voice from heaven—saying, this is my beloved Son, in whom I am well pleased."

Like as in the days of Joshua the river overflowed "his" banks sweeping downward in a tawny stream to the Dead Sea. Along its margin on either side, is a belt of tangled woodland, of willow, and slender poplars and mighty reeds. From a sky like copper shines the fierce sun. Sweltering pilgrims hasten to dip head and feet in the water of the stream. Some seek sequestered nooks, glad to bury themselves beneath the waters, finding that what they had thought to do as a sacred privilege has a pleasant amount of earthly comfort in its composition.

Among the trees along shore we cut sticks. We gather reeds from the thickets as souvenirs. We fill cans and bottles procured for that purpose, with water of the river which we will carry half way around the globe to distant homes. Finally we turn regretfully, feeling that it was good to be there, and toil across the barren plain above, in the hot afternoon sun, to Jericho, where we spend another night and in the gray of the next morning, climb up out of the valley to the mountain heights of the Holy City.

THE SAMARITAN BROTHERHOOD.

I DO not crave the earth entire, but among the regrets of my life is one that I could not be with the "Samaritan Brotherhood" in its long ride to the north. For pictures thanks are due to Rev. J. G. Hamner, Jr. As for the story— is it not told delightfully by the honored president, Rev. Dr. Brett, in his "Narrative?" The soul of the poet speaks in his closing words :

"In those sun-filled days and moon-lit nights, over steaming coffee, and amid the smoke of Turkish tobacco, in friendly chat, as we rode side by side, or tender confidences, after we had lifted our souls together in praise and prayer, friendships were formed, and loves enkindled which shall be eternal. It will be a strange coincidence if we twenty-five should ever meet in one place on earth. A common faith and hope, however, give the assurance that, some day, we shall meet in the New Jerusalem, on Canaan's happy shore, and there, as we recount the experiences, gay and sad, of life's long pilgrimage, we shall often talk of that blessed week spent together in the 'Land of the Book.'"

From the secretary of the brotherhood comes a sketch of the pilgrimage, just touching a suggestive bit here and there :

MY DEAR MR. STODDARD :

Of the various "side-trip" parties from the Friesland none could congratulate themselves more heartily on using time and money to advantage

THE SAMARITAN BROTHERHOOD.

1. Rev. J. Garland Hamner, Jr.
2. Rev. Newell M. Calhoun.
3. Rev. Calvin A. Hare.
4. T. M. Irvine.
5. W. P. Glover, M. D.
6. Rev. W. T. Thompson, D. D.
7. Rev. John H. Logie.
8. Rev. Henry Quigg, D. D.
9. Rev. Daniel H. Martin.
10. Rev. Wm. Plumer Jacobs, D. D.
11. Rev. S. C. Caldwell.
12. Henry D. Moore.
13. Rev. J. Garland Hamner, D. D.
14. Henry H. Dawson.
15. Samuel Clark.
16. Rev. Worley Brighton Slutz, D. D.
17. Rev. John H. Prugh, D. D.
18. Rev. Alonzo Monk, D. D.
19. Rev. A. J. P. McClure.
20. Rev. William Dallam Morgan.
21. Henry C. Hines.
22. Rev. S. L. Morris, D. D.
23. George P. Smyser.
24. Rev. Cornelius Brett, D. D., Prest.
25. Samuel Jacob, Secy.

than did the " Samaritan Brotherhood," consisting of seventeen ministers and eight laymen, who shortened their time in Jerusalem to two days that the remaining five days of their time in the Holy Land might be spent in a horseback ride through Samaria to the Sea of Galilee and thence to meet the ship at Haifa.

We started from Jerusalem, Tuesday, March 5th, at 2 P. M., under the guidance of Chaleel E. Awad, dragoman. The pack train, carrying stove, bedding, luggage and provisions, consisted of twenty-six donkeys in charge of Simon Tomeros, cook, and eight or ten muleteers.

Clattering out through the Damascus gate, where Saul of Tarsus went forth "breathing out threatenings and slaughter," we go, the walls and towers of the City of Zion glorified under the afternoon sun as we look upon them from the hill Scopus. To the west is Nob, where David seized the sword of Goliath; to the east a little farther is Gibeah. At the base of a hill we pass through Er-Ram (Ramah), and, in the distance, 3,000 feet above the sea, we behold Mizpah of Benjamin. At 6:15 we draw up in the open court of the Latin Hospice at Ram Allah and make it headquarters for the night. The grateful glow of good feeling that comes from rest and a good supper leads the tired riders before rising from their seats to formally organize "The Samaritan Brotherhood." A very pleasant visit is paid by members of the party to the Friends' Mission House, in charge of Mrs. Huldah Layton, of Philadelphia, and her native helpers.

At 6:30 next morning all are in their saddles. The first stop is at El-Bireh, notable for the tradition that here was the spot where Joseph and Mary, missing the 12-year old Jesus from the caravan, turned back and "sought him sorrowing." A few minutes farther on we leave to the right Bethel, so full of historic associations. Within sight is Ai, and farther on we come to the Robbers' Cave and Spring marked by ruins of Crusader times. We dismount at Shiloh, and inspect the few huts that remain to remind one of the departed glory of the great city that once proudly stood here. At 12:20 we stop for lunch at the Khan El-Lubban, where the neighboring village women have come for water. Lebonah of Judges is in sight. The plain of El-Makhna is reached at 4:30 and the sun is about to set over Mount Ebal as we alight at Jacob's Well. To the north, perhaps a mile away, is Sychar, and half way between is Joseph's tomb. The adjoining fields are in wheat, as they were when Jesus sat at the well and spoke of the harvest. We pass through the amphitheater between Mounts Ebal and Gerizim and draw up at Nablous, the ancient Shechem, for the night.

The first interesting point in the morning is Sebastiyeh, the ancient City of Samaria, against which the prophets uttered the curse of God for its wickedness, and which has had an eventful history. Passing Dothan, where Jacob's sons fed their flocks, we meet a caravan of camels on their way to Egypt, going the same route that Joseph was carried. We pass where of old there were " mountains full of chariots and horsemen," and spend the night at Jenin, the " fountain of gardens."

In the morning we cross the Kishon by an easy ford. To the northwest is the city of Nazareth, and the outlines of Mount Carmel are visible. The

Mount Tabor and the Plain of Esdraelon.

broad plain of Esdraelon is dotted with villages and to the east may be seen the peaks of Gilboa, Hermon, and Tabor.

The plain of Esdraelon is the battlefield of the ages. In the northeast Mount Tabor rises solitary to about the height of 1,000 feet, and commands the most extensive prospect in the Holy Land. In this immediate neighborhood Saul fought with the Philistines, and David continued the warfare. Here Pharaoh Necho, of Egypt, won the battle of Megiddo, and King Josiah fell at the hands of his enemies. Here Saladin contended with the valiant Crusaders ; and, in 1799, Napoleon, the Man of Destiny, fought against the flying squadrons of the Turks. Mount Tabor competes with Mount Hermon for the glory of being the place of the transfiguration. An old church in ruins marks the summit.

We pass through Jezreel and Shunem and Old Testament stories are suggested on every side. We leave witch-haunted Endor to the east and, crossing a northern spur of Tabor, reach long before sunset, the Horns of Hattin, where the whole of Lake Galilee is visible at a glance. We can never forget the matchless beauty and impressiveness of the view.

We descend to Tiberias, spend the night, take a boat ride to where the River Jordan leaves the sea, and after several hours amid the scenes of Christ's mightiest works go forward to Nazareth, which we reach before twilight, meeting beyond Cana, on the way, the Galilee section of our friends. After a night and a morning at Nazareth, we go over fairly respectable roads to Haifa, arriving on schedule time, to learn of the Friesland's mishap at Port Said, and in consequence spend twenty-four more enjoyable hours awaiting her arrival.

For two days out from Jerusalem the riding was decidedly rough, leading over a mountain path traversing gullies, limestone bowlders, and solid stretches of rock which the horses, single file, managed to get over safely in some miraculous way, but the rest of the trip was easy and a source of constant delight.

Palestine is a land of contrasts. Turn to the 29th chapter of Deuteronomy, read from the 21st to the 29th verse, and realize that "the stranger that shall come from a far land" finds the prophesy literally fulfilled as to the part there spoken of, while the northern portion might "blossom as the rose" were the withering curse of Turkish misgovernment lifted from it.

An American is impressed with the small area of Palestine and its places of interest. Accustomed as we are to large bodies of water the designation "sea" of Galilee is especially deceptive. Its entire length is only thirteen miles and its width does not exceed six. It appears to be merely a widening of the River Jordan, which would be called with us a large-sized creek and which entering the lake at one end leaves it at the other. The lake is 820 feet in depth at its deepest. Its surface is 681 feet below the level of the Mediterranean. The water is fresh and sweet, the bottom and shores pebbly, and to this day, as in the days of the Apostles, abounds in fish. It is also notorious for sudden and severe storms. The craft in which we had our ride was an open boat propelled with sails and oars, probably the "ship" of the times of Christ. On this occasion the crew consisted of five scraggy and half-clothed natives of Tiberias.

How different the bleak and barren hills of Judea, cheered here and there by struggling fig and olive orchards or an occasional vineyard, from Samaria, with its abundance of flowers, its luxuriant grain-fields, its birds and its beasts, its men and its women. Mental photographs come crowding back as we recall the many incidents of the time.

A modern Jacob lies on his native earth, his pillow a stone, dreaming perchance of such stairs as those whereon his ancestor saw

> " Angels ascending and descending, bands
> Of guardians bright, when he from Esau fled
> To Padan-Aram, in the field of Luz,
> Dreaming by night under the open sky,
> And waking cried, 'This is the gate of heaven.'"

A Modern Jacob.

We compelled a hawk that was attempting to fly away with a reptile to drop its prey, and found it to be a writhing black-snake five feet in length. We saw numbers of storks, a herd of gazelles bounding away from us, a fox scudding to its hole, lizards, a pet coney at Shunem, domestic sheep, dogs, cattle, donkeys, camels and interesting fauna at every turn.

We see again the ancient types of plowmen at work, the watch-towers, the shepherds, the "green pastures and still waters," until old Canaan seems familiar as the well known parts of our own more blessed America.

SAMUEL JACOB.

The Rev. Dr. Prugh writes enthusiastically, delightfully, lovingly of the trip :

"The advantage of such an overland trip to the student of Biblical history is incalculable. While Bethlehem and Jerusalem appeal to you with peculiar pathos, superstition has played such an important part in the edifices erected over the spots made sacred for all times and all people, and so much filth and wretchedness meets your eye on every hand that there steals over you gradually a feeling of sadness and disappointment. But when you climb the old hills of Judea and go down into her valleys ; when you ascend the mountains of Samaria and cross her great plains ; when you ride the waters of sweet Galilee, and cross old Jordan, you are conscious you tread the same paths which the Saviour trod, and you look upon the same beautiful scenes. The hills and plains, the sacred lake and river of Palestine, are unchangeable. And as we slept in the village where lived Samuel's parents, as we passed by Mizpah and visited Bethel, Shiloh and Jacob's Well, Shechem. Samaria and Shunem, Nain, Nazareth and Capernaum, Mt. Tabor, Mt. Gilboa, Mt. Hermon, the plains of Jezreel, Esdraelon and Lake Galilee, and recalled anew the sacred history of these places, the Scriptures unfolded themselves to me with new meaning.

We had been warned to prepare for rough weather, and friends had assured us that six days of continuous horse-back riding would subject us to so much hardship that we would get no pleasure or profit out of the trip. ' The Samaritan Brotherhood,' however, was composed of such genial, companionable men, the weather was so much like that of summer time, the places visited were so big with interest, riding a spirited Arab horse was so thoroughly intoxicating, that when we cantered across the end of the plain of Esdraelon, and dashed into the little town, and dismounted at the foot of Mt. Carmel, and I patted ' Saladin's ' arched neck for the last time, I did so with the feeling that those six days in the saddle were among the happiest and most thrilling and profitable of my life."

Jno. H. Prugh.

*Saladin—
arching
his
neck.*

The Sea of Galilee.

The view is taken from a point near where the River Jordan
begins its course to the Dead Sea. The buildings on the left are
old Roman baths. At the right is Tiberius.

THE GALILEE SECTION.

AFTER landing the Port Said contingent at Jaffa, the "Friesland" carried the "Galilee Section" north to Haifa and returned to Jaffa once more to pick up the main party which had spent the week at Jerusalem and in going down to Jordan. To Rev. W. A. Robinson, D.D., I am indebted for the following account of the trip from Haifa to the Sea of Galilee :

The Galilee section, consisting of twenty-five or more, duly mounted on the fiery Arabian chargers of which the Land of the Prophets boasts, left Haifa, at the foot of the Carmel range, March 8, at about one P. M. Many more horses had been brought down from Nazareth for our use than was needed, but they with their owners formed a part of our cavalcade, and Mr. Clark had to pay for the supernumeraries. The surplus furnished an opportunity for the ladies of the party to suit themselves—if they could—by swapping until at last they settled on the right one. Any unoccupied horse they wanted to try, Mr. Gimel saddled for them, and even then some of them didn't ride to Galilee "on flowery beds of ease" Among the ladies who were plucky enough to take this trip, were Mrs. Knapp, of Bridgeport, Miss Allen, of New York (who was a famous horsewoman and rode without tiring the day through), Miss Burritt, of Bridgeport, Mrs. Fred. Gallagher, of Cairo, Ill., Mrs. and Miss Hedges, of Urbana, O., Mrs. Scudder and daughters, Mrs. and Miss Forman, of Jersey City.

We were a desultory company, and a jolly, stretching out for a mile or two, as carriages, palanquins, donkeys and horses filed through the valley of the Kishon, thence across that famous and mighty (!) river, over hills covered with scrub oaks, past the village of Sisera, where His mother looked through the lattice in a vain waiting for His coming in that fateful long ago, and finally out onto the great plain of Esdraelon, which stretched before us, a very Dolly Varden in the variety of colors which clothed it. The little farms which were tilled by the villagers through whose mud towns we passed every three or four miles were under a high state of culti-vation and presented the appearance of a variety of vast rugs, artistically arranged. It looked indeed as if the Almighty had emptied his paint pot upon the valley. We entered Nazareth by moonlight at about eight o'clock and were quartered quite comfortably at three hotels, where we had a good supper of soup, meat, rice, pigeons, oranges, lemonade and coffee cake. We enjoyed it.

Some of the company did not sleep much that night because others slept so enthusiastically, but, nevertheless, the early morning found us all astir, some to find their way, before breakfast, to Mary's well, the single well which supplies this quaint town of ten thousand people. Here we found a score or more of women with water jars on their heads, while from all di-rections they were coming and going, stopping a moment, perchance to greet each other and exchange the morning gossip, which answers there in place of the regular morning paper. After breakfast, we went reverently to the Church of the Annunciation, where we were shown the spot where the angel stood, the pillar from whence he came, where Joseph stood and where Mary stood when the annunciation was made. We also went into the little grotto where the Holy Family lived and the cave kitchen where they cooked, and went through the stone doorway through which they would naturally pass in going to the well. Thence we went to the Chapel of the Carpenter Shop, to the synagogue where our Lord preached his memorable sermon (*i. e.*, the site of the synagogue) and also to the hill from the brow of which his enraged townsmen would have hurled Jesus to his death if he had not conveyed himself away.

In the morning we got a fairly early start for Tiberius. The way led over the hill to Cana, where we lunched in the rain. Here, in the midst of the squalid mud village, we visited the church which, it is claimed, is on the spot where Jesus turned the water into wine. In confirmation of this we read over the entrance, "*Naptae Factae Sunt in Cana Galilee et Erat Mater Jesu Ibi.*" We also visited another chapel which claims for itself the same honor in a Greek inscription. The ride to Tiberius was through a country dotted with flocks and herds. We saw but two fences, one of stone and one of thorns. Orchards of fig, pomegranate and olive trees

A Threshing-Floor.

flourished in beauty and fruitfulness at frequent intervals. Imagination and fancy were both busy as the dragoman said, "We are now riding through that cornfield where Jesus and the disciples went when, 'being ahungered on the Sabbath, they plucked the ears of corn.'" Later, pointing, our guide said, "Yonder are the horns of Hatton, from which our Lord delivered the 'sermon on the mount!'" A pleasant episode about this time was the meeting between our section and the "Samaritan Brotherhood," which had come from Jerusalem direct on horseback. We halted and talked but a few minutes and then hastened on. About 5 P. M. we caught our first glimpse of "Blue Galilee," and an hour later were filing through the narrow streets of the only city on the lake which existed in the times of our Lord, of which there is no mention made of his having visited.

We were not uncomfortably quartered at the hotels provided for us. We had fish for supper which we had no reason to doubt had been caught from Galilee that morning. A stroll of two miles down the beach brought us to the hot springs and afforded us a view of the ruins of Herod's Palace. On the shore we gathered quantities of shells. The Feast of Purim followed the day of our arrival, and the night was filled with Fourth of July noises which we were told were made by the shooting of Haman. They gave him "Jesse" sure enough! We were told the King of the Fleas dwelt here but we did not make his acquaintance. The morning was ushered in with thunder, lightning and rain, but nothing daunted, we took boat and rode over rough Galilee to Bethsaida, where we lunched and from which we looked away to the place where Capernaum once stood. We were carried by the brawny boatmen out to the boats, which could not come nearer than 50 or 60 feet of the shore. We landed at Magdala, the reputed home of the Mary who wet the Saviour's feet with her tears and wiped them with the hairs of her head—a dirty village of 300 people and one palm tree. Here we mounted our prancing steeds, and rode up the steep ascent which headed us again for Nazareth, in a blinding rain storm. After spending the night at Nazareth. we pushed on for Haifa the next morning. Two and a half miles out we halted and Gimel pointed to the Carmel of sacrifice across the plain of Jezreel, and thence to Jezreel, twelve miles away. To our left as we faced Carmel was Little Hermon and Tabor; the City of Nain, Endor, Shunem and the Gilboa mounts, where Saul and Jonathan fell.

We reached Haifa in time to ride to the top of Mount Carmel, from which we had a wonderful view of the valley and of the sea, over which a rainbow of matchless beauty and perfection trembled upon the face of a storm, then made our descent, and after an absence of three days and nights found ourselves once again safely aboard the "Friesland."

W. A. Robinson.

NORTHERN PALESTINE.

Monday, March 11th, 1895.

A WEEK and a day after landing at Joppa the Friesland with the main party on board sailed away again, pointing northward. In the middle of the afternoon we dropped anchor in the harbor at Caifa. Caifa comes nearest to having a natural harbor of any place in Palestine. Here Mount Carmel pushes its rocky head out into the sea, protecting a little section of water from the force of the south and west winds. The town displays a reasonable amount of commercial prosperity, and some hopeful signs of refinement in special quarters, which you look for in vain in southern Syria.

On the side of Mount Carmel are monkish grottoes, one of which is said to have given shelter to the Holy Family after the return from Egypt. On its summit is a monastery which is the fountain head of the Carmelite order. To Mount Carmel came Elijah, and the priests of Baal and the people with them, to test the question as to whose god was the true God. The prophets of Baal placed their offerings on the wood of the altar and called on the name of Baal, that he might send fire to consume it. And when they had called from morning until noon in vain, Elijah mocked them, suggesting that possibly

Baal might be talking, or on a journey, or peradventure sleeping, " and they leaped upon the altar which they had made, and cried aloud and cut themselves after their manner till the blood gushed out upon them." And, continuing, they prophesied until the time of the offering of the evening sacrifice, and yet " there was neither voice, nor any to answer nor any that regarded." And then Elijah prepared the altar of the Lord, and put the wood in order and laid thereon his offering and called the people to pour water over it all. A second and a third time they poured on water, and he prayed the Lord God, " and the fire of the Lord fell and consumed the burnt sacrifice and the wood and the stones and the dust and licked up the water that was in the trench." And Elijah brought the prophets of Baal down to the brook Kishon and slew every mother's son of them. And thus endeth the first lesson.

And again the prophet stood on the top of Mount Carmel and prayed for rain (for famine threatened the land). And when he had prayed he sent his servant to look out toward the sea. And the man, when he had returned the seventh time, said, " Behold there ariseth a little cloud out of the sea like a man's hand." And the heavens grew black with clouds and there was a great rain—possibly such as we saw from the mountain top, which gathered and broke over us and passing, swept upward along the coast and out to sea, to build a wondrous arch in the clouds which we accepted as a promise of good to come. Here at Caifa, those who came from Joppa by ship and those who had journeyed from Galilee and Samaria by land, met, and once more with a united party the Friesland sailed away out into the night.

208

*Caifa
from
Mt. Carmel.*

Morning found us anchored off Beyrout. Beyrout impressed me favorably. The towns give indications of being more enterprising as we proceed northward. They have a cleanliness and thriftiness specially noticeable after our experience in southern Palestine. Beyrout shows signs of an advanced civilization, and although the streets are full of things oriental, has in places much of the appearance of a European town. It has upwards of a hundred thousand inhabitants and is the most important commercial town of Syria. There is a good artificial harbor with stone piers built out to enclose a section of the sea. Twelve Arabic newspapers are published here. The American (Presbyterian) mission in Syria has its headquarters in Beyrout and is a potent factor in the work of civilization on modern lines. Much of the prosperity and refinement of the section is undoubtedly due to the work of this organization. There are also Scottish, British, German, French and Italian missions and charitable institutions and schools here. Its stores are attractive and appear to be doing business on legitimate lines, and we actually got a delectable course dinner here at a moderate price. Many fine residences are seen in large tree-shaded grounds or with pretty lawns in front.

The principal business appears to be silk culture. The mulberry is common for shade and ornamental purposes and furnishes food for the silk worm. Outside the town are groves of mulberry trees. The trees are of varying sizes, usually from six to eight feet in height. The tops and branches are cut back close to the body, which sends out fresh shoots every year. When they have been stripped of their leaves they are in turn cut off, the result being a big knob at the top of a slender trunk, from which shall spring a mass of new shoots the next following season.   The silk worm is kept in carefully guarded buildings in racks or on trays, where they are supplied with the fresh leaves and allowed to feed until, in the course of nature, they prepare for the transition from the poor grub to the butterfly state.   The moth lays its eggs the latter part of summer, attaching them by a gummy substance to whatever object may be nearest.   The worm hatches out the beginning of the next summer, its shape that of a little gray caterpillar, which appears to have no object in life for a time except to eat, and is content to remain where born if food sufficient is supplied.   It eats of the mulberry leaf voraciously and increases rapidly in size until it is about three inches in length.   At the end of about two months it ceases to eat and begins to spin its cocoon, forming with the spinnerets at its head a continuous double thread from the viscid substance which fills the glands (and which now constitutes a considerable part of its body), and winding this thread round and round its lessening form by adding layer after layer to the inside, until the substance out of which the silken thread is spun is exhausted and the shrunken body lies quiet within.   Experts know by touch when the work is done.   A little less than a week is taken in the spinning of the cocoon which, when completed, is about an inch in length.   If left to itself now it would in two or three weeks eat its way through its covering and come out in its moth form, but the operation would render the silk worthless by cutting the thread, and to prevent this they are subjected to a dry heat, which kills the worm.   Having served the purpose of their lives, from man's point of view, their life is taken and the silken winding sheet which they have spun is unwound from the useless body.

In one of the large establishments devoted to that purpose we saw the process of unwinding. Seated at a long table, in a big room, were nearly a hundred girls and women. Deep pans, let into the table, were filled with water, which was kept at a high temperature by steam passing through it, and in these were masses of the cocoons. The heat softens the glutinous matter so that the outer ends of the threads are loosened, to be picked up by means of a small bundle of twigs to which they adhere, and gathered in a bunch at the side of the dish. Four of

Silk Weaving.

Unwinding the Cocoons.

these threads are gathered into one and passed over a glass rod above the operator's head, then on to a reel which extends the entire length of the table, and kept turning steadily by hand power. As the reel turns the four cocoons from which the thread is unwinding bob and dance about in each pan. When but three cocoons are seen to be in motion, another strand is added deftly to the main thread, and thus continued until all are wound off and appear on the reel a shining mass, seeming like fine wire and yellow as gold.

Silk weaving is carried on in the commonest sorts of sheds, in certain quarters bordering on the streets, where boys and men may be seen working at the rudest of looms, from which, however, are turned out remarkably beautiful fabrics. The weaver sits with his feet in a little pit in front of a swinging frame, which contains a series of reeds like a fine-toothed comb. Through this "comb" the warp is strung, the portion nearest the weaver to be wound around a roller as the weaving progresses, the ends of the warp farthest away passing over another roller, or over a number of wheels, up somewhere at the side of the building, held taut by weights suspended on the gathered strands. The shuttles, carrying the filling of various colored silks as the pattern demands, are shot swiftly back and forth between the spread warp, by quick motion of the hands, the upper and lower warp quickly reversed by means of the rude harness, operated by treadles in the pit, and the shining threads pressed home by the swinging beam brought quickly against them. Fabrics made of the raw silk, usually striped white and gold, are comparatively inexpensive and worn by the common people generally.

A railroad is being built from Beyrout to Damascus. The

212

Cedars of Lebanon.

valley through which it runs and the enclosing hillsides are like a grove with mulberry trees. The verdant valley and sunny hillsides, the square buildings in warm reds and yellows and the mountain sides were very like an Italian scene in form and color, as we saw it that sunny afternoon in March. Beyond, far away at the north, are the snow-covered heights of Lebanon, from whose sides came the cedars which Hiram, king of Tyre, sent in floats to Joppa for the building of the Temple.

At night a reception was tendered the Americans by the Masonic fraternity of Beyrout. It was graciously American in appearance, gorgeous with red, white and blue bunting, and American flags, twined with the colors of the country. The best families of the Syria came to take part, and we understood it was considered a Great Event. A delightful repast was served and a native band, composed half of male and half of female performers, with the Friesland band, furnished music representative of the mixed nations. The dances were "mixed" literally of native and American brands, each very interesting to the other and sometimes funny. Conversation between native and visitor was limited somewhat as to words, but smiles passed current and good fellowship was interchangeable and fully understood.

Somewhere about midnight we sailed away. We have reached the limit of our journey toward the East. Westward, toward home, lies all the rest.

ASIA MINOR.

Friday, March 15th, 1895.

MORNING finds us anchored in the bay of Smyrna along with a number of British ironclads, which have presumably dropped in as a suggestion to the Turk that his some what out-of-date manner of converting Armenians to the Mohammedan way of thinking by cutting their throats, may inadvertently be carried a little too far. We *had* hoped that, not only Britain but even our own, and other nations with powder to burn, would do something more effective than simply stroke the Turkish cat and purr. But then we were only just common private citizens and could hardly be expected to understand affairs of State. Of course, viewed unofficially, it seemed that the Armenians who had been so unfortunate as to have their heads cut off should have some redress, but as they had utterly failed to notify us through the proper channel, we could hardly be expected to take cognizance of unofficial rumors of alleged peculiarities in a Friendly Power. It really made some of us quite provoked, and relations were strained to such an extent that I have no doubt if the Sublime Porte had approached us then and there, it would have been made to feel our serious displeasure. However, as it discreetly kept its distance, and none of the unfortunate creatures came near with complaints, we in time regained our wonted tranquillity, and were enabled to preserve uninterruptedly pleasant relations with the natives. Americans are unquestionably born diplomats.

Smyrna is one of the oldest cities of Asia Minor, and one of the largest. Here is the rush and roar of a great town, with its conflicting interests and trade, in which is a curious blending of European methods with the ways of the Orient. Here the natives wear stockings, suggestive of the colder climate, and heavy shoes, instead of the makeshift slippers seen in Palestine.

Along the water front is a broad esplanade with fine buildings on its far side, many of them elegant and imposing structures. The doors and windows are particularly noticeable for their beautiful iron fret-work wrought in graceful and intricate patterns. The newer buildings are of marble and of stone, green, gray, and chocolate colored, laid in regular order, or like the blocks in a crazy quilt, of every color, artistically mixed to blend harmoniously, each color outlined in white cement. Back on the hill are round structures of brick and ruined castles crowning the heights.

Smyrna is associated in my mind—presumably from trade advertisements—with rugs and figs. The former were much in evidence and many of the party indulged their fancy and sunk considerable sums in their purchase. The latter we filled up with. Smyrna has all the thrift and stir of Beyrout but not the easy going ways of the Syrian towns. You are dealing with a sharper civilization, more polished perhaps, but in trade suggestive, some way, of Ali Baba and the Forty Thieves. The narrower streets in the heart of the old city are covered over with rude, shed-like structures, or with awnings. Its bazaars are vast aggregations of many kinds of business, in niches,

215

in boxes, and on stands devoted to some specialty in linen or silken fabrics or of metal goods in bronze, and trinkets of gold and silver and brass, each one guarded by one or more watchful attendants, who importune you with tempting offers, which you are assured are ruinous to the dealer but where it is unsafe to offer one-third the amount named unless you are prepared to accept it at that price. Through these narrow streets go little donkeys and great two-humped camels with bales of silk and crates of spices or fruits in bulk, as they have been brought in from far away places.

The valley through which we go out of Smyrna on the way to Ephesis is like a garden with vineyards and olive groves and fig trees; with spreading fields of vegetables and springing grain. Farther along it spreads out into a considerable plain, the fields divided by mud embankments or by lines of irrigating ditches. Wild poppies show in patches of bright red, and flowers of yellow, of pink and of purple, in great variety, carpet the uncultivated ground. Across the country go big, noisy, solid-wheeled carts drawn by oxen. Long lines of camels, carrying great bales of goods, are seen coming cityward from the region outside. Flocks of sheep, guarded by herdsmen, appear on plain and hillside when the cultivated land is left behind, and the country generally has an appearance of thrift and prosperity. Even the mud houses of the laborer appear quite comfortable and homelike when compared with the dwellings of a like class seen in Southern Syria. At ancient Ephesis, 54 miles from Smyrna, the railroad ends.

Ephesis once had a trade greater than any other city in Asia and to its harbor came ships from all the known world. Now the harbor is a swamp, the highest tides only reaching places

where in its palmy days came the trading vessels of all lands. Once it had the most magnificent of public buildings and the most wonderful temple the world ever saw, considered then as one of the seven wonders of the world. "Great is Diana of the Ephesians," cried the people to silence Paul when he preached against their idolatrous worship. To-day the outline of its foundation can not be traced even! You see only an irregular depression in the surface, some portions deeper than others, filled with stagnant water; marble columns, fallen, with here and there perhaps a fragment of some marble capital. The tomb of St. Luke; the church of St. John; the prison of St. Paul—are matters of name rather than of fact. Extensive ruins are there, however, scattered about the hillsides and on the plain. Some are mere masses of brick and stone, others have well preserved walls, with domes and towers of stone, and of bright red, fresh-looking brick, the color of which age does not seem to dull. In the hillside is the cave and the church of the Seven Sleepers. There are extensive ruins along the promon-

217

The Hill Citadel.

"Where Storks build their Nests."

tory which juts out into the old harbor and a mediæval castle crowns a hill, the walls seemingly firm as the hill itself. We moralize over a mass of brick and mortar which at one time formed a portion of a great arch, now being riven asunder by the slow pressure of a growing tree which has sprung from some tiny seed that found lodgment in an unguarded crevice. We wonder of the time that has elapsed since water ran in the channel we trace from far away along the winding hillside to cross over the great arched aqueduct to the citadel. On the tops of these broken arches storks build nests and raise their young, unmolested by the people, who believe the birds in coming bring good luck. And these columns and arches, whose history goes back to the days of Paul, have built into them, with the rougher material, sculptured marble of still older ruins, in quantities that lead one to wonder what mighty buildings could have existed then that should make works of art common as the roughest stone.

Backward glancing the mighty past rises. The spreading bay is like changeful silk with its shifting sails and flaunting flags. The plain below throbs with the life of a great city. The hills round about rise in fluffy, vine-covered terraces, on which stand marble villas tipped with bronze and silver and with gold. The summits of the hills are crowned with lordly castles, while like a dream in their midst stands the beautiful temple, serene in its unapproachable splendor.

"Great is Diana of the Ephesians!"

Look again! Nature, aggressive, unresting, has reclaimed her own. The space which the ocean once took away is hers once more. She drapes the crumbling ruins with lines of grace and spreads her carpet of richest verdure across the dead city's level. The olive and the fig and the vine of the hillside yield up their fruitage; the sunlit-earth trembles with rich promise to man. And the women who, on bent knees and with faces to the earth, creep in lines across the lowland, plucking out with earth-smeared hands the evil tares from the precious wheat—what think they? Of the vanished glories of Ephesis, or of their own estate in which they exist but as useful animals? And are they thinking—as animals—of that on which they will be fed when their work is done, or of something higher—of their half-brutal loves, which prove them human; of earthy things just touched with things divine—who shall say? Their field seems narrow but, in their narrowed vision, may it not be filled with light ineffable, far more satisfying to them than the whole earth to those who have reached the mountain's top and standing there but faintly grasp the greater fact that they have only touched the threshold of the great Unknown.

Saturday, March 16th, 1895.

BACK in the shadowy age of myth Greece quickened into life as fox-fire breaks the darkness of some dreary swamp. While the children of Israel were making bricks of mud in the valley of the Nile, Athens was shaping figures in imperishable marble. In days when the ancient British savage was painting his body blue with woad—before even nations which now control the earth were born—Athens had reached the zenith of her glory and shone resplendent on the heights! Then came the decline, and when the day was dawning on a new western world the light was fading here, and Athens the Beautiful in its debasement became a vassal of the sensual Turk—its governor a eunuch!

Yesterday we sailed all day through the beautiful Ægean Sea, threading our way among submerged mountains, whose tops rise up out of the blue waters like towers, their summits crowned by gray castles, while clustering villages cling to their seamed sides or fringe the water line, as shell-fish hang along some half-sunken ocean pier. No wonder the people who lived on these islands became heroes and pirates and patriots, for every island was a fortress and its master a king.

Early in the day we approach the main land and, passing

through the narrow entrance to the inner harbor, anchor before the ancient city of Piræus, the seaport of Athens. It is a comely city we see here. Back of it rise rounded hills and low mountains; on their sides gray villas and castles and little villages. Piræus exists because of Athens. It is the landing place simply, but, like those who serve royalty, great because

Piræus.

of its connection with greatness. Of old, diverging lines of walls extended from Athens to Piræus on the west and Phalereus, a little to the east, affording a covered way to and from the sea. Athens lies back there five miles away, white and gray, and above it rises the Acropolis, crowned with rare Minerva's perfect temple.

How different land and people here from what we saw yesterday, and the days before. Not so picturesque perhaps; not so virile; not throbbing so with intense animal life, but a land and people shorn of their crudities by long ages of polishing, differing from the others as an ivory statue differs from the rude totem of the Alaskan Indian. The newly discovered sense of the beautiful, born in the awakening savage, displays itself in raw color and angular form: here you hardly realize the existence of color at all until you analyze the seeming neutral tint and find it the solar spectrum itself! Here is the refinement of art which conceals art. Here forms of beauty are the rule; the uncommon is common. In the plethora of perfection even the uneducated eye unconsciously detects the discordant note, if any, and is hurt by its presence.

What effect has art on a people? Unquestionably we are influenced for good or evil by our environment. The man who lives among brutes becomes brutish. The priest who sheds blood in sacrifice will lose his natural horror of blood and learn to value life itself lightly. Beautiful flowers bring thoughts of better things. Association with forms of beauty lead to unconscious grace and a love of those things which the senses approve. Perfection? Far from it. Judged by his own standard, the Greek is found wanting. Common clay could hardly hope to reach the high plane of the gods and goddesses of ancient Helas, but the legacy of the beautiful past is with the Greek of to-day, and he is a nobler creature because of that past. The natives of the Orient will tell you that the Greek is entirely dishonest and the Thief of the World. I think, however, a part of this is due to pure envy, because he is the smarter thief when he makes theft his business. He is more gifted than his noisy brother of the far East, and when he does cheat you he does it in such a pleasant, gentlemanly sort of way that you feel it is better to be diplomatized out of a dollar by him than to be beaten out of a dime by a howling, gesticulating, low-down Arab or an oily, unclean beast of a Turk.

It is not safe to accept noise and bluster as proof. Flitting writers sometimes—too often, I fear—play to the gallery where they find the boxes unresponsive. They lay sweeping condemnation on peoples, and arraign, breezily, on hearsay, conditions which they can not possibly understand, trusting that no one will think to investigate. It is so easy to make faces at the chained tiger, even to twist the lion's tail when at a safe distance!

Greece is but a tiny spot on the great earth. Among kingdoms she is of little note; her powers are hardly worth considering; her credit, nothing. As a money-maker she has proved a dismal failure, yet her chief city stands peerless, crowned with a noble past. She has been plundered—legally perhaps, but plundered all the same—of the greater part of her gems by friends in her days of necessity; but much is still there, and although the jewels stripped from her white breast are now the priceless treasures of other nations, her glory stands forever. Athens belongs—not to Greece alone but to all the earth, for she is the fountain-head of all that is most beautiful in poetry and art and the common mother of earth's most noble thought.

The city of Athens is pleasant to look upon. It is red-roofed and gray-walled. Its public buildings are works of art, as might be expected of its people; its private places, however expensive or rich in decoration, are chaste in form, with a unity of design which does not exalt one portion to the debasement of another. The streets are broad and clean, many of them paved with white marble and with curbing and sidewalks

of the same. Royalty is gentle. Tradesmen are courteous without being servile. Even the street hawkers, who sell you alleged pilfered bits of the Acropolis in minature monuments of many colored stones, have a self-respecting air which challenges admiration and checks a disposition to dicker. Its stores are models of their kind. The dress commonly seen on the street does not differ materially from that of Paris or London, or New York—except in occasional instances. That which attracts most attention and seems most foreign there is really the national Albanian dress seen on some visiting countryman or on the king's special guards.

Some of the customs strike a westerner as curious. Along the clean streets, with slow step, comes a procession. It is a funeral *a la mode*. The paid bearers wear uniforms of lace-bordered caps, and skirts. The coffin is formed of two half sections. The upper half, draped with flowers, is carried upright between two men at the head of the procession. Then come bearers with the lower half, on which rests the body, on which also rest large masses of beautiful flowers. The body is richly dressed and the flesh painted to give the appearance of life. Even in death their devotion to art cannot be forgotten. Following the coffin are friends on foot, and after them comes the empty hearse drawn by four horses.

And what is this which approaches? Is it a man? It is a man! It is one of the king's guards. See how it is dressed. Quilted skirt, like a ballet dancer; scarlet cord with tassel, gartering white stockings at the knees; red shoes, turned up at the toes and with big balls of red cotton at the tips; corded cap; brass buttons and short sword.   And in this figure—we may be looking at a descendant of some ancient Spartan!

But the chief interest at Athens is in the dead past, in its philosophers, its poets, its orators, its warriors—heads of classes that have never been equalled—so great that the universal world claims them as its own.   Here Homer wrote his "Iliad" nine hundred years before the Christ.   Here immortal Demosthenes displayed the power of oratory never approached since—unless perhaps by the local lecturer who shows you about and spouts in shaky English to the exhaustion of his noble theme.   Demosthenes spoke 385 years before Christ.

Prison of Socrates.

Before Demosthenes came—more than a hundred years—Socrates was convicted of telling the truth unnecessarily about his neighbors, so that, much as they admired the old philosopher, they felt obliged to request him to shut up or make way with himself.   He preferred death, and found it in a dose of cold hemlock, glad possibly of an excuse for going where his sharp-tongued wife could no more find fault with him for want of fire. The prison in the rock where he was confined before his death is shown, the front barred for some unexplained reason.

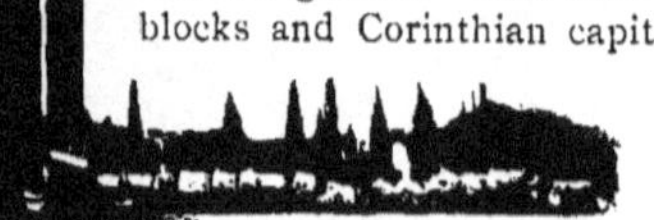

Of the Temple of Jupiter enough remains to indicate its matchless grandeur in the days when it stood complete. A number of the columns stand in a group, supporting massive girders.   One column lies as it fell, with fluted blocks and Corinthian capital prone along the ground.

At the theatre of Bacchus are broken statues and fragments of figures innumerable. Tier on tier, in widening rings, rise the

Theatre of Bacchus.

stone seats in the circling hillside, as they were two thousand years ago. The marble seats of the nobles and the throne of royalty is here, but all horribly suggestive of an ice-cold, cast-iron sort of luxury beside which a common chair with a cushion would be a welcome substitute. Herod's theatre gives the best idea of the ancient play-house. It is a semi-circle cut out of the rock of the Acropolis. The massive walls, in which were the rooms surrounding the stage, are still well preserved, and the great stage itself with its tiers of platforms affording space for the multitude that engaged in the grand tableaus and spectacular displays of those ancient days.

Temples are on every hand. Every profession had its titular god, every god its temple. In Egypt the gods have wives and children and brothers and sisters and mothers-in-law and cousins several times removed. At Athens a god who was any sort of a god at all insisted on owning a shrine and running it without any other members of the family to interfere. They had a god for every profession, condition, and time and— for fear they might inadvertently overlook some deserving little son-of-a-god—a special altar dedicated to the "Unknown God," who probably got the sweepings. But this

Theatre of Herod.

The Acropolis.

The Parthenon stands centrally at the highest point of the Acropolis. A little to the left on the far side is the Erectheum with the Caryatides. At the left is the Propylæa and its approach. The Theatre of Bacchus lies at the extreme right, and Herod's Theatre, nearest of the ruins, at the base of the rock. Just outside the limits of the picture at the left is Mars Hill.

Mars Hill.

extra gave to Paul the opening he was quick to seize upon
when he told the scoffing Athenians, ''whom therefore ye ig-
norantly worship, him declare I unto you.'' Paul's temple was
the one which all the arts of Athena could not raise. Its roof
was the blue dome of heaven, its floor the common rock, his
pulpit Mars Hill. Mars Hill is but a rough, rocky knob on the
side of the Acropolis hill, with an open space all round, where
now, as in the past, an orator with good lungs might make
himself heard by all the populace.

The Acropolis can be gained from one side only. At all
other points it presents vertical walls. The slope, as you look
up toward the entrance, is flanked on the left by Mars Hill, on
the right by the theatre of Herod. An impregnable fortress
against which mortal valor could not prevail in the old days,
it remained for the vandals of the days of gunpowder and shot
and shell to disfigure its more than earthly beauty. Up the
slope to its grand portals and through its columned propylæum
to the inner height, where of old rolled chariots; climbing the
steep slope of rock within, marked with cross-ruts cut to give

the horses foot-hold and showing still the marks of ancient chariot wheels, we go and stand in the court of the temple where Art was religion and so-called Reason reigned supreme.

Ruins only, but such ruins!

One feels like uncovering before the shrine of the heathen goddess. From the casket most of the jewels have been taken, but not all. England grabbed the Elgin marbles when the world was indifferent—not knowing they were in the market—then the world awoke and cried "stop thief." But I suspect the chief regret of those who shouted most was that England had got the start of the rest, and there are believed to be others who would willingly bear the name to possess the treasure.

Portions of the grand temple yet remain. There are sculptured figures there that are above price. On one side stand the matchless Carytides, where they stood by the gilded fane when the Christian religion was but a dream among savages. Five are patrician. Who shall say they are not silent in their outraged dignity at the presence among them of the plebeian face which came to take the place of the one which was stolen. They are scarred and maimed and broken but beautiful beyond compare. Here are the ruins of the temple of Wingless Victory, from which victory has flown—for lack of wings could not hold her in the roofless ruin.

There was also an old building up there, which they called the "Parthenon,"—but it looked draughty and unsafe, and I don't think anybody lived in it anyway.

CONSTANTINOPLE AND THE TURK.

A T Piræus we were told the ship would not go to Constantinople! Asiatic cholera had broken out there in its most virulent form—or was momentarily expected to break out—and the fierce, ravening microbe was said to be lying in wait to pounce upon any one rash enough to enter the Golden Horn. For had not Piræus (and also the island of Popycock, or something thereabout) quarantined against vessels coming from Constantinople? Was not such evidence convincing? The fact that the ports mentioned were jealous commercial rivals of the Levantine capital and in the habit of doing this very thing at intervals did not count. And when we suggested that we had already landed at Piræus, and didn't care a rap about the other place, the triumphant fact remained and settled the question against us. It was really absurd for us to argue that we would be justified in taking the risk simply because other vessels on like quest were coming and going! Any way, whether Asiatic cholera was there, or had been, or was going to be, the captain didn't consider it safe, and had set his face as a rock against the senseless desire of the Westerners to rush in where captains fear to tread. We remembered that the Azores had dropped out of the itinerary because the ship was behind her schedule time. As to Malta, the Friesland was of the kind that pass in the night. The island of Rhodes had also been skipped—same old reason. It was now planned to skip Constantinople—that place of paramount interest—on general principles, according to general belief!

At this point the Westerner got down and "kicked." It was not *his* fault that the anchor had been weighed and found wanting. *He* did not run the ship aground at Port Said, nor was he responsible for the cost of getting her off. Even the fact that she consumed more coal while running than when lying still was not thought sufficient reason for breaking contracts. He had paid for going to Constantinople and he proposed to *go* to Constantinople or know the reason why. He had his ticket—printed plainly in good old fashioned English. The manager held the company's contract, specific, voluminous —with certain provisions, however, which left it completely at the captain's discretion and on shipboard the captain is King. It was a triangular question and the captain sat serenely on the apex!

The Westerner held a mass-meeting and adopted resolutions. He used some pointed language (which is ordinarily printed in dashes), and proposed to take it out of the manager. The manager, with the prospect of being crushed between the upper and the nether mill stones, was not happy, but finally cast in his lot with the Westerner and cabled the ship's owners at New York.

The owners ordered the captain to take us to Constantinople.

Our way that night and the next day lay through the beautiful Grecian Archipelago and up the Dardanelles—that narrow strait down which come pouring the swift waters of the Black

Sea, gathered from many streams of Europe and Asia and of Asia Minor.

In the steely blue of late afternoon the sun shows us, picked out in lines of light, excavations which they tell us reveal the ruins of ancient Troy. In fancy we picture the mighty walls, the swarming populace, matchless Helen, Paris, and of course the wooden horse. Here, across this narrowest part of the Hellespont, Xerxes stretched his bridge of boats, and here, perhaps, Leander swam from shore to shore to meet his priestess and confess—and once too often swam, else the story would

In the Dardanelles.

never have been told, for the achievement did not seem so very difficult as we looked upon it. I am not so sure that I would not have undertaken it myself under certain conditions. I am quite positive that there were a number on board our ship who would have ventured if perchance their individual Hero had stood waiting on the other side, instead of separated from them only by the arms of a steamer chair—*that* even at times seemed a cruel, cruel distance. Do not believe that the days of chivalry have entirely passed away. Leander's case was lifted out of the ordinary—not because of what *he* did, but because his Hero showed her woman's nature by electing to join him in his watery grave rather than to live out her life without him.

It is nearly sunset when we come to anchor in the narrowest part of the Dardanelles, where long black guns lie on the green slope of substantial earthworks guarding the way to Turkey's capital, and wait until the Turkish inspector finds time to come out and satisfy himself that we are proper persons to enter the Sultan's possessions, then we steam slowly ahead into the night and onward through the little sea of Marmora.

Constantinople is covered by a luminous fog, when in the morning we creep slowly up through the Bosphorus. Later the sun burns his way through, and dissipating the mists shows us the city which promised so many interesting things. There is something uncommonly attractive about this place. So little is positively known—or at least is known so doubtfully; so many things are hinted at that are delightfully near the improper; the Sultan himself is so charmingly wicked, and we, being Americans, are to be granted unusual honors, and have fluttering hopes of being able to clasp the royal hand. And it is hinted also that the ladies of the party—being Americans— are to be invited to a special reception to be given by the ladies of the royal harem, and, being women, very naturally have a desire to see how a man with fifty—or is it five hundred?— wives, will behave in company. But alas, through the irony of fate it is not to be, for the ship is late.

Unusual courtesies have been extended in many places because of the far-reaching links in the chain which binds together the members of the Mystic Brotherhood. At the Bermudas arrangements had been made for a public reception, which failed only because the ship did not reach her appointed place.   At Cairo it took the form of a banquet and an excursion on the Nile.   At Jerusalem sessions of the Mother Lodge were held in King Solomon's ancient quarries, followed by a reception at the leading hotel.   At Beyrout a ball and banquet were given.   Here the arrangements were in the hands of Oriental brethren high in authority, and was to include a banquet, a visit to the royal treasure-house and an audience with the Sultan himself some time during the stay.   But the management on shipboard—which did not take into consideration the American disposition to rebel—had spoiled it all.   The report of the existence of Asiatic cholera at Constantinople was made an excuse for cancelling all arrangements there and notice to that effect was wired on while yet the members of the party rested in blissful ignorance of the fact, content with the assurance that all possible efforts would be made to accomplish the desired end.   As a result, when the Friesland finally sailed up the Bosphorus she came as an unexpected guest, who, having first declined an invitation, arrives but to find the dinner cold and the servants off on a holiday.

And this is why the Americans did not clasp the hand of the Son of Heaven or the ladies see the inside of the royal harem!

We are not disappointed, however, in finding Constantinople an interesting city.   It is beautiful to look upon as we see it first from the water, with many stately blocks lifting their fronts like steps, one above another as the hills rise from the waters' edge; white palaces and mosques with moon-like domes and slender minarets, all gleaming brightly in the morning sunshine as the fog parts and rolls away.   Pera, Galata and ancient Stamboul, three cities in one, form modern Constantino-

235

ple. Between Galata, the higher city, and Stamboul, the older,
extends the Golden Horn inland, a harbor free from the swift
current of the Bosphorus which sweeps past outside. It is
alive with moving craft and crossed by bridges on boats, the

Stamboul and the Golden Horn.

lower one, leading to Stamboul, presenting a scene of shifting
forms and colors like a kaleidoscope. Stamboul juts out into
the strong current of the Bosphorus and is of chiefest interest.
Among the many minarets we can see rising the flattened
dome of St. Sophia.

The streets of Constantinople! Ah its streets! Occasionally
is one seen broad and clean, but as a rule they are narrow and
undeniably dirty. Things are there that were better removed.

Galata from Stamboul.

The people are evidently not hampered by obnoxious sanitary regulations.

The dogs of Constantinople are the most notable feature of the streets, and are as offensively characteristic as anything Turkish can be. I expected to find them there but I had the impression that they existed on sufferance only. Instead they are honored guests. I supposed they were simply tolerated; I found them fixtures by rights which no Mussulman questions, and with privileges which a common human being could not indulge in without risk of the bastinado. They are a public charge, fed at public expense, or from funds provided for that purpose as one might endow a chair of dogology in some college. They have no fear of, and but little interest in, man or woman, except as a medium through which their food is supplied. They roam their several beats at will or lie sleeping, stretched in sunny places, or wake to snap at pestiferous flies, while pedestrians step over or around them in the most matter-of-fact manner possible, never seeming to think of suggesting that they get out of the way. The people there are high steppers generally. They become so of necessity—in stepping over the sleeping dogs. I fell easily into the habit myself, and could step over one almost as unconcernedly as could a native born. The dog doesn't mind unless you step on him, or hit him in passing. When this happens he seems to be surprised, and may whine or snarl after you have passed. Whatever the standard of honor among the dogs themselves, it is evident they do not expect ill

238

*Dogs
of
Constantinople.*

treatment from the human animals with which they occupy the
street in common. They have something the appearance of
the fox about them, of tawny yellow generally, although mixed
black and white is not uncommon. They are intensely clannish
in their habits. They live and die in the street or section
where they are born. Ordinary dog-courtesy does not seem to
prevail among the pampered sons of the streets of Constantinople. Every dog has its place as well as day, and every other
dog sees that he is kept in it. If by chance, or in search of
adventure, one happens to stray beyond the limit of his beat,
the members of the family into whose territory he has ventured
quickly unite in apprising him of his mistake and it is sometimes
a question if he escapes with his life.

I think the secret of the dog's immunity from human perse-
cution here, where they are so obviously a nuisance, is not, as
sometimes explained, because they are the city's scavengers,
for they probably bring more filth than they remove, but in
every dog the faithful Mussulman sees a possible reincarnation
of a former friend. It is believed that Mahomet will himself
some day come back to earth in form of a dog and an injury to
one of these might in the course of events be a dishonor to the
Immaculate One. I am inclined to think there may be something in the belief. By inverse reasoning it seems quite prob-
able that the reincarnation business works both ways, and that
the soul of a dog looks out of the eyes of the average Turk—
and rather a low-down breed of dog at that.

In the streets are people of many nations, exceeded in variety
nowhere perhaps outside of Cairo or Algiers. Along its quays
go porters bending low under immense loads of materials which
in the West would be handled on drays. Bread and cake,

Off his beat.

239

*A
Street
Car.*

Turkish sweets, and things which the small boy loves, are hawked about the streets with senseless cries interminable. In public places are seen the long haired dervishes, barefooted, dignified, begging their bread, for to beg is a part of their religion.  Men with jars, or water bags, strapped to their backs, representative of some public benefactor who has set aside a fund for this special holy charity, are dispensing water to those who will partake. They have different cups for different people and beliefs—the common, the not so common, and the special; the latter for the Muslim, who would consider himself contaminated by putting his lips to that which a Jew or a Christian had touched.

In public places are monoliths from Egypt and marbles filched from Athens. In the mosque of St. Sophia the Turk has carefully destroyed every form of Christian life, and obliterated or covered over all paintings or suggestion of its Christian builders.

St. Sophia is the most notable mosque of the city and every visitor goes there. The name has survived although the original church, built by Constantine about 325 A.D., was destroyed. Another St. Sophia, erected on the same spot, shared the same fate in 415 during the reign of Justinian, who at once became sorry that he had permitted it, and set about erecting another in expiation, building it in its present form. The cost was enormous. The effort seemed to have been to make expense a prime object, possibly with a thought of atonement or perhaps in that wanton spirit which led the Egyptian queen to dissolve and drink the pearl. It is estimated to have cost upwards of sixty millions of dollars. Into its building and furnishing went the choice things from despoiled temples of the

A Public Offering.

Mosque of St. Sophia.

known world. The art treasure of captive nations and the priceless jewels of pagan peoples were here gathered to do honor to dominant Christianity. The dome of the tabernacle was of pure gold, surmounted by a gold cross en-crusted with precious stones. Its sacred vessels were of gold, the altar of molten gold, into which had been cast pearls and sapphires and diamonds, seemingly simply with a view to enhance the cost. It is of magnificent proportions. The dome rises a hundred and seventy-five feet above the floor. Two mosques like the Mosque of Omar, one standing on top of the other, might almost rest beneath this great concave.

In 1453 the Turk took possession and turned the Christian out. He appropriated the available gold and jewels for that which in his eye seemed better uses. He covered the mosaics of the interior with plaster—for the painted forms of living things were an abomination in the eye of the Mussulman. Under the plaster of St. Sophia to-day are the mosaics of the early Christian church. In the name of Art at least it is to be hoped that some day a more tolerant religion may bring its ancient beauties to light.

Before landing I had been advised by the manager that I must not carry my kodak ashore! The sub-manager asserted that the police would seize and smash the machine on sight! The local manager came up with suggestions that an attempt to take pictures would quite probably breed a riot! I went ashore with fear and trembling and called on the American consul. He thought I might venture, but suggested, diplomatically, that it would be well not to take a brass band along, and if I got into trouble to send for him. So I went snapping about with a special guide. I was specially warned against photographing the dogs or Turkish ladies, but the dogs didn't object and I doubt if the ladies would if they had known— it's their owners you must look out for. I secured a good assortment of dogs but don't think I captured any ladies worth mentioning. The only ones I got near enough to to photograph (except one dilapidated specimen who was distributing dog-meat) were carrying fat, black-eyed babies, and were, I suspect, only nurse girls. The valuable ones were in closed carriages or at home behind bars.

Every one who visits Turkey proposes to investigate the multo-marriage muddle prevailing there. It usually ends in glittering generalities or in a rehash of sensational reports and suppositions. I regret that, although we spent an entire day there, I was unable to sift the system to the bottom. This question of questions is a question to which it seems impossible to get a satisfactory reply. It is a subject about which you are not encouraged to talk among those who are qualified to speak intelligently. You are trenching on delicate ground. It seems to be the great object in a Mussulman's life, and yet you must ignore its existence except in a general way. You are left in doubt whether it is considered a sacrament too holy to be discussed between men ordinarily or the other extreme, about which coarse men may talk but gentlemen never, unless perhaps muddled with drink—and, as to become drunken is a great sin in a Mohammedan, *this* road to knowledge is practically closed to the investigator. There seemed to be but one satisfactory way out of the difficulty—to set up an experimental establishment in the interest of science; but time was not allowed for this even, and the cloud of ignorance still remains as dense as ever.

" He takes a fresh one every Easter," said my guide, an intelligent Jew, jerking his head over toward the Sultan's palace.

The Sultan may be able to do this, because he doesn't have to buy Easter hats for Number One ever year; but there are two sides to the question. Some who are nearer to his majesty than my friend of the street intimate that it is not because he is such a dash of a fellow but that it is an established custom which it would not be safe for even his royal head to defy. There are other interests than his own involved, for every new wife brings a new family of relatives, which must be provided with offices or created nobles or something of that nature. This absolute despot is the slave of his people, to the extent at least that he is expected to take " a fresh one " once a year, and the young woman who can be worked off on the somewhat overloaded head of the government is a valuable piece of property.

I was unable to get a shot at any members of the royal harem, but secured by purchase a picture which is called " The Queen of the Harem." It is a fake, of course, because the Turk able to own such a piece of property as that would not put it on exhibition. It is interesting, however, as illustrating the supposed butterfly existence of a creature whose life of sunshine is never disturbed by wordly cares. The Oriental values his women highly according to established standards, and treats her as well as he does any other domestic animal contributing to his pleasure or profit. Why not? She is useful in many ways. In the lower walks she is the bearer of burdens. The wealthy ornaments his house with her in number as his means permits. It is true she has not the freedom of a slave even. She is guarded jealously, night and day, as a

"The Queen of the Harem."

formless thing without knowledge of right or wrong—as incapable of resistance where her master, man, is concerned, and
not to be trusted in the slightest degree.   He credits her with
a certain kind of intelligence—that she should know good from
evil—but finds it safer to turn the key on her all the same.   It
is understood generally that she has no soul of her own—or at
least is not responsible for it in any future state—but is thought
to possess a rudimentary sort of a one, sufficient for reincarnation purposes.   *That* much would seem necessary, for the Mohammedan's paradise would be a dreary place indeed without
her.   It would be the play of Hamlet with the Royal Dane
left out.

Religion has a strong hold on the Turk.   He prays on his
knees at stated periods—on the stranger without ceasing.   The
humblest rascal on the streets makes much of his faith.   He
will drop your much valued kodak—and himself also—to the
ground without warning when he hears the muezzin's call for
prayer.   This faithfulness to religious form is not confined to
the humble.   It is a matter of state.   When the Sultan goes
to pray it is a national event and calls for the whole army and
a lot of brass bands.

Watch the devout Mussulman prepare himself for prayer in
the mosque.   He washes his feet as a necessary, preliminary
part of the proceedings.   If the foot basin is not convenient he
makes use of the drinking fountain—
he is not particular—the build of his
bloomers enables him to perform feats
impossible in the Western dress.   His
ablution performed, he gets down on
hands and knees on the rug and in al-

ternate bowing and rising, with recitation of prayers, makes his way like a measuring worm to the sacred east. His prayer consists almost entirely of passages from the Koran, which he has learned and repeats, parrot-like, the import of which he need not necessarily understand.

The followers of El-Islâm charge it as a sin against Christians that they keep no fasts and are undeserving of the delights of the next world, as they deny themselves nothing in this. The Muslim is consistent in that *he* does deny himself certain pleasures at certain times. For the entire month *Ramadân* he fasts during the day, neither eating nor drinking from daybreak until sunset. It was during this month that we were passing through Mohammedan countries and from Cairo to Constantinople could note the usual practice among the faithful. We saw even policemen going about the streets telling their beads to keep their minds out of their stomachs!

The Mussulman believes that his is superior to all other peoples or religions. Whatever his sins, he is foreordained to be saved, albeit he may tarry in purgatory for a time. He may do evil, but the evil is weighed with the good and is not counted against him if the good he does bears down the scales on the other side. He recognizes but one God. Adam, Noah, Abraham, Jesus and Mohammed were prophets. Mohammed, the last, was the greatest of all and the appointed mediator between God and man. It would seem that a religion which so reveres created life that it is thought to be a sin to imitate its form even, would have some regard for human creatures. It might be trusted to treat Christians as the equals of the street dogs at least—but it doesn't.

It may not be best to provoke comparisons, in view of the

blood shed by early Christians when they were on top. They acted according to their light. It may be said of the Muslim that he also is acting according to his light now, but the difference is that the Turk is still groping along with the old tallow-dip in these days of the electric search-light, which rivals the sun. Mahomet preached conversion by the sword. His followers to-day continue to practice what he preached and follow with a quick jab of the pike—as a saving ordinance—to make angels of the converts before they have time to fall from grace.

After making all due allowance for a fanatical, half-savage people in rebellion against established authority, there is little doubt but that the Turk—equally savage and fanatical—has, by his inhuman acts, forfeited his right to existence among civilized nations, and the best thing that could possibly happen for all parties concerned would be for the combined powers to run him into some asylum for insane criminals and parcel out his possessions among themselves, not forgetting to set aside a goodly slice for poor little Greece.

It is not a question of religion simply but of humanity.

Naples and Vesuvius.

NAPLES.

March 22d, 1895.

WAVERING and uncertain is the shore-line of the Bay of Naples when we look upon it first in the morning. Towering cumuli hang on the shoulders of Vesuvius—seen dimly at times, in the center of a lurid vortex—then they are torn asunder and the sun, as if forming a part in the grand display of nature's mighty forces, flames out across the volcano's smoking head. Later the mists sweep upward and away, and the golden glory of the peerless bay rests before us as pictured in fancy for long expectant years—a sheet of shimmering turquoise held within a circling shore that stretches like a sharp edged sickle in a gradually widening curve far away into the blue distance, its gleaming edge sharply defined in light, its ribbed back studded with emeralds and rubies and pearls.

About us lie white-hulled ships and rakish steamers, and clumsy craft, filled with natives who come to offer help, to sell, and to solicit under various guises. We are in the land of song and musicians are about us in the boats below—fierce looking men and black eyed women and girls with viol and guitar and mandolin—singing brightly (although for a fact there seems rather too much tremolo at times, suggestive of the bleating of a shivering goat, to suit my unappreciative ear) and watching sharply for the coins which the voyagers toss down to them.

Here we, who have formed the big family of the Friesland for so long a time, are to separate and go our different ways back to our homes. Some will continue with the ship around Gibraltar, through the tempestuous Bay of Biscay and the English Channel to Antwerp, thence back to New York ; others—and they the great majority—by varying lines across Europe to regain the ship at the Flemish capital, while still others will return by other ships and other lines across the ocean to their western homes. Those who are to continue on the Friesland land first, that they may make the most possible of the limited time allowed them on shore and get back to sail again in the afternoon ; others who are to spend but a short time in Naples come next, while a third lot, composed of such as are to proceed leisurely across country, generously give way and land last.

It is with mixed feelings that we bid the " Friesland " good-bye. Not all of pleasure has been the time spent on board, but it has been our abiding place in time of danger, our *home*, and is endeared to us by ties stronger than we suspected until called upon to part, and many an eye moistens and many a throat fills with a stifling lump as her lessening bulk grows dim with distance. Dear old Friesland ! Staunch, steady, reliable. We did not fully appreciate all of your good points while with you. It wanted the experience which we later had of the long, slim, screwy, wriggly ocean liners, where speed was the great de-sideratum, to give us a lasting sense of the comfort of your broader hull. You did not fail us in our time of need and the recollection of unpleasant features which were unavoidable has vanished, and in place remains abiding love.

We run the gauntlet of the custom house (where nothing seems contraband but tobacco, which is made to suffer for the sins of all) and disperse, some to find quarters in hotels, some to go about the city in carriages, some to Mount Vesuvius, some to prowl about buried Herculaneum and uncovered Pompeii.

In the breaking up, a trio went out together, held by congenial tastes—Æsculapius, the Prince of Michigan, and the Man-with-the-Kovered-Kodak. The first, a traveler of old, was an adept in looking out for Number One—and knew ways that redounded to the advantage of numbers Two and Three. He was a vast, bristling, symbolic American Kick where he thought imposition attempted, but the men and maids of his section of the ship found—when old ocean seemed yawning to engulf them, and they themselves but an aching void—that he was soft as a baby and helpful as a blustering cherub, scattering sunshine, powders and pills in his pathway, without money and without price.

The Prince was built substantially—else he never could have lasted back to land. He started in with all known aids to comfort. He was filled to the brim with pertinent poetry; with history of things past, and with forecasts of things to come. He laughed at the demon *mal de mere*, for had he not the means by which it could be exorcised? But the storm struck—and the fabric fell! Then he gave up his firmly established theories—in fact he gave up almost everything that was not fast internally—and smiled like a seraph through all, rejoicing that he still lived. On land he shed light and gladness wherever he went. His other unattached belongings he also shed, from Gibraltar to the Golden Horn, and then laid in a fresh supply to distribute through Europe. He was solid as a rock—gentle as a girl. His laugh was infectious—exhilarating as a tonic tornado; women trusted him as a father confessor; the church welcomed him on sight, yet—it is a curious fact—when any new and particularly atrocious story got about, somebody would be sure to say "it's Loud's latest." His accomplishments included what he called "Michigan French," and brought order out of many a verbal chaos. It passed current in Algiers; the donkey boys understood it in Egypt; it worked well in Jerusalem; classic Greece felt its power; it conquered Rome; it wormed its way through Switzerland; it was even understood in Paris! I believe with English and Michigan French one could travel anywhere.

The doctor also was something of a linguist. His vocabulary was not large but it was forcible. It was glorious to see the natives jump when he, bringing his umbrella down with sounding raps, to punctuate his words, would shout:

"Hi! you there, Cha'ley! Mush *daw* de crap-*poo*—wot you *'bout*, bring us something to eat—coffee, beefsteak, anything-yougot—Bif—*stek*, caf-*faa*, moo-*tan*. Un-stan—an' be quick about it." And we usually got it.

In Cairo he added "coochy-coochy" to the formula. At Naples he worked in "macaroni spaghetti" in a most effectual way and later drew on his fund of apothecary's Latin in a way to make classic Rome howl.

As to the Man-with-the-Camera? Modesty sits on top the struggling tribute. Anyway he couldn't have been a very bad sort or the other two wouldn't have stuck to him as they did.

The streets of Naples are full of life and color—of color such
as the Italian loves—wondrously harmonious at a distance,
horrible in its discordant combinations of rank greens and blues
and browns and reds and yellows near by—as displayed in the
fabrics with which the people cover themselves.   The men and
women of the Bayside streets are such as come to us in the new
world.   Men; small of stature, muscular, low-browed, black-
bristled, brass-bejeweled; women; black-eyed, frowzy-headed,
heavy bodied, beaded and banded, bewrapped, bescarfed, and
wadded; early ripe and quickly aged, seeming old with years
while yet the glorious women of England and America are but

"Spaghetti."

gathering perfection of form
and sweetness.

Here are fruit stands, junk
dealers, fisher women, peddlers and beggars.   Makers
of macaroni are alongside the
open ways, and masses of
spaghetti, hanging on poles
in folds like skeins of yarn,
its loops scarce clearing the
filthy pavement, are not particularly comforting to lovers
of the glutinous stuff.   Here come loads of garden truck, piled
high on long-poled, springless carts, drawn by horse, or dog, or
donkey, or by the long-horned Roman cow—either alone or all
in combination—it matters little what the combination, so long
as the motive power is secured.

Some fine horses are seen and a lesson taught.   The Italian is
merciful to his beast, and instead of the horrible iron bit

255

with which the horse of Palestine and Arabia and the United States and some other countries, is tortured, they use a band of leather or metal fitting around over the nose, with bars projecting on either side, at the ends of which are rings where the guiding reins are attached, leaving the mouth free for purposes for which nature intended it. Draught horses, particularly ones attached to carts, have heavy saddles strapped to their backs, rising from which are highly ornamented single or triple horns of wood, leather or metal, studded often with brass nails and further ornamented with tufts of hair or gaily colored ribbons.

The milk peddler, with his leisure-loving cows or droves of goats with tinkling bells, comes through the streets ready to draw a fresh supply for you while you wait—presumably unadulterated, although it is asserted that some of the wily sons of Sunny Italy have learned to carry water in bags to mix judiciously with the foaming liquid by means of a rubber tube which passes down their sleeve.

Venerable padres, clean-shaven and well-fed, in black gown and furry hats, are often seen. Soldiers—horse and foot—are common about the streets, and not a bad looking lot of men, albeit picturesque fellows with felt hats weighted down on one side by a mass of fluttering cock's feathers have a somewhat festive appearance.

Often among the common surroundings are seen beautiful pieces of sculpture, uncared for and seeming of little note. In the better quarters the public buildings are works of art. The museum contains the finest collection of bronzes in the world and many noted master-pieces by celebrated sculptors. It contains also—most interesting of all—the great collection of

256

A Milk Train.

marbles and mural paintings recovered from Herculaneum and Pompeii, some of which speak better for. the art education of the people who lived in those days than for their morals.

The prevailing architecture of the city, aside from its public buildings, which are palaces, shows a tendency skyward, a general look of being squeezed thin with a multitude of excrescences in shape of small balconies, the railings of which are usually hung with things to dry; of a network of clotheslines crossing over narrow streets like cobwebs in a dusty garret, and on these lines flapping garments in variegated colors and forms answering purposes at which you wonder and may sometimes guess. Outside the denser portions of the city the buildings are squatty, square-topped and decaying, giving one the impression of dry-goods boxes piled irregularly, picturesque enough but not notably clean or attractive. At many points along the street which follows nearest to the circling shore—a dirty way of shops and stores and swarming, ill-appearing natives—are arched openings through which we get glimpses of imposing gateways of iron and stone, and beyond, white walks, spreading lawns, waving trees, marble statues and playing fountains, the way suggesting the seaweed slime that might cover the entrance to some pearl lined shell.

The Padre.

T HE way to Vesuvius leads along shore to the east and
through the outskirts of Naples by a narrow roadway
running between solid stone walls that are pierced by
occasional arched gateways in which hang heavy doors Farther out the way becomes more open and the ascent precipitous.
On all sides are vineyards, the vines trained on poles and over
trellises eight to ten feet in height. Fig trees are here—naked
yet, for the season is early—and apricot, covered with masses of
fragrant bloom. A company of musicians with flute, guitar
and mandolin tramp beside our slow-moving carriages, playing
airs which were popular in the streets of New York when we
left home, evidently thinking—and judging rightly—that the
familiar sounds would open our purse-strings wider. They
sing the words with varying success, remarkable, however,
when we remember they were acquired phonetically, and are
as nearly correct no doubt as the American girl's rendition of
the Italian songs which she may reckon among her other accomplishments.

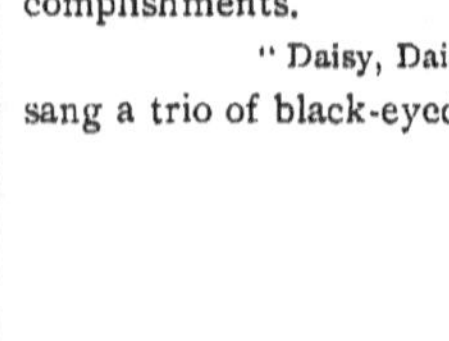

" Daisy, Daisy, give me your answer true,"
sang a trio of black-eyed girls for us the following day, in words

as purely English as one usually hears in American streets, and yet they had no knowledge of the tongue as a spoken language, and the words they sang were no doubt as meaningless to them as were the words of that other strictly English gem which in response to an encore they gave us in

"Ta-ra-ra, boom de-aye!"

Ragged urchins caper along beside us and turn cart-wheels, and when we stop, promptly stand on their heads and wave their feet around in the air and shout for lira. On these unsuspecting creatures we unload our "neat little paper boxes." Round-faced peasant women, with full arms and with bundles or baskets balanced on their heads, are coming down as we go up; venders of lava jewelry offer us rare bargains by the way and beggars ask alms picturesquely and artistically. Methods differ. The Egyptian begs sullenly, like a beast; the Arab demands bakshish as a right; in Palestine the beggar whines and snivels; in Spain he wriggles and howls. But the Italian mendicant makes begging an art; he smiles and coaxes and wheedles—and succeeds where the others fail.

Occasional glimpses are caught of Vesuvius as we proceed, capped always with its canopy of smoke or steam rising, now in a great white plume, now as a spreading palm, now a streaming banner whipped in the wind, now a spouting torrent of black smoke streaked with fire. Above the vineyards are oceans of lava sweeping around islands of ver-

For Centesimo.

259

On the Lava Beds.

dure. As the lava cooled in its flow, so it lies now, in knotted lines, like sprawling roots of trees; in black strands, like the arms of an octopus; in masses, like the interwoven bodies of slimy serpents! Above the slag rises a mountain of cinder.

Where the cinder meets the lava, still 1,500 feet below the summit, the winding carriage road ends and the inclined railway begins. Here are substantial stone buildings, refreshment rooms, and bazaars where lava jewelry is offered for sale—brooches, bracelets and necklaces of various shades combined, each article marked with the year of its eruption. A connoisseur will, ordinarily, tell the date by its color. A wholesome lunch, served daintily, is not the least pleasant feature to be remembered.

"*One-seventy-five* for little lunch like *that !*" shrieked the woman who kicks. "It's an im-po-*si*-tion! I won't *pay* it; they told me it would be only thirty-five *cents.*"

"It *ees* zat, mad*am* ah—one lira, seventy-fife centesimo—terty-fife cens America-lady's money."

For a fact it *is* somewhat startling at first to have your bills rendered in detail and footed in round numbers, but when you get accustomed to the fact that each unit represents only the fifth part of a cent it is rather soothing and makes one feel pleasantly like a modern sort of Crœsus.

Two parallel tracks of iron resting on high wooden rails run up and over the shoulder of the mountain between the lower and the upper stations. On each rail a car sits astride, and, made fast to them, are endless wire cables, working over drums in the power-house, so that when one car goes up the other comes down. As we ascend the black lava-land, the vineyards, sprinkled with red-roofed buildings, the blue circling bay, all

seem dropping away, while the horizon rises with us like the rim of some vast concave in splendor of color rarely seen.

At the upper station, guides stand ready to throw you a rope and tow you up, if you will, through the yielding cinder to the summit, three or four hundred feet higher, to point out what you cannot help seeing and to dilate on obvious facts in the most non-understandable of Italio-English.

"Gentle*man*, *S-s-s-t!* Wanty guide? *good* guide. Sho-we Vesuve! Go roun de crate! Tecky you down in de hell? *S-s-s-t!*"

You wonder if he really means it! If not he must have blundered on a fact. It smells like it any way. It looks as you imagine the infernal regions might look—a black gulf filled with billows of steam, out from which come sounds of muffled thunder, of roaring and hissing, of the spluttering of bubbling matter with hot blasts as from a furnace, flashes as of lightning, and fumes of sulphur, stifling and unbearable, to breathe which is like breathing flame. At intervals come outbursts of super-heated air, which seem to eat up vast areas of vapor as a flash, revealing the depths, black and hideous, save where internal fires shine through. The edge of the crater is like iron that has melted and cooled in globular lines. Outside, it rounds off irregularly and slopes sharply down, covered with slag and cinder. The inner edge is broken away like the shell of a decayed tooth, with vertical walls, ragged and black, with spots of red like blood, others of bright yellow sulphur, saturated with moisture and crumbling to the touch. Within the crater, near to one side, is a huge cone of scoria formed around

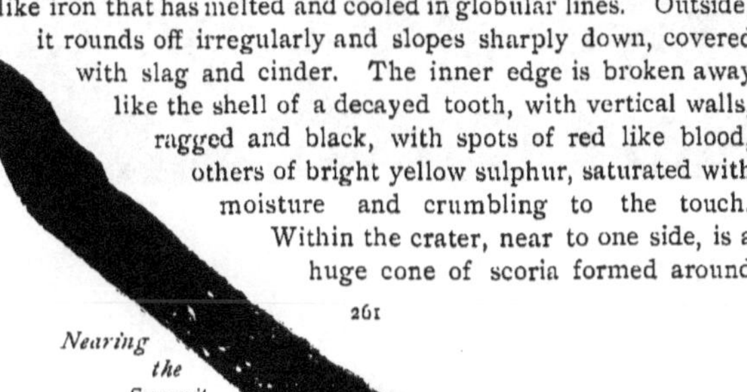

261

Vesuvius.

the main vent, from which masses of red-hot lava are thrown at frequent intervals hundreds of feet into the air. You can hear the bubbling of the liquid fire in the bowels of the mountain, and the roar of escaping steam. The ground beneath you shakes with the beating of earth's mighty heart of fire. It is never entirely at rest. By day it sends forth white steam in infinite form, or inky smoke that darkens the surrounding land. At night it flames, and blazes, and paints the clouds with blood. Some day a greater force than common, seeking vent, will send this matter that now chokes the outlet into space, or rend the mountain asunder, and descend in a river of fire to overwhelm villages, as it has done in the past, when, as now, perhaps, the people who lived in its shadow, in their familiarity, lost all fear of the monster. At every eruption masses of scoria are thrown high into the air, some to descend again into the opening from which it was ejected, some in a shower around its mouth, some in arching lines like the flight of a rocket, to fall outside the crater. The very timid do not linger near; others venture within the line of falling matter but keep a watchful eye aloft. Guides, ever on the alert, pounce upon some choice piece of slag while it is yet red in its heart, press a coin into it and bending its sides, cup-like around, before it has cooled, sell it to visitors as souvenirs of Vesuvius.

Some go down into the crater beside the cone—and pay the guides an exorbitant price for towing them up through the yielding ashes, which gives way beneath the feet like the steps of a treadmill. I start down and am held up by one of the natives, who insists on his right to convoy idiots into what he considers dangerous places. When I persist

In the Crater.

263

in declining his services he throws up his hands in intense disgust and with the gesture responsibility in results. I find that it is not such an easy task after all. The place is filled with stifling fumes of sulphur, but by advancing when the swirling clouds of steam clear away; by covering mouth and eyes with a handkerchief, and by dropping low to the ground when necessary to get an occasional breath, I work my way to the lowest point. Here, in one of the side vents, molten lava bubbles and sputters, and from it at intervals rushes volumes of steam, hissing and roaring fiercely, pierced with sharp tongues of blue and yellow flame. Fire and water, nature's warring forces, to whose agency all change is due, struggle against each other here, as they have struggled from time when time was not, teaching in language which can not be misunderstood the utter insignificance of puny man. I am glad enough when I finally reach the top once more and stand on the solid rim.

It is a glorious sunset that follows. I do not wonder that enthusiasts rave over the Bay of Naples under such conditions. Downward the black mountain melts into an ocean of purple haze through which the white road doubles upon itself like a satin ribbon. Low in the west hangs the sun, like a globe of mild fire. Among the vines beyond the lava belt, rubies and gold gleam in a thousand house-tops; silver and gold are the villages below; pearls and opals strew the circling shore. Red land and turquois water fade away in the distance, uniting at last in one common, iridescent line where the purple horizon joins the golden edge of the mighty vault that arches above.

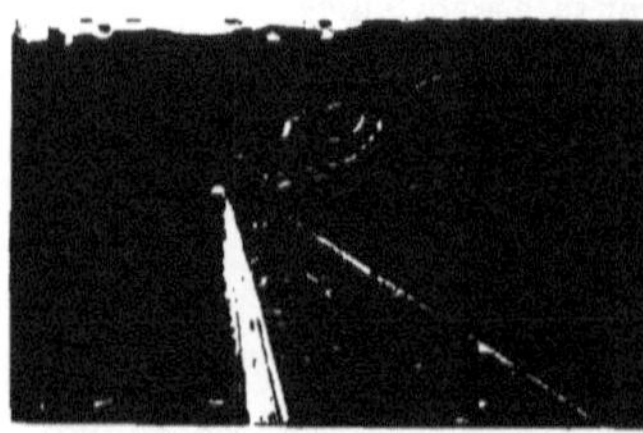

*Down
the
Mountain*

HERCULANEUM AND POMPEII.

FROM the heavens also in the year 79, while yet men lived who had walked and talked with the Christ, came a like horror of fire and brimstone, of burning lava and of ashes, and utterly blotted out the cities of Herculaneum and Pompeii.

They called it by another name then and it reached the surface at a slightly different point, but it was the same wicked old Vesuvius that now threatens the people who rest under its glowing torch. More than half a hundred times since that awful day has it broken out afresh, carrying death in its train. Houses and people are destroyed, but the survivors come back to gather up what may have escaped; to plant again the fig and train the vine; to sing their songs and warm themselves, fascinated in its baleful light, loving yet fearing, knowing full well that some day it will again bring destruction on the land, yet hoping that it may not be in their time. After them—who cares?

Herculaneum and Pompeii were lost to history—as other cities that once rested on the slope of the volcano may have been lost—their existence even forgotten. Later, accident revealed them and systematic digging has since brought parts to light.

A Street in Pompeii.

It calls for a guide, a torch and two francs to get any sort of an idea of Herculaneum. The ruins rest deep under a bed of hardened lava. Only small portions have been uncovered, and can be seen only in their mine-like obscurity under the modern town of Resina. Portions of a great theatre, capable of seating ten thousand people, are shown; a prison also; a temple and public and private houses. No one knows the extent of the old city. Its uncovering is like quarrying through hard rock.

Pompeii is farther away, distant from Naples about fifteen miles following the coast eastward, and five miles perhaps in an air line from Vesuvius. A large part of the city has been uncovered and the work of excavating is still progressing systematically if slowly. Sundays it is open to the people. On week days an admission fee of two francs is charged and an official guide is sent to conduct parties and to watch that no vandal hand may destroy or remove the treasures.

My impressions of the Silent City are so contradictory that I find it difficult at times to accept facts and figures—sometimes doubt what is real and what fancy. St. Peter's at Rome and St. Paul's at London are disappointing at first sight. They do not impress one with their size, seeming to lack the grandeur—which, however, is sure to come in time. Unlike St. Peter's, the forms of Pompeii gave me an impression of greatness out of all proportion to actual measurements. Its most imposing temples do not hold their own under the rule; its noblest columns are not great in feet and inches. Beautiful and symmetrical as they may be and all their lines admirably proportioned to space, they would appear almost insignificant if placed beside the Temple of Jupiter at Athens or among the ruins of the Acropolis. It is solid, heavy, squat; a city built for eternity.   Two stories in height is the limit generally, built perhaps to withstand the earthquakes which threatened, not dreaming that destruction could come from above.

They may have been a luxurious people there in those days but they certainly were not effeminate.   How much comfort could a Modern take if obliged to sleep in beds like stone troughs, and get down on his elbows on lava benches to scramble for his food?   We are told they were immoral, as indicated by the signs on the streets and the frescoes on the walls. They were not *saints!*   They were half way back to the days of the prophets and patriarchs, who were not altogether saints themselves, according to the record.   They lived nearer to nature than now and did not veil their common thoughts in fine metaphor or attempt to conceal what everybody knew. Heathens?   With all their knowledge of art and the sciences they were not so far removed from their ancestors of the swamp as to be entirely free from the fetish worship of things unclean. There are pictures on the walls in some quarters which are anything but refined, it is true, but I warrant worse may be found in any city in the world with a population such as had this city of the past when surprised by death.   The difference

is that here it has been protected and studied by wise people—in the interests of antiquarian research of course—who brush the dust of ages off the carefully preserved indecencies and give edifying dissertations on the lamentable

268

*Ruins
uncovered
in 1895.*

depravity of the Ancient, when, if they would only come down
out of the clouds, they could easily find better—or worse—subjects under their very learned noses.   In defense of Art, which
needs no defense, I must say that all the " works " of this character to be seen were very crude indeed, and I believe the prom-
inence given the subject is out of all proportion to its merits.
On the other hand the statues which stood in the temples and
in the public places of Pompeii might well veil their faces with

shame if confronted by some of
the things now in the Louvre or
in the Ducal Palace at Venice,
and even St. Gauden's " Diana "
would hardly pass muster among
the daintily draped goddesses
found here.

They were a roystering set in
those days. War was a pastime,
gladiatorial contests their recre-

A Theatre.

ation, their amusements generally of the heroic order.   The
amphitheatre outside the city walls would seat twenty thousand
spectators. Within the city is the Tragic Theatre and the
Comic Theatre.   In the Civic Forum they met for games, for
semi-religious ceremonies, and to discuss matters relating to
the public weal. Their courts of justice were open to the air
and sunshine.

The streets are as the streets of old-world cities generally;
some broad, some with little more than space for a single chariot
to pass along. Nearly all are paved with large blocks of lava,
irregular in size and shape but closely fitted at their edges.
At the sides are raised foot-walks and at intervals stepping

269

*Stepping
Stones.*

stones on which footmen might cross over the roadway. Deep wheel-ruts between these stones indicate the wear of past traffic.

They may have had printed signs but the ones seen to-day are of stone or terra-cotta, and of the symbolic order. A money chest was the sign of the banker; a bundle of grain indicated a bakery; a goat was the accepted symbol of a dairy (having presumably some relation to butter), while a coiled serpent gave notice that within might be found the dealer in drugs. Shops were there in abundance, with materials and tools of the trade indicating their line of business. The fuller, the brewer, the wine merchant, the inn keeper, were all represented. Bakeries were there with hand-mills for grinding the grain, and ovens, in some of which were found well preserved loaves of bread.

The pavements of many houses were beautiful in mosaics of white and colored marble. Frescoes were on many walls but they were not as brilliant as I had been lead to expect. They were in dingy terra-cotta reds and yellows, preserved in their present condition through the long years, more I imagine by volcanic mud and ashes than for any remarkable preservative virtue within themselves. The finest have been removed bodily to the museum at Naples with the statuary and other valuable works of art.

A stone watering-trough stands at the street-side, the pavement at its front worn deep by iron-shod hoofs. The stony mouth of the sculptured face, through which the water once poured, is worn away until now the opening is around on one side—worn by the lips of the street people who quenched their thirst in the refreshing stream long ago.

270

A Watering Trough.

The water system was no doubt very complete. Fountains are common in public courts and dwellings. Baths were not looked upon simply as a sanitary necessity but as a pleasure. Bath-houses are common—double walled for heat and steam, with facilities for hot and cold water, plunge and spray. That the thrifty plumber had his innings is no doubt true, though his ablest ally—frost—is not so effective here as farther north. Lead pipes are seen in many places and specimens of work which would not do discredit to the artisan of the present day. These pipes were formed of sheets of lead 3-16 of an inch or more in thickness and from four to six feet long, bent round until they came together, the edges turning sharply outward, affording a broad, flat surface where they were joined together. Their diameter varied from one and a half to five inches. I was told there were "wipe-joints," supposed to be a modern acquirement, there, but I saw none. A specimen of the pipe in my possession has become oxidized until only detached globules of pure lead are present, held together by the deteriorated matter which still preserves its cylindrical form.

For objects in detail and things of special interest you should consult the local "Guide to Pompeii, illustrated." I did. From it I gathered vast store of knowledge and, incidentally, some fine examples of Anglo-Italio literature. The writer tackles subjects with exceedingly Pompeiish touch and goes into details in matters which the average writer skips. I select a few gems and quote for *belles lettres* as well as for information.

The Outer Walls.

271

" Very important was also here the discovery of a deposit of vegetal coal the same used now-a-days, that till now vas not thought to the at Knowledge of the ancients, while it was employed by the manifacterer of cups."

This is a tragedy all the same.

" The proximity of the two skeletons and the leauness of the ill formed child leads to suppose being of a motter running away and beering in her arms her dear chid, which could not escape by it self, owing its miserable health.   They fled from the danger escaping by the windou of their own dwelling-house, for not finding another evasion in these supreme moments, when the rain of ashes was going to burg them in their house."

Here is a graphic description of a fresco of the Judgment of Solomon.

" The third of these pictures has given much to study for its subject. There is represented a solemn judgment like Salomn's — We give of it the following description, in order that evergone may have an exact idea of it.

" The scene shows a royal palace having in the centre a great pedestal before a pavilion.   Upon this pedestal is an old man sitting and having a sceptre in his hand, and assisted by two ministers, with a group of soldiers behind him for denoting the royal dignity. Opposite the king is a large tripoded table, upon which lies a naked little bay, while a soldier is going to strack the baby with an hatchet blaw, and near the table a woman looks indifferently the cruel deed, which the soldier is executing — Beneath the throne is another woman kueeling, who prays with lifted arms the sovereign for obtaining a great grace, that perhaps of saving the baby from death."

A Roman Hat-rack.

Our author dips into natural history.

" Round the *podium* we see some animals; viz: a haughty cock stopping at the sight of a stork pecking a toad."

He touches on mythological things.

" Two Nereids crossing the ocean, one upon a marine bull the other upon a hippocampus guided by a Cupid."

The following would be intensely interesting if one could only understand what the writer was driving at.

" Opposite the entrance we observe the damaged picture of Apollo, woh, having rejoined Daphne, presses her in his arms, while the Nymph fallen upon her kulls endeavours to repel the loving deity's embraces. An *Amorino* keeping her veil makes her shawn quite naked."

Incidentally we find reference to "A fish pond for keeping geese." That gentlemen were sometimes annoyed by the pestiferous dun may be inferred from the following :

" Near the *peristilium* there is a secret door which served for exit to the master of the house to aidvo the expectation of importunate people."

Come with me into one of these Pompeiian homes. We pass the watchful *ostiarium* at the *vestibulum*, and threading the labyrinthian *perystilum* cross the mosaics of the *atrium* to where gold fish sport in the alabaster lined *impluvium*.

"SALVE:"

The *tablinum* is open to us! In the *triclinium*, as *locus consularis*, we are fully loaded and later convoyed to our respective *cubicula*. But—if tempted to venture into the *apodyterium—cave canem*, for *frigidarium* would be ours or thumped *crani*, until we wished *thedevilhadum* the *wholedurncaboodleum*.

I suppose they were built that way and wouldn't have enjoyed living as we do.

Out on the side toward Vesuvius is the Herculaneum gate. Beyond is the Street of the Tombs. Beside the gate is a niche where, tradition says, the Roman soldier stood at the time of the destruction of the city, until death released him.

In the museum at the *Porta della Marina* rest mute evidences of that dreadful day of the past. Domestic gods and do-

273

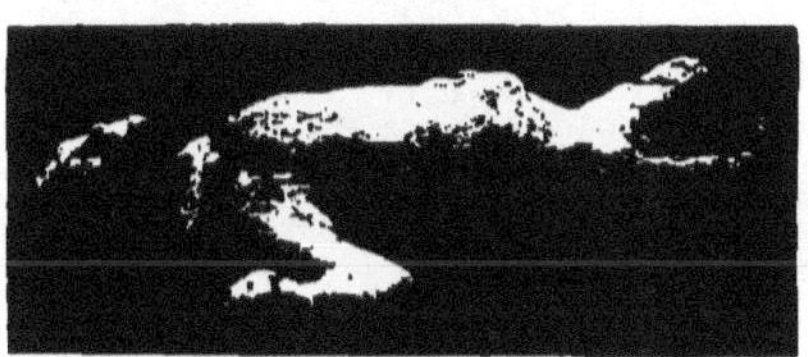

Plaster Cast in Museum.

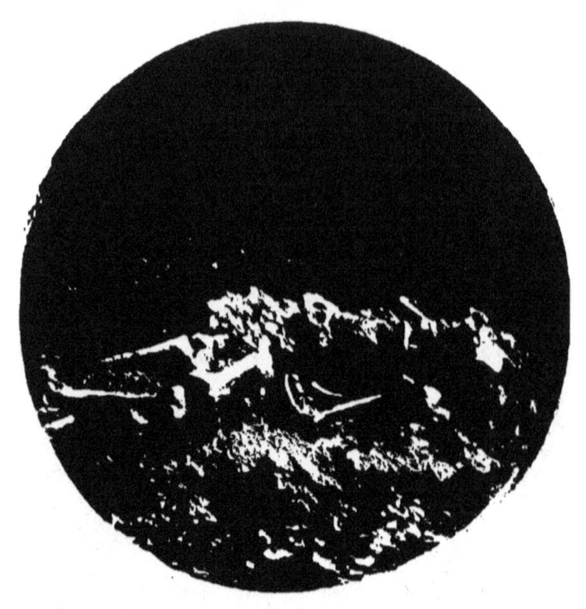

A Story of the Past.

mestic utensils, tools of the mechanic, the arms of men of war, ancient locks and hinges, woods and fabrics, bread and fruits. Skeletons of horses, dogs, cats, rats and domestic fowls, are here with human bones, gathered as the work of excavating has progressed. Human skulls are on shelves and the semblance in plaster of human forms, and the forms of animals, are in glass cases through the centre of the room. A hound with

white fangs and bronze collar-rings; men contorted, as if defying fate; yielding women, face downward, mutely telling the story of their fear, are there—caught in the descending mud and ashes, which formed a matrix about their bodies as perfect as if cast in molders' sand. Into these moulds plaster was poured to take the place of the vanished body, and hold firmly, although in misshapen place, the bones and metal ornaments which once formed part, or decoration, of the living creature.

But the sight most strange to me of all, and grewsome, was through the grated window of a stone dormitory, whose heavy roof had withstood the weight of ashes cast upon it—of a human skeleton lying as it has lain since that awful time eighteen hundred years ago, unshrived, untouched, white and ghastly on its mother earth.

St. Peter's.

BLESSED is he who can enter Rome to know its beauties and recognize its good, with enmity against no class or custom, creed or country ; who can understand the loveliness of the saints yet not forget the grandeur of the pagan ; who can honestly dissent yet as honestly admire those who in purity of life and purpose pursue another road to heaven—to such, Rome will yield rich tribute of enjoyment. To the narrow minded ; the imbittered, who are troubled with dyspepsia and think it religion ; who can not see good in any belief differing from theirs—plenty of material will be found to prove that Rome is full of evil. Whatever is sought in reason may here be found. Whatever the affinity—be it for good or evil—that is in cosmopolitan Rome, as well as in Paris or in New York. If purity of faith and devotion to religion be sought—it is also there. Bigotry and intolerance may stand at its side, for evil always attaches itself to successful good, but the just-minded find good in all religions—the best takes little note of creeds. May not even the heathen, bowing low before gods of wood or stone, if it lead to good, gain equal blessing with him who with greater light proves his claim from Holy writ—who can tell ?

"He that is without sin among you, let him first cast a stone."

Arch of Constantine.

The Roman Catholic faith dominates all others here, as might be expected where the head of the church is. Intolerant ? So is every successful religion. Throbbing with the hot blood of martyrs, it has sent its children out to the uttermost parts of the earth, to court hardships, to welcome death if necessary, in its name. It is the Mother Church, to which all Christian faith might well look with reverence, even though differing from it in what many consider essentials. In form, in spirit, and in earthly temple, the Roman Catholic religion is grandly present here.

From a distance one is, in a measure, satisfied with what he may know about Rome—possibly regards himself complacently as possessing a knowledge thoroughly sufficient for all ordinary occasions. *In* Rome the multitude of half-remembered shapes of men and events rising out of the misty past humbles him, for Rome seems to fill all history and all time.

We reached the Eternal City by train at night, and drove through streets ablaze with electric lights to our modern hotel. Yet, surrounded by things modern, we have but to step out into the public square to find ourselves confronted by things that were old when the apostles who had known Christ came preaching a new doctrine. The principal streets are as the streets of almost any modern city. Its manners are the manners of other old world places except in minor things. The under ways must be visited for character. Newspapers are not often thrust into your face ; the demand for news is not an absorbing passion here ; instead, the sellers of baubles and trinkets, and dealers in mosaic jewelry and ornaments besiege you on every side. English is spoken in many of the stores and at the principal hotels—after a fashion. Attendants are found using familiar words with varying success.   To write it is not so common, yet some of the natives believe they are accomplished in that direction.   Pinned on the door of the lift—there are no elevators in the old country, they are "lifts"—was the following:

> " The lift not go
> up.   of cause
> they are no water."

Such is quite commonly the condition of " lifts " in Italy.

Every cab driver assumes to be a guide.   Occasionally he has a smattering of English and always a firmly rooted belief that he knows where you should go, what you should see, and the order in which you should see it, without regard to limitation of time or any opinion you may have formed as to the importance of subjects—and he is not to be dissuaded from his course.   Licensed conductors are a higher class.   They guide parties on various rounds and give exhaustive talks on various subjects.   Itineraries are arranged by them which enables you to do the town in a week (or a shorter time if you desire) and see the more important objects to the best advantage.   For one who has little time to spare—or even with time unlimited—they offer the most satisfactory way of gaining the first general outline of what there is at Rome.   L. Reynaud, our conductor, is a " Licensed Lecturer on Roman Antiquities," and a better could not be asked.   The best hand-book, and sufficiently comprehensive, is Hare's " Walks in Rome," in two small octavo volumes of 300 pages each, containing not only the author's opinions, but also the opinions of noted travelers on important subjects, for the convenience of such as are in doubt about their own.

*The
Lecturer*

From the mass, special pictures stand out clearly before me—many of them unimportant, some but the whimsical thought of the hour—the yellow Tiber, winding through the city ; the wine-boats beside ugly warehouses ; grim St. Angelo ; the

Castle St. Angelo.

dome of St. Peter's rising beyond the sunny bridge.

You should spend a week with the " lecturer," according to the itinerary laid down, then, book in hand, wander at will, devoting hours to important points, to fix in mind the great events of the past in their true time and place, with the visible outline of the ruins of to-day before you. Go into the streets and see where ancient column and marble facade does duty as part of some modern shop; climb the Palatine Hill to what was once the Palace of the Cæsars; lose yourself in the vast ruins of the Coliseum and from some crumbling height picture it filled with men,

"While stands the Coliseum, Rome shall stand;
When falls the Coliseum, Rome shall fall;
When Rome falls the world."

with Roman maids and matrons drunken with the sight of blood, whose delight it is to see men kill men; picture the helpless Christians down there in the arena, torn by half famished beasts or tortured by barbarian slaves when beasts, less bloody minded than their masters, refused to do their part. Go to the Roman forum and wonder at the ruins of its heathen temples; see where great Cæsar fell when Brutus' dagger found his life; where Mark Antony stood over the dead body and changed the mood of a tiger populace with the matchless craft of his eloquence; find where the she-wolf suckled the helpless twins; follow the furrow turned by Romulus, outlining the ancient city's wall; go out along the Appian Way, with its great tombs and towers; bury yourself in the black catacombs and ponder the lives of the persecuted who found their only safety there; study the old masters for the perfection of Divine Art in gross ideals and compare with the spiritual beauty of the purer modern—and then, after a time, you will know something of the greatness of Rome.

Rome is a city of churches. Full forty are in the name of the Mother of Christ. In most of them the traveler may witness forms of devotion at almost any hour, and every day in the year. Sometimes one hears people loud voiced in their assertions that old-world churches are show-places simply—but then these same people were also loud voiced through ignorance of what was becoming when in those very churches.

St. Peter's does not impress you with its magnitude as you approach. As the foot-hills dwarf the far away mountain peaks, so the grand facade of St. Peter's hides its mighty dome. When told that the cross is 434 feet above the pavement— nearly as high as Cheops lifts his head above the sand—it is

St. Peter.

hardly to be believed. At first the puzzled judgment accommodatingly decides that the people scattered about on the plaza are minute pigmies instead of full grown men and women. Perhaps you catch a glimpse of some human mite beside one of the great figures that guard the bulwarks above, and learn that there are people who are born and eat and sleep and work and die, perhaps, away up there in a little village on top of the great roof, having little in common with the earth except its toil—and after a time you begin to realize that it is because St. Peter's is great in all its parts that it seems but little out of the common.

Enter and the same disappointment as to size goes with you. But you see that it is grand and beautiful and rich in color from variegated pavement away up into the misty dome. Human creatures are the only tiny things there. Its saints are colossi; its winged cherubs giants ! From where you stand, up to the dome, is more than 400 feet. The scribe pictured up there does not suggest great size, yet he holds in his hand a pen seven feet in length. The place is so vast that you may wander about for hours, interested in its beautiful marbles and the grand pictures, and yet not see it all. At times there are echoes which cannot be traced, as the mysterious whisperings of a great cavern ; at others space seems to absorb sound, and it may happen that you step suddenly from silence into a mighty volume of organ tones and voices, bursting from some seemingly unimportant recess, and find yourself standing in a congregation of worshipers.

Under the dome is the grand altar where the pope only, or a cardinal proxy, may say mass. Over it is a canopy of bronze resting on four great twisted columns, beautiful as that perfect one shown in another part of the cathedral which they tell you once formed a part in Solomon's Temple. Under the canopy is the tomb of St. Peter.

The patron saint sits enthroned near the central shrine, with two tall tapers before him on either side, a substantial halo on his head and his right hand uplifted, with fingers formed to bless. The right foot is extended and the historical big toe is worn away to half its original length by the lips of visitors, the process of reduction hastened by those who surreptitiously wipe it off with pocket handkerchief, or convenient coat-tail, before saluting with a kiss.

Here was the circus of Nero. Nero, the fiddler, who loved light better than darkness to such a degree that he rolled Christians in pitch and touched them off when he walked here o' nights—that he might not stub his imperial toe. Here, tradition says, St. Peter suffered martyrdom, and was buried. Here in the year 90 was founded an oratory by the Bishop of Rome, who had been baptized by St. Peter and from him received the authority to make or unmake, which has been handed down through long lines of popes to the present time. Here in 306 Constantine the Great built a basilica. In 1450 steps were taken to found a cathedral which should exceed in size and beauty all others in Christendom. In 1506 the foundation was laid, but little progress was made until 1546, when the superintendency devolved on Michael Angelo, then 72 years of age. To the genius of this man—sculptor, painter, architect, engineer—is due the greater credit for the building of St. Peter's, although the plans of many men have shaped it. Michael Angelo died in 1564, leaving the work unfinished, but it was completed by his pupils practically as planned by him.

In 1626 it was dedicated, after being 176 years in building. Its cost was enormous. To meet the cost indulgences were sold, which led to the reformation.

The Vatican is a vast angular aggregation, appearing flimsily French as compared with the grander bulk of St. Peter's, with little seeming thought of a symmetrical whole. It contains eleven thousand rooms, and shelters upward of two thousand people, including the papal guards, workmen and servitors. It is the palace of the pope, and here, with all the wealth of the world at command, the supreme pontiff lives the lonely life of an ascetic, content with the meager necessaries which might be expected as the portion of the humblest priest.

In the Vatican are acres of paintings and miles of frescoes. Many of the rooms seem to exist simply to afford four walls and a ceiling for the display of works of art. Michael Angelo's famous fresco of the "Last Judgment" is in the Sistine Chapel. I must confess I could not grasp the alleged unearthly grandeur of this painting. I could, in a measure, feel the might of St. Peter's great dome ; I could see, in the statue of the Madonna supporting the dead Christ, beauty of form and the awful mimicry of death, and in the mother the tearless woe of the living. I could recognize the majesty of his "Moses" —although the irreverent mind must always associate the blowing wind with the great law-giver's coiling whiskers—but the "Last Judgment," so-called, was clearly above the sculptor and architect. He could depict earthly things but not heavenly. It is a jumble of figures—strong in individual cases and wonderful in display of physical development, as might be expected of the sculptor, but often strained in posture and grotesque rather than grand. Where else, except in a caricature, would it be thought necessary for a saint to bring his own bloody skin in one hand and in the other the knife with which the deed was done, to show the nature of his martyrdom ? As a whole it is without unity of design and is entirely lacking in any controlling presence such as one might expect to find dominating all. It is pandemonium instead—a sort of go-as-you-please affair—in which the saints, shorn of all dignity, are clamoring as wildly to get their reward as are the damned to escape theirs, and between them the Supreme Judge of the universe—a god of anger—has lost his head and stamps his foot and threatens with uplifted hand to strike—like any ordinary clay ! Fear and hate are there but not love, or pardon, or the bliss of the redeemed. It shows a wonderful drawing of straining, tortured human beings but of the peace and harmony of heaven gained there is no thought. One is not surprised to see the damned, naked and writhing, where asbestos clothing would be of so little avail, but raw, beefy saints and angels, and nude Mothers of Christ, and Deity itself, convulsed with passion, naked and capering—is inexpressibly shocking. No wonder the reigning pope, even in Michael Angelo's time, ordered that the nakedness of the sacred women be covered. It was not prudery—it was only common decency. The good work might have been continued farther to advantage. Much can be forgiven of art, but it doesn't seem right to strain at poor, dusty old Pompeii just because it happens to be a back number—and Pagan at that—and swallow the Last Judgment whole.

In other rooms are frescoes and paintings by great artists, a number by the greatest of all—Raffaelle. Here is his masterpiece—the " Transfiguration "—faded, cracked and dim, yet claimed by many to be the greatest picture in the world. (See page 126.) As an example of the master's skill in *chiaroscuro* it is above praise. You stand in amazement to see the extended hand of the figure nearest stretched toward you, seemingly outside the frame itself and other hands and arms reaching upward away from you a measurable distance, while Christ, and Moses and Elias seem actually floating in space, entirely free from the canvas on which they are painted, clothed in garments filled with radiant light! Yet the figures themselves are unetherial as the laborers on the streets—heavy bodied, big boned, with the bulging muscles of the bearer of burdens. You look in vain for the grandeur of divinity in the Master, or spiritual grace in the attendant saints.

There are no patricians among Raffaelle's ideals. He recognized no higher personality than was represented in the physical development of the prize-fighter. It does not lessen the painter's honor that his figures are of this class. A great artist may be depended on to give the accepted highest type of his age and country in his heroes, without regard to the dress they may happen to be masquerading it at the time. Particularly would this be true in his conception of Deity, and no doubt we see in the "Transfiguration"—not Jews but the people of Rome in Raffaelle's day. They were a noisy, emotional, gesticulating set. Every one is talking—nearly all pointing at something or other, like ghosts in a nightmare—and every mighty muscle in every frenzied figure is straining wildly for diverse ends. About the only ones in the whole lot who are not doing something uncomfortable are the fellows in the bushes —who are respected uncles or something of the cardinal who ordered the job—who know they have no business there and

The Laocoön.

are trying to explain how it all came about. Raffaelle is not to blame for this. It was the style then when Tragedy ranted, and gnashed its teeth, and dragged its toes across the mimic stage to make meaning plain to a people who were thought not capable of understanding ordinary emotions. Crowds do not act that way in these days. It makes you tired. You *do* wish that the saints, at least, would stop paddling for a little. I am glad I saw it, but I could not stand it long. There is more real repose in a red-hot American game of foot-ball than in this painting of the Transfiguration.

Is it sacrilege to suggest that in art—outside the representation of the human form—even Raffaelle was not infallible? His trees or bushes, or whatever they are meant for in his master-piece, would hardly pass on the cheap window shades of fifty years ago. And see his "Miraculous Draught of Fishes," where Christ and two of his disciples are in a little boat, which is further filled, full to overflowing, with nets and fishes of various kinds! Any schoolboy would see at a glance that the least of the three massive figures, with their development of mighty muscle, would be about all the tiny craft could carry, yet, with all its contents, which at a low estimate must weigh nearly half a ton, the boat sits on the surface of the water like a dry leaf, with scarcely any displacement at all!

In the galleries at the rear of St. Peter's are hundreds of bronzes and marbles, famous in history and familiar to students of art the world over. Here "The Gladiators" stand face to face; here is the "Apollo Belvedere," most beautiful of manly forms; here the "Torso Belvedere," a fragment only but a poem in muscular development, and—most wonderful of all, and horrible in its human agony of face, of straining

"The River Nile."

muscle and distended vein—that Pagan figure of which Pliny wrote, the Laocoon, struggling in the folds of the twining serpent.

In one part of the Vatican a considerable number of work-men are employed in the making of mosaic copies of paintings. Of such are the pictures in St. Peter's and the long line of the popes, heroic size, in greater St. Paul's, the latter costing, as they told us where we watched them at the work, 2,000 liras each. Other work done here is for anybody's money who may wish to pay the price. In the city elsewhere you will find dusty little workshops where mosaic jewelry—the kind with which the street Arab lies in wait—is made, and the better ones, where skilled workmen put the labor of days into the space of a watch crystal, who, with the genius of the true artist, are yet common workmen earning from six to ten liras per day. It is interest-ing to watch the artist at his work. He sits with the design which is to be copied before him, and a flat stone, or metallic surface, as a foundation on which the mosaic is to stand. Quantities of artificial stone, or opaque glass, of every con-ceivable shade and color, in form and size like large knitting needles, are there. These he breaks into suitable lengths with a pair of tweezers and places upright, one by one, in their place, according to the subject, pressing the ends down into a thick cement which is applied to the plate as needed. The colored bits, as furnished the artist, serve for broad shades and large subjects. Where finer gradations are required, as in a miniature or for the petals of a flower, he heats the sticks and draws them out into threads of any required thickness, copying with marvelous exactness the original that has been placed be-fore him. When his work is done, and the cement thoroughly hardened so as to hold the bits of stone in place, the surface—which at this time consists of a multitude of jagged points—is ground smooth and polished after the manner of polishing marble generally. The result is a picture in colors that will not change or grow dim, and everlasting as the stone itself.

In the convent of the Capuchin monks we saw the most curious freak in the religious world. One is in doubt whether to laugh at its absurdity, or be shocked with the ghastly spectacle. In the vaults of the convent, in earth brought from Jerusalem, the Capuchins bury their dead. Later, as room is needed for new comers the oldest buried are disinterred, and the bones, stripped of all flesh, strung together in particular cases in the semblance of the living form, with cross on breast and flowers in the bony hands, are given a place of honor in some niche, or, lacking the special honor, in fragmentary condition become ornaments and decorations for the walls and ceilings. Here we saw hundreds of human skulls, and cords of human bones artistically arranged and in graceful designs—really artistic and beautiful as a  whole if you could only for the moment forget the material out of which they were composed.

The monk who showed us around took much pride in the exhibition, but I felt all the time that he was mentally sizing us up and considering the desirability of our bones for ornamental purposes, picturing our skulls in some arching fire-place or a string of our vertebra for festoons and pendants. After we had slipped the expected fee into the extended hand of our guide the Prince asked in his choicest French that we might

*The Monk
who
would n't
be
Photographed.*

Cappuccini Cemetery.

St. Paul's-outside-the-Walls.

take his picture, to remember him by, but he slipped into his hole like an agile gopher, and only stuck his head out just for a second, radiant with a most unsaintly grin to think that he had outwitted us after all!

St. Paul's-outside-the-Walls stands on the campagna where he of Tarsus suffered martyrdom. It contains the pillar to

The Cloisters of St. Paul's.

which he was bound, and the block on which he was beheaded. Where his head struck when severed from the body—bounding thrice—three fountains gushed forth. Over each was erected an altar. It is said that the water flowing from the fountains comes from one hot, from the second lukewarm, from the third cold! St. Paul's is magnificent in colored marbles with gold and bronze decorations. It is one of the most magnificent

Interior of the Coliseum.

church interiors in the world. The cloisters about the quadrangle show a series of beautiful columns of varied forms. The
court itself is a wilderness of small trees and plants and flowers.

Need I tell of the Coliseum ? It divides with St. Peter's the
first thought that comes of Rome. Five years before the destruction of Pompeii its building began. When the foundation
of St. Peter's was laid it had passed to ruins. It is an elipse
620 feet the longest way, 525 the shortest, its height 157 feet.
Like the Pyramids, its raising was with the labor and sweat and
blood of captive Jews—brought from Jerusalem by Titus. It
had seats for 87,000 people. Portions could be covered with
canvas, as protection against sun or storm, by means of ropes
stretching across from wall to wall. The arena, which gave
room for hundreds of gladiators and wild beasts to engage in
death struggles for the amusement of the people, could also be
flooded for naval battles, although how, without filling the subterranean ways with which it is honeycombed, authorities neg-
lect to state. Perhaps the question was not worth considering.
The personal comfort of wild beasts and slaves and Christians
and other vermin did not cut much of a figure with the Noble
Roman so long as they had life enough to work and fight. It
has been a circus, a citadel, a shrine, in different eras and a
stone quarry for ages, yet its mighty bulk stands to-day the
grandest ruin in the world.

Westward from the Coli-
seum, beyond the Roman
Forum with its beautiful
ruins, is the Capitoline Hill
where Romulus staked out
his personal claim after he

In the Roman Forum.

had done plowing—the hill of kings and the place of the temple of Jupiter.

In the Capitoline museum, from out the chaos of marble, one figure stands forth and will not down—

The Dying Gaul.

> " I see before me the gladiator lie:
> He leans upon his hand—his manly brow
> Consents to death, but conquers agony,
> And his drooped head sinks gradually low,—
> And through his side the last drops, ebbing slow
> From the red gash, fall heavy, one by one,
> Like the first of a thunder-shower ; and now
> The arena swims around him—he is gone,
> Ere ceased the inhuman shout which hailed the wretch who won.
>
> He heard it, but he heeded not—his eyes
> Were with his heart, and that was far away ;
> He reck'd not of the life he lost, nor prize,
> But where his rude hut by the Danube lay,
> There were his young barbarians all at play,
> There was their Dacian mother—he, their sire,
> Butchered to make a Roman holiday."

In the ancient church of Ara-Coeli we saw the dearest of little saints—Il Santissimo Bambino. Bambino is Italian for baby, and this little saint represents the blessed Saviour. From Christmas to Epiphany it is shown lying in a manger, or in the mother's lap, with Joseph standing, and the cattle, and the wise men from the East. At other times it is kept in its cabinet shrine and brought out only to be seen by pilgrims, or that the sick may touch it and be blessed. It is wrapped in silken vestments with gold and silver tinsel, a crown on its head, and sparkling with jewels worth a king's ransom. It has its attendant priests, servants of its own and a carriage in which it goes to visit the sick. Of old it was sometimes left with the suffering, that it might impart some of its miraculous virtues to them, but now it never goes out except under guard.

Once upon a time there lived a bad, bad woman with streaks of goodness, as was common in those days, who thought to get the precious Bambino and keep it as her own, that she might be blessed forever. So with much cunning she made a doll exactly like it in size and appearance and, when everything was prepared, feigned sickness and sent, begging that Santissimo Bambino be brought and left with her for a little lest she die. And when St. Bambino came, and the holy father who brought him had given the woman his blessing and taken his departure, and she had said many prayers—for she was a very devout woman—she rose and stripped the rich wrappings and trappings off the little form and gently put him away in a warm bed and covered him up, and put the silk and the gold and the silver and the jewels upon the doll she had provided, and put the jeweled crown upon its head—for she was an honest woman and would not keep any of the valuable things—only just St. 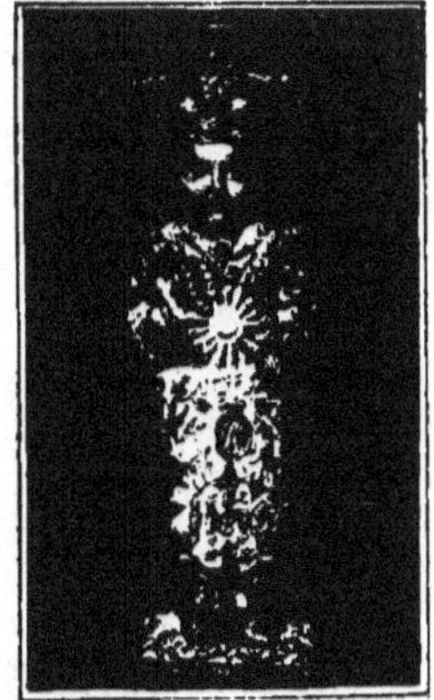 Bambino himself—and carried it all the way up, giving glory in a loud voice all the time for her miraculous cure. And she gave the pseudo Bambino into the hands of the priests to be placed in the *presepio* instead of the true St. Bambino which she had locked up in her own house, and the holy fathers did not know of the deceit that had been practiced on them! But in the night the wind began to moan as if in pain; there were whisperings in the air and hurrying sounds as of searchings all about, and signs of an approaching tempest. Out in the dark-

ness a belated greyfriar, hastening to find shelter, told later how the heathen gods and goddesses that stood in the portals of the *musce* first laughed and wagged their heads in secret glee, and then suddenly shrunk and cowered as if under the lashings of unseen spirits, and the bronze wolf howled, and the great gilded horse of Marcus Aurelius reared and nearly unseated his kingly rider, and even Castor and Pollux were fain to shield their dazzled eyes from the forms of light which descended bearing something in their arms, even to the door of the church. Then the holy father, unable to bear more, covered his face with his cowl and sank swooning to the earth. Within, the waiting priests were troubled—they knew not why—and borne down as with the weight of prayers unsaid. And as the horror pressed on their souls they gathered fearfully in the church while thunders crashed above the golden ceiling and the curious columns shook, and lightning, blazing through the painted windows, made the rain pouring down the outside seem as blood streaming from the sacred heart, until with a crash more deafening than all others, and a blinding flash, came a terrific shaking of the church doors as if struck by giant hands. Then came a lull and in it they heard a soft knocking, and they that were kneeling low saw under the bottom of the door two wee, pink feet, and opening it quickly beheld the true St. Bambino, naked and dripping with the rain yet with a glory about his head a thousand times more beautiful than was his sparkling crown, and a smile of heaven on his cherub face. And they bore him in wonder to the inner sacristy. And when they would have destroyed the false one He would not have it, but turned his troubled face away and they remembered all at once what the Christ had said about little ones who had not yet learned to know good or evil, and later, when they gathered in council to decide what punishment should be meted out to the wicked woman, He put good thoughts into their heads—for even a saint can forgive much in a woman who makes an idol of him, sinful though it be—and they said, "forgiveness is better than justice; she sinned because of her belief in Him." So they took the little figure that was so like the true Bambino and had for a time filled his place and sent it back to the woman, with a blessing. And she took it in her arms and cherished it, saying to herself, "that which has, though only for a time, been as the blessed Christ, must retain some of His virtues ever after and, though the form differ, yet is the symbol the same forever."

But little Saint Bambino never goes out alone now, or ever remains away unless under the guard of faithful keepers.

The Appian Aqueduct.

Out along the Appian Way we go to see Rome from the distance. Straight away it runs, veering neither to right or left, with its solid bed, the model for good roads for more than two thousand years. On either side are the round towers and crumb-

303

Keeper of the Keys.

ling tombs of ancient Romans. Along this way went out the hosts of Rome to conquer the world. Here they came marching back, arrogant in the pride of their victories, with kings dragged at the tail of the victors' chariots, with long lines of captive slaves and with the rich spoils of conquered nations. Here also came St. Peter, and St. Paul.

Across the campagna runs the great Roman aqueduct which in old times brought water to the city. In places it stands firmly in an unbroken succession of arches, at others but a trace is left, yet sufficient to indicate its course, stretching away until dim with distance.

We go to the catacombs, penetrating deep into the hills—how far we cannot tell, but at best only through an infinitesimal proportion of the labyrinth where in the early centuries the persecuted Christians burrowed like moles in the earth, finding in them a refuge in life as well as death, and homes and temples in which they worshipped. These dark streets are at varying levels, sometimes as many as five lines running and crossing over each other in a single system, their length, if extended in a single line, sufficient to reach from the southernmost point of Italy to the mountains of Switzerland.

One of the sweetest recollections that remains with me of Rome is of the gentle, white-haired keeper of the keys, who, with blinking eyes, as if unused to the great light, came with us out into the beautiful sunshine, to give us his parting blessing and God-speed.

FLORENCE.

FROM Rome, the frayed strands of travel diverge still wider, later forming little knots in Florence, under Pisa's leaning wonder, in naughty Monte Carlo, or eastward to Venice, then through Switzerland to Paris and the north. Groups of old friends—old friends though the age that had made them so was less than two full moons—were to come pleasantly together at widely separated places with little surprise, drawn by a unity of purpose to centers of interest where such meetings seemed the most natural thing in the world.

Up along the yellow Tiber, over sunny plains, went we three who journeyed together. The sun shone lovingly ; the buds of the grapes were swelling big with spring. At stations along the way natives brought gourd-like bottles filled with wine, which they offered for half a franc. Many indulged—some pronounced the substance better than vinegar! Broad, smooth wagon-roads crossed at intervals, usually at a different level, or if at grade, closed with double gates. Towns were built on the hills with solid walls around them and church or cathedral spires rising from their center. Here and there were higher

306

hills that might be called mountains, their sides rendered unscalable by heavy masonry, their summits capped by mediæval
castles—abandoned now, so far as could be seen.   At night we
reached Florence.

Florence is a beautiful city; a clean city; a city rich with
works of art.   It emerged from the dark ages in a Kilkenny-cat
sort of condition between Guelph and Ghibelline, and even
when the Guelphs had finally swallowed the Ghibs they were

Florence.

not really happy, but immediately set about swallowing each
other.   Out of this came Dante, who wrote of heaven and
hell with muse sublime, and, after the manner of his time, gave
to his friends all the fat offices in the Halls of Light and con-
signed the enemies of his house to the other place.   In a narrow street is the house of the Divine Poet.   In the public
square he stands—a colossal statue.   In the church of St. Croce
is a monument erected to him, although his body lies at Ra-

venna.   In this church also is the tomb of Michael Angelo, and Galileo, and also of Amerigo Vespucci, who
may be remembered as one of the first of Americans,
although he didn't know how to spell his own name.

Through Florence runs the Arno, crossed by bridges six.
The view from Monte alle Croci, shows at the left the Pitti
Palace and the covered bridge crossing the Arno; centrally the
tower of the Palazzo Vecchio;
at the right the Campenile and
the great Cathedral.

The covered bridge is picturesque with its stores and gold-
smiths' shops, and above, in an
unbroken line, the long gallery
of paintings ·which unites the
galleries of the Pitti Palace on
the one side and the Uffizi Gal-

Ponte Vecchio.

At the Loggia Dei Lanzi.

lery on the other.   At the Palazzo Vecchio is the principal
public square of the city, faced on one side by the Loggia Dei
Lanzi, which of old afforded the magistrates a cover from which
they could get in touch with the great public, now adorned
with sculptured masterpieces, which in some places would be
sheltered and behind barred doors.

The Cathedral front is one grand work of art, so harmonious
as a whole that one loses thought of detail in individual works
in its massing of beauty.   It impresses you as a perfect whole
and you find yourself searching for defects as a welcome
change.   The need of a bell gave excuse—although excuse is
never needed for such works of art—for the Campenile, which
stands beside the Cathedral, rising in slim purity of marble, to

308

Palazzo Vecchio.

The Campenile.

perpetuate the genius of Giotto as a whole, and of many others less noted in detail of statue and embellishment. Fronting the Cathedral is the Battistero, octagonal in form, originally a Pagan temple. It is specially noted for its bronze doors, which Michael Angelo said were "worthy of being the Gates of Paradise!" (didn't I tell you back in Rome that Michael's conception of heavenly things was of the earth, earthy?) These bronzes are indeed remarkable, showing in bas relief the Creation, the Expulsion from Paradise, and other scenes of Bible history.

While it was yet dark in the morning we were called, the call followed quickly by our breakfast of hot coffee and rolls, that we might eat, as is the custom, and gain strength for the arduous duties of dressing, and with the early light we were speeding away toward the City of the Sea.

The Cathedral.

On the Grand Canal.

VENICE.

A COUNTRY stretching away in gently rolling green—
clumps of white buildings here and there on its swelling
surface, and occasional strips of water between, marks
our way. Now the pungent odor of salt meadows comes to us;
now tufted marsh with spaces of black mud, evidently subject
to frequent inundations; now broad rippling lagoons; now
unbroken water on either side, and on a long stone-bound embankment we go, to rest finally at the edge of a city. The
station is substantial enough but we miss the usual roar of a
great town. There are no thunderous trucks rolling along
rocky streets, no ear-deadening stages, no nerve-racking cabs,
no cable cars, no pavement-destroying, filth-breeding horses
here. We are in a city where the only beasts of burden are
men and women. Its carriages make no noise, for sound is
muffled in the yielding waters through which they glide.
Movement here is a poem and travel restful to all the senses.
There are hotel runners, it is true—and some of them noisy
enough—but it is all curious and picturesque and tempered by
a sense of harmony which belongs to no other city in the world.
We soon find our man, and, in one of those long black gondolas,

go out across the Grand Canal, leaving it for narrower ways, to cross it once more, and yet again to find it out on its seaward side where, near the grand piazza of St. Mark's, we find delightful welcome in Hotel Britannia.

The days that followed have left their impression as days of delight. Much of the pleasure was perhaps due to the sunny comfort of our inn, with its dainty service, suggestive of our western world; much in the delightful ways of this old city of the sea, with its atmosphere of rest; its suggestions of indolent enjoyment; its freedom from the jar and turmoil of busy thoroughfares; its silent nights, broken only by soft sounds, as the gentle lapping of waters, the muffled swish of the gondola's sweep, the faint music of lute or of human voices.

In ancient times a timid people fled to this cluster of low islands to escape the persecutions of more warlike tribes, and, becoming a sea-going people, cunning in trade, developed finally into a powerful and war-like nation, and "Venezia" became mistress of the sea. The main thoroughfare is the Grand Canal, which, like a big reversed letter "S," divides the city into two unequal portions. Narrower canals subdivide it into more than a hundred islands, which are bound together by bridges of marble, and cut through by narrow alleys and arcaded streets, through which the footman can make his way. It is a solid city to the water's edge, with stone foundations, although originally built on piles which are in some instances still to be seen. The Grand Canal is edged with palaces built by the merchant princes of old, some of which are now places of trade, workshops, and private residences where ladies go calling or shopping in gondolas. Here government officials sail literally in "ships of state." Some of the palaces are yet occu-

pied by their patrician owners, while some of the finer ones now serve as hotels.

Through the Grand Canal and to the outer islands, at short intervals, run modern steamers, which are here called "tramways." Freight barges, propelled by long sweeps, go up and down, and larger craft with brilliantly colored sails, dot the surface of the lagoon. Along the Grand Canal are lines of tall piles against which gondolas may rest. Many are carved and painted in lines, and spiral bands of yellow, red and blue. Gondolas are everywhere. There are two thousand licensed gondolas in the city, which pay the municipality a license fee of twenty-five francs each per year. Five hundred of these are private, the rest for hire. By an ancient law they were all painted black, and custom has continued the color. They are

usually thirty-one feet in length, covered centrally with the house, which can be closed by doors and curtains at will in bad weather, or taken off, as is common when the days are pleasant. The average cost, with house complete, is five hundred francs each. The tariff for service, fixed by law, is five francs per day. An English-speaking guide can be had for the same amount, although an additional fee is usually given. Antonio Barcellona, guide and courier, accompanied us and was eminently satisfactory.

The Rialto Bridge is covered with shops and stores, which are a source of considerable income to the city, each paying as rental about a franc a day. Near by is the Merchants' Exchange of Shakespeare In an old building here is pointed out the win-

The Rialto Bridge.

dow behind which Shylock lay in wait for his victims. Near by are the Jewish quarters of the city.

The fish market is near this point. Here I saw more strange forms than I had any idea existed among the food-fishes of the world. I suppose such places are very necessary, but its fragrance is not of the kind that I enjoy. The city did not present evidences of extreme poverty common to great cities, in any place we visited. Perhaps we did not find our way into its worst. Living—such as it is—is not very expensive there. I saw men selling the laborers' common dinner in the public mart for twenty centimos (four cents). It consisted of a handful—a half dozen or so— of fish about a finger in size, salted and fried in grease, and about two pounds of what looked like hard-boiled corn-meal cake, cut from the solid mass of two or

three hundred pounds heaped up on a dirty table—by sawing
out the required quantity with a string, as I have seen people
cut through bars of soap.

From the Rialto to St. Mark's runs a series of the more interesting commercial streets and arcades of the city, in some
instances being entirely covered over. They are brilliantly
lighted at night, some places requiring artificial light all the
day.

St. Mark's is the great square of the city—a center of open
air amusements and of business in the dainty unnecessaries of
life. On three sides are palatial buildings, forming a continuous line, pierced at intervals by narrow arcaded streets. Arcades along the sides and end give space for fine bric-a-brac,
gold and silver ornaments, watches, diamonds, jewelry and
works of art. Little tables, grouped on the open plaza, are
often spread with most delightful things to eat and to drink.
A pretty feature of the plaza is its great number of doves,
which descend in flocks to be fed, seemingly without fear,
alighting on the shoulders and heads and the extended hands of
those who come to feed them. On the east is San Marco Church,
unique of architecture, suggestive of Constantinople and the
East, and glittering with its exterior of mosaics, which cover a
surface of more than an acre in extent.

We climb to the top of the Campenile to look out over the
city and lagoon, and outward beyond the islands to the blue Ad-

riatic; we admire the winged lion of St. Mark, the
clock of the square where two bronze men with
sledges strike the hour on the great sounding bell.
We enter the Ducal Palace; we are shown the hole
in the wall where, in the days of the inquisition, a

San Marco Church.

slip of paper dropped into the Lion's Mouth by some name-less coward might blast a hero's life; we go through the halls of the Tribune, the place of the mighty Three; the dungeons of the condemned; the galleries of statuary, and the Council

The Doges' Palace.

Hall where hang the portraits of seventy odd doges, and which holds Tintoretto's "Paradise"—the largest oil painting in the world. We also go through the Bridge of Sighs, which, figur-atively, drips with blood-curdling traditions of unjust con-demnations and death. Ruskin, speaking of this bridge, de-clares it to be of no merit—but then Ruskin never *did* see much merit in anything he did not himself specially discover. Our Howell calls it "that pathetic swindle"—although how anyone can call it a swindle with a palace and a prison, and the bridge

The Bridge of Sighs.

itself in evidence, is more than I can understand. In rebuttal are the words of our guide, who showed us where the victims went and where they took their last sad look at the sunlight through the grated windows, and heaved sighs and groans, and the very stone floor worn into deep ruts by falling tears—which ought at least to be convincing to any one with a heart.

Prettier subjects are the fair Venetian lace makers, at work on fabrics fine as cobweb almost, and dainty as a dream. A bit shown us—which would later grace the shoulders of royalty, had taken a year's time to make, and the price—fixed unalterably by the time devoted on it—is at the rate of a franc a day. The most expert of the girls here receive for their work a sum not to exceed seventy centisimos a day, and this after serving a long apprenticeship; but then they live very cheaply here.

Among the stateliest of church buildings is La Salute. It stands on the Grand Canal, a noble dome, unhampered in its lines by extended facade—as is too often the case in the great cathedrals—its octagonal sides with the heavy figures and grand portals, adding grace and strength without dwarfing the higher parts.

We leave Venice at night, its innumerable lights in wavering lines coming down to us across the Grand Canal, with the music of tinkling guitars and mandolins, and with soft voices of singers from afar.

Beautiful Venice! Dream of rest. A poem art thou among the cities of the world.

SWITZERLAND, PARIS AND BEYOND.

WE are among the mountains. Across the plains of Lombardy we came early in the morning, hastening northward toward the snow-topped Alps. Como, its shores rising steeply from the water's edge to be lost among the clouds, is passed; the border line is reached, and the Swiss customs officers go through the form of inspecting our baggage in a manner void of offense. The railroad men—and the people generally with whom we come in contact—impress me with a sense of their sturdy independence not common among those who serve in the East, yet with a rare courtesy, respecting the slightest wish of others. They are a thrifty people, as indicated by their well ordered homes and the bits of soil gathered on the mountain sides, which show evidence of careful cultivation. A thorough people—the small streams are bridged with solid stone arches, where, under like conditions in America, a couple of sticks and a plank thrown on would have been thought sufficient. A liberty loving people, yet placing the state above the individual to the extent that a man may not cut a tree on his own land without due notice given and permission secured.

Lake Lugano.

The roads we cross are smooth and even, suggesting the delights of a tour awheel. Fences are of granite slabs, set upright, edge to edge. Rocks on the valley's side are shored up with solid masonry to guard against a possible fall, where Americans would take the chances of its inopportune descent—and compromise with the widow. The railroad service is admirable; the stations and coaches are most comfortable; the road-bed perfect, with electric signals throughout.

The building of this road over the bulwarks of the Alps was a stupendous work—a marvel ef engineering skill. It traverses the sides of vertical cliffs; it crosses over mountain torrents on great stone bridges; it doubles in confusing loops upon its course; it bores its way into the mountains in a spiral, as one might turn a corkscrew into the yielding cork, to come out again along the dizzy cliff as if for breath, then plunge again into the mountain for another circle, until the higher level is reached. Then it goes, nearly ten miles, straight through the solid rock in the great St. Gothard tunnel, to come out beyond the glacier's foot on the north, where, with snow lying about us, we lunch in two languages, then descend by more loops and more spirals to the valley below.

Backward, the sunny valley shimmers in the spring-time warmth. Above, the mountains lift their glittering crests against the deep blue vault. In their laps rest mighty glaciers;

Near Altdorf.

adown their sides is the track of the avalanche. We do not
wonder that the Switzer learned to so love his country that
death itself might well be risked in its defense. It was the ex-
ultant spirit of the mountains that created a William Tell!
We pass Altdorf, where the tyrant Gesler ruled and where Tell
taught his countrymen what might be ventured in Freedom's
name. Here are two fountains where, tradition says, father
and son stood—the boy, unflinching in his perfect confidence,
with apple poised on head; the man, with cross-bow leveled, to
send the unerring dart. Here also stands a statue raised by
his admiring countrymen in honor of the sturdy mountaineer.

We touch the Lake of the Four Cantons at Fluelen; leave it
again at Brunnen; see the purple shadows creep down the
eastern slopes while the sides of the mountains beyond shadowed
Art are bathed in red
gold, then turn west-
ward, and, circling
about The Rigi as the
day ends, reach Lu-
cerne to find welcome
at "The Swan" and
—appropriately
enough—sleep on

Art.

mighty feather beds under soft puffy coverlets of eiderdown.

No fairer town exists than Lucerne as it appears to us. It is
just awakening from its winter's sleep. The large caravansa-
ries—which will be filled later with summer visitors from every
part of the world—give no sign of life as yet; the great Stone
Lion of Lucerne is still swathed in his winter garb. But everything is fresh and clean; a sunny spot with a faint touch of

Lucerne.

winter still remaining, and a bracing air from the mountain tops that are white on every side.

In our descent from the higher Swiss highlands travel is a continuous pleasure. We admire the thrift of the Swiss peasant-

At Basle.

ry. Farm lands are productive and farm buildings suggestive of home comfort as a New England home. Forest planting is encouraged and groves are seen in all stages from the knee-high nursery plats to heavy timber lands.

At Basle we touch the German Rhine—yellow and swelling with the spring floods—and visit the old Cathedral with its noted cloisters and see its other worthy sights, then westward through forfeited Alsace and across France.

The surface grows level now, with spreading, unfenced meadows and grain lands. The buildings are of stone, red tiled and picturesque. Villages are at intervals on the higher ground, solidly built to the edges like patchwork of grey blocks let into the surrounding mosaic of green. And now we are in the glare and noise and bustle of a Paris night!

325

The Morgue.

Paris. Beautiful, gay, wicked Paris! Some one has said that the good all go to Paris when they die. We are unwilling to run the risk of waiting. Yet we do not see it all. It is borne in upon us as an inspiration that at some later day we may come again. We stroll through public gardens; we pace

The Grand Opera.

noted promenades; we steam the bridges of the Seine; we omnibus the boulevards; we spend delightful moments in the flower markets; we loiter in the Latin Quarter, and find it most disappointingly respectable! A glimpse we have of public squares; of heroic columns; of the Arc de Triomphe, with its suggestions of the Man of Destiny, followed by a little revery in his stately tomb. There is a peep at the Windmill and a sickening moment at the Morgue—each in its way an admission of life's utter failure; a race through the palace at Versailles; a time all too short among the paintings of the Louvre; an evening at

326

In the Latin Quarter.

the Grand Opera, filled with harmony divine—then we melt away into the night and the English Channel.

London! We are as drops in the turbid river that sweeps under its heavy bridges; as shells on the shore at Jaffa; as sands that pile up against the pyramids. We go through its great Tower; we see some of its treasures; we stand in its sacred places; we read on its marble tablets the names of the illustrious dead!

And is it all a dream—that stony face of Egypt looking out from its unknown past; the strange people of the Orient; the land where the Saviour walked; Jerusalem; Athens; Imperial Rome! the new friends who have come into our lives never to go out again?

There are wonderful pictures, as of a hand long since dead, and though they fade, yet will they never pass entirely away, but rise before us to the end of time.

Well: Let it remain a dream. Westward lies our way. Beyond the fog, where the sunshine lies brightest, where Old Glory is floating, where old friends are waiting—there is our home.

In the Straits of Messina.

L. Melano Rossi,
Manager, Paris.

J. Tschetinian,
Secretary.

F. C. Clark.

THANKS:

To F. C. Clark, organizer and manager, for personal as well as general favors. No one could have planned better. The things whereat we kicked were often the result of forces beyond his control. To make up, he assumed expenses not called for in the bond, cheerfully paying the fiddler for music of others' ordering.

Master of diplomacy he. When held accountable for adverse weather, he willingly accepted the responsibility and promised to have it changed—when anyone, by the exercise of a little judgment, could clearly see that it was all the captain's fault!

He was a good fellow anyway—broad-minded and liberal to a fault. With present knowledge I would not ask for a better if the trip were to be made again.

329

G. K. Turnham,
Manager,
London, Eng.

MORE THANKS·

To Messrs. Brown, Chew and Jacob, and to Rev. Doctors Brett, Prugh and Robinson, for valued suggestions and literary assistance.

To Doctors Bell and Fletcher, and to Messrs. Hamner and Batsford, for photographs, some of which appear in this volume.

To Messrs. Little and Hamilton, Doctors of Medicine; to Messrs. Kuhns and Martin, Doctors of Divinity, and to Messrs. Loud, Merritt, Downer and Irvine, Doctors of Laws, for helpful sympathy, physical assistance, cash, rugs, powders, pills, advice, etc., as may be severally due to each.

And to the representative from Florida, the man from Seattle, the judge from the Province—in short to you who have thought kindly of me, one and all, I give thanks. To mention by name all whose faces come to me as I write, who contributed to the pleasure of the trip—although perhaps they knew it not—would exhaust a large part of the passenger list.

That you may find some little pleasure in going over old scenes with me again is the sincere wish of your Fellow Voyageur.

*The Representative
from Florida.*

"The
Solid
South."

The
Grand Army
of
The Republic.

Our Clergymen.

The Doctors.

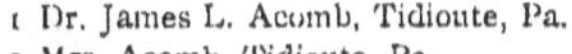

PASSENGER LIST.

1 Dr. James L. Acomb, Tidioute, Pa.
2 Mrs. Acomb, Tidioute, Pa.
3 Mrs. Dora C. Adams, Frankfort, Ind.
4 Mrs. L. M. Aldrich, Washington, D. C.
5 Miss Elzira Allen, New York.
6 Mrs. F. Armstrong, Bridgeport, Conn.
7 Col. B. F. Atkinson, Fort Smith, Ark.
8 Mr. R. W. Austin, Chicago, Ill.
9 Mrs. Clara M. Ayers, Concord, N. H.
10 Mr. Dwight M. Baldwin, Red Wing, Minn.
11 Mr. J. S. Bailey, Westport, Pa.
12 Mr. James E. Batsford, Waterloo, N. Y.
13 Mr. Ezra D. Barker, New York.
14 Rev. Otis W. Barker, Newton, Conn.
15 Mrs. Ida Haight Barber, Cleveland, O.
16 Dr. Henry S. Babbitt, Dorchester, Mass.
17 Mrs. Babbitt, Dorchester, Mass.
18 Miss Grace Babbitt, Dorchester, Mass.
19 Mr. Elwood G. Babbitt, Dorchester, Mass.
20 Miss Nellie G. Bates, Pittsburg, Pa.
21 Mr. Dayton Ball, Albany, N. Y.
22 Mr. Henry D. Ball, Albany, N. Y.
23 Mr. Jas. R. Barrett, Henderson, Ky.
24 Mrs. Barrett, Henderson, Ky.
25 Mr. Henry Barrett, Henderson, Ky.
26 Miss Susie Barrett, Henderson, Ky.
27 Mr. W. H. Beach, Jersey City, N. J.
28 Mr. Theo. H. Benedict, Danbury, Conn.
29 Mrs. Benedict, Danbury, Conn.
30 Mr. Wm. M. Bell, McKeesport, Pa.
31 Dr. J. R. Bell, Cleveland, O.
32 Rev. R. W. Beers, Waterford, N. Y.
33 Mrs. Beers, Waterford, N. Y.
34 Hon. Morris B. Beardsley, Bridgeport, Conn.
35 Mrs. Beardsley, Bridgeport, Conn.
36 Rev. J. C. Bigham, Pittsburg, Pa.

333

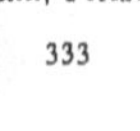

37 Mr. Frank M. Bingham, New York
38 Mrs. Ellen M. Bettes, Rockford, Ill.
39 Mr. Wm. M. Blackstock, LaFayette, Ind.
40 Mrs. Blackstock, LaFayette, Ind.
41 Mrs. A. B. Blodgett, Syracuse, N. Y.
42 Mr. Henry I. Bosworth, Elgin, Ill.
43 Rev. F. R. Brace, D.D., Blackwood, N. J.
44 Dr. F. Standish Bradford, Morristown, N. J.
45 Mrs. Bradford, Morristown, N. J.
46 Rev. Cornelius Brett, D.D., Jersey City, N. J.
47 Miss Maude Brett, Jersey City, N. J.
48 Hon. A. T. Brinsmade, Cleveland, O.
49 Mrs. Brinsmade, Cleveland, O.
50 Mr. Oliver L. Briggs, Boston, Mass.
51 Mrs. Briggs, Boston, Mass.
52 Mrs. H. T. Browning Howell, Mich.
53 Mr. Derrick Brown, Poughkeepsie, N. Y.
   Mr. Charles DeW. Brownell, (see No. 101.)
54 Mrs. Dr. Phœbe A. O. Briggs, Troy, Kan.
55 Dr. E. P. Buffett, Jersey City, N. J.
56 Miss Mary L. Burritt, Bridgeport, Conn.
57 Mr. II. F. Cady, Omaha, Neb.
58 Mrs. Cady, Omaha, Neb.
59 Miss Hattie F. Cady, Omaha, Neb.
60 Rev. S. C. Caldwell, Hazlehurst, Miss.
61 Rev. Newell M. Calhoun, Canandaigua, N. Y
62 Miss Isabel Campbell, Brooklyn, N. Y.
63 Mrs. E. N. Carpenter, Ridgefield. Conn.
64 Miss Helen Carpenter, Ridgefield, Conn.
65 Mr. S. Chew, Camden, N. J.
66 Mr. D. J. Chamberlain, Elgin, Ill.
67 Mrs. Chamberlain, Elgin, Ill.
68 Mrs. C. D. Chamberlain, Elgin, Ill.
69 Mr. Samuel Clark, Newark, N. J.
70 Dr. A. L. Clark, Elgin, Ill.
71 Mrs. Clark, Elgin, Ill.
72 Hon. Alexandre Chauveau, Quebec.
73 Mrs. Chauveau, Quebec, Can.
74 Mr. D. M. Clewell, Ravenna, O.
75 Mrs. R. L. Cochran, Franklin, Pa.
76 Dr. Wm. J. Conan, Superior, Wis.
77 Mrs. Conan, Superior, Wis.

78 Mrs. Marguerite Cook, Elgin, Ill.
79 Mr. David C. Cook, Jr., Elgin, Ill.
80 Mr. Geo. E. Cook, Elgin, Ill.
81 Rev. J. A. Cosgrave, Pittsburg, Pa.
82 Hon. C. E. Cowgill, Wabash, Ind.
83 Mrs. Cowgill, Wabash, Ind.
84 Mr. Stuart C. Cowgill, Wabash, Ind.
85 Rev. E. M. Cravath, D.D., Nashville, Tenn.
86 Mr. Horace Croll, York, Pa
87 Miss Mary D. Croll, York, Pa.
88 Mrs. A. M. Crosby, East Glastonbury, Conn.
89 Miss A. B. Crosby, East Glastonbury, Conn.
90 Col. J. H. Cunningham, Boston, Mass.
91 Mr. Dexter J. Cutter, Dorchester, Mass.
92 Mr. A. W. Cutting, Wayland, Mass.
93 Mr. Junius Dana, Wooster, Ohio.
94 Mr. F. J. Darlington, Westchester, Pa.
95 Mrs. Darlington, Westchester, Pa.
96 Mr. Samuel Davidson, Hamilton, O.
97 Mr. Henry H. Dawson, Newark, N. J.
98 Mr. E. DeCamp, Ovid, Mich.
99 Mrs. DeCamp, Ovid, Mich.
100 Mr. Frank DePuy, Wabash, Ind.
102 Mrs. D. D. Dickey, Pittsburgh, Pa.
103 Hon. Azro Dyer, Evansville, Ind.
104 Mrs. Dyer, Evansville, Ind.
105 Mr. Chas. N. Dietz, Omaha, Neb.
106 Mrs. Dietz, Omaha, Neb.
107 Mr. Geo W. Downer, Cleveland, O.
108 Mrs. E. S. Duchesnay, Quebec, Can.
109 Mr. John A Dunn, Gardner, Mass.
110 Mrs. Dunn, Gardner, Mass.
111 Miss Annie E. Earle, Jersey City, N. J.
112 Miss Sarah Eastman, New Haven, Conn.
113 Mr. John Edelstein, Jersey City, N. J.
114 Mrs. Edelstein, Jersey City, N. J.
115 Miss L. Edelstein, Jersey City, N. J.
116 Dr. Henry Oliver Ely, Binghamton, N. Y.
117 Mrs. Ely, Binghamton, N. Y.
118 Col. Dudley Evans, New York.

335

119 Miss Lula Ezell, Okolona, Miss.
120 Mr. H. W. Fanker, Harmony, Pa.
121 Mr. S. E. Fay, Athol Centre, Mass.
122 Mr. O. A. Fay, Athol Centre. Mass.
123 Mr. John Farrell, Pittsburg, Pa.
124 Mrs. Farrell, Pittsburg, Pa.
125 Miss Ann M: Farrell, Pittsburg, Pa.
126 Miss Alice N. Farrell, Pittsburg, Pa,
127 Miss Nettie E. Foote Catskill, N. Y.
128 Mrs. L. E. Ford, Flatbush, L. I.
129 Mrs. Ruth A. Forrest, Logansport, Ind.
130 Dr. Samuel R. Forman, Jersey City Heights.
131 Mrs. Forman, Jersey City Heights, N. J.
132 Miss May A. Forman, Jersey City Heights.
133 Dr. C. I. Fletcher Indianapolis, Ind.
134 Mrs. Fletcher, Indianapolis, Ind.
135 Mr. Arthur B. Foster, Cleveland, O.
136 Mrs. Foster, Cleveland, O.
137 Mrs. W. J. Friday, Pittsburg, Pa.
138 Miss Cora J. Friday, Pittsburg, Pa.
139 Miss Jennie M. Frost, Jersey City, N. J.
140 Mr. C. Fred Galigher, Cairo, Ill.
141 Mrs. C. Fred Galigher, Cairo, Ill.
142 Rev. J. F. Gallagher, Newcastle, Pa.
143 Mr. John T. Gawne, Cleveland, Ohio.
144 Mr. Enoch Gerrish, Concord, N. H.
145 Mrs. Gerrish, Concord, N. H.
146 Mr. D. L. Gillespie, Pittsburg, Pa.
147 Mrs. Gillespie, Pittsburg, Pa.
148 Dr. W. P. Glover, Macon, Ga.
149 Mr. E. L. Graves, Cleveland, Ohio.
150 Mrs. Graves, Cleveland, Ohio.
151 Miss Jennie M. Graves, Cleveland, Ohio.
152 Mr. Eugene S. Graves, Cleveland, Ohio.
153 Miss Fannie R. Gray, Jersey City, N. J.
154 Mrs. L. W. L. Goff, Appleton, Wis.
155 Hon. John D. Gougar, LaFayette, Ind.
156 Mrs. Gougar, LaFayette, Ind.
157 Mr. John B. Grant, Schoharie, N. Y.

158 Mrs. Grant, Schoharie, N. Y.
159 Hon. H. L. Gregg, Delanco, N. J.
160 Mrs. Gregg, Delanco, N. J.
161 Miss Maude M. Griswold, Chicago, Ill.
162 Miss Grace Griswold, Chicago, Ill.
163 Mrs. S. S. Grubb, Baraboo, Wis.
164 Mr. Alfred A. Guthrie, Albany, N. Y.
165 Mr. Keith Guthrie, Albany, N. Y.
166 Miss Harriet L. Hall, Columbus, Ohio.
167 Mr. A. P. Ham, Boston, Mass.
168 Mr. Geo. Hamilton, East Liverpool, Ohio.
169 Dr. W. R. Hamilton, Pittsburg, Pa.
170 Mr. G. W. Hamilton, Covington, Ky.
171 Mrs. Hamilton, Covington, Ky.
172 Miss Annie S. Hamilton, Covington, Ky.
173 Miss Katharine S. Hamilton, Covington, Ky.
174 Mr. Samuel Hamilton, Pittsburg, Pa.
175 Mrs. S. Hamilton, Pittsburg, Pa.
176 Mr. L. B. Hamlin, Elgin, Ill.
177 Rev. J. Garland Hamner, D.D., Lamington, N. J.
178 Rev. J. Garland Hamner, Jr., Newark, N. J.
179 Miss Maude F. Hanna, Columbus, Ohio.
180 Mr. J. M. Harris, Vermont, Ill.
181 Mrs. M. T. Harris, Vermont, Ill.
182 Mr. Gilbert Hart, Detroit, Mich.
183 Rev. Calvin A. Hare, Indianapolis, Ind.
184 Mrs. Mary E. Hartwell, Cambridge, Mass.
185 Mr. J. M. Hastings, Pittsburg, Pa.
186 Mrs. C. W. Hawley, Bridgeport, Conn.
187 Miss Mary W. Hawley, Bridgeport, Conn.
188 Mr. C. S. Hedges, Sag Harbor, N. Y.
189 Mrs. S. H. Hedges, Urbana, Ohio.
190 Miss Louise Hedges, Urbana, Ohio.
191 Miss Louise B. Henderson, Philadelphia, Pa.
192 Mr. W. F. H. Herrman, New York.
193 Mrs. C. S. Herrman, New York.
194 Miss Grace Herrman, New York.
195 Miss Laura Herrman, New York.
196 Mrs. E. Edgar Heston, Cranford, N. J.
197 Mr. Geo. E. Hibbard, Boston, Mass.
198 Mr. Henry C. Hines, Newark, N. J.
199 Mr. Chas. P. Hohlstein, Buffalo, N. Y.
200 Mrs. Hohlstein, Buffalo, N. Y.

337

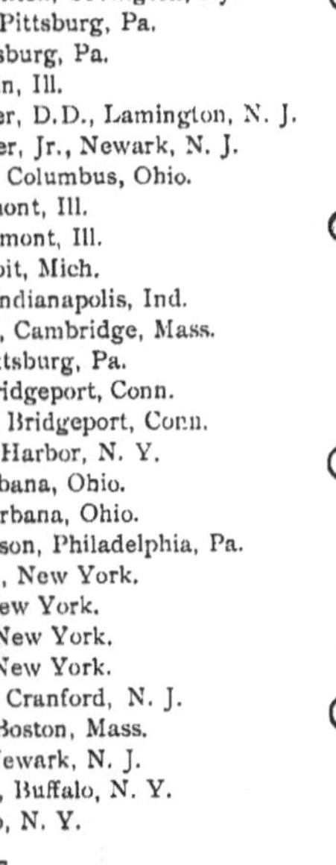

201 Mr. Samuel Holmes, Montclair, N. J.
202 Mrs. Mary E. Homan, Elgin, Ill.
203 Miss C. A. Howard, Washington, D. C.
204 Mr. Mathias Hoelscher, Pittsburg, Pa.
205 Mrs. Blackburn Hughes, Charleston, S. C.
206 Dr. F. B. Hyland, Soughton, Wis.
207 Mrs. Hyland, Soughton, Wis.
208 Mrs. H. B. Ives, New Haven, Conn.
209 Mr. T. M. Irvine, Cleveland, Ohio.
210 Mr. Samuel Jacob, Wellsburg, W. Va.
211 Rev. Wm. P. Jacobs, D.D., Clinton, S. C.
212 Mrs. W. Wilson Jefferies, New York.
213 Hon. L. T. Jefts, Hudson, Mass.
214 Mrs. Jefts, Hudson, Mass.
215 Rev. J. G. Johnston, D.D., Port Richmond, S. I.
216 Mrs. E. P. Jones, Findlay, Ohio.
217 Miss C. F. Jones, Findlay, Ohio.
218 Rev. Herrick Johnson, D.D., LL.D., Chicago, Ill.
219 Mrs. Johnson, Chicago, Ill.
220 Rev. David Jones, New Brighton, Pa.
221 Rev. Geo. W. Judson, Orange, Mass.
222 Mr. L. D. Kellogg, Westfield, Mass.
223 Miss Louise J. Kerr, Hartwell, Ohio.
224 Hon. John Kimball, Concord, N. H.
225 Mr. H. M. Knapp, Bridgeport, Conn.
226 Mrs. Knapp, Bridgeport, Conn.
227 Mr. Geo. Krouse, Jersey City, N. J.
228 Mrs. Krouse, Jersey City, N. J.
229 Rev. H. W. Kuhns, D.D., Omaha, Neb.
230 Mr. John B. Kurtz, Baltimore, Md.
231 Mr. E. H. Lamberton, Franklin, Pa.
232 Mrs. Lamberton, Franklin, Pa.
333 Miss Mame Lamberton, Winona, Minn.
234 Rev. Franklin N. Lapham, Elgin, Ill.
235 Mrs. Mary A. Lauer, White Haven, Pa.
236 Master Claude J. Lauer, White Haven, Pa.
237 Miss E. C. Lawrence, Syracuse, N. Y.
238 Mrs. D. Y. Leslie, Buffalo, N. Y.
239 Dr. Geo. W. Little, Glens Falls, N. Y.
240 Mrs. William Loeffler, Pittsburg, Pa.
241 Miss Flora C. Loeffler, Pittsburg, Pa.

242 Hon. Jas. E. Long, DuBois, Pa
243 Miss Annie Lord, Stamford, Conn.
244 Mr. Jas. H. Love, Jersey City, N. J.
245 Rev. John Henry Logie, New York.
246 Mr. H. N. Loud, AuSable, Mich.
247 Rev. C. S. Lucas, Allegheny, Pa.
248 Rev. Daniel H. Martin, D.D., Newark, N. J.
249 Mr. Wm. A. Marshall, Oakland, Cal.
250 Mr. M. P. Mason, Carthage, N. Y.
251 Mrs. Mason, Carthage, N. Y.
252 Mr. William J. Matheson, Brooklyn.
253 Mrs. Matheson, Brooklyn.
254 Miss Anna E. Matheson, Brooklyn.
255 Master Hugh Matheson, Brooklyn.
256 Master Malcolm Matheson, Brooklyn.
257 Mrs. Anna M. Matheson, Brooklyn.
258 Rev. Alex. Milne, Columbus, Ohio.
259 Mrs. Milne, Columbus, Ohio.
260 Mr. T. F. McCauley, Washington, D. C.
261 Dr. J. B. McCaw, Richmond, Va.
262 Dr. Walter D. McCaw, U. S. A., Rio Grande, Texas.
263 Rev. A. J. P. McClure, Wyncote, Pa.
264 Mr. Elbridge McFarland, Gulf Mills, Pa.
265 Hon. Henry F. Merritt, U. S. Consul, Barmen, Ger.
266 Rev. Alonzo Monk, D.D., Macon, Ga.
267 Mr. W. G. Moore, Haddonfield, N. J.
268 Mr. Henry D. Moore, Haddonfield, N. J.
269 Miss Minnie A. Moore, Haddonfield, N. J.
270 Mrs. Mary T. More, Catskill, N. Y.
271 Rev. Wm. D. Morgan, Baltimore, Md.
272 Rev. S. L. Morris, D.D., Macon, Ga.
273 Miss Lulu Mowry, Englewood, N. J.
274 Miss Mary C. Murphy, Pittsburg, Pa.
275 Mr. J. H. Neff, Kansas City, Mo.
276 Mr. Geo. N. Newbery, Troy, Pa.
277 Mr. J. W. Newell, Leadville, Col.
278 Mr. Sam'l A. Nightingale, Providence, R. I.
279 Dr. F. E. Noble, Jersey City, N. J.
280 Rev. John H. Norris, Pittsburg, Pa.
281 Mrs. Jas. S. Noyes, Jersey City, N. J.
282 Mr. H. H. Otis, Buffalo, N. Y.

283 Mr. Edwin Palmer, Albany, N. Y.
284 Mr. Solon Palmer, Jersey City, N. J.
285 Mrs. Palmer, Jersey City, N. J.
286 Mr. Winfield Scott Palmer, Glenburn, Pa.
287 Miss Grace A. Parker, Worcester, Mass.
288 Mr. Lewis Parker, Trenton, N. J.
289 Mrs. Parker, Trenton, N. J.
290 Mr. St. Clair Parry, Indianapolis, Ind.
291 Mr. James Parsons, Brooklyn, N. Y.
292 Miss A. H. Patterson, New York.
293 Mrs. L. L. Peck, Bridgeport, Conn.
294 Miss Sarah E. Pence, Pittsburg, Pa.
295 Mr. Douglas Perkins, Cleveland, Ohio.
296 Mr. John H. Phillips, New Haven, Conn.
297 Mr. Leland B. Potter, Scranton, Pa.
298 Miss Mary L. Price, Columbus, Ohio.
299 Rev. Jno. H. Prugh, D.D., Pittsburg, Pa.
300 Rev. H. Quigg, D.D., Conyers, Ga.
301 Rev. P. J. Quilter, Carnegie, Pa.
302 Dr. G. G. Rahauser, Pittsburg, Pa.
303 Mrs. Jennie A. Reeve, Poughkeepsie, N. Y.
304 Mr. Edward B. Reynolds, South Bend, Ind.
305 Mr. Ethan S. Reynolds, South Bend, Ind.
306 Mrs. Reynolds, South Bend, Ind.
307 Mrs. Annie F. Richardson, Stoneham, Mass.
308 Mr. Henry W. Riddle, Ravenna, Ohio.
309 Mrs. Riddle, Ravenna, Ohio.
310 Mr. Jacob Ringle, Jersey City, N. J.
311 Mrs. Ringle, Jersey City, N. J.
312 Rev. W. A. Robinson, D.D., Dayton, Ohio.
313 Mr. W. L. Robinson, Chicago, Ill.
314 Mrs. Robinson, Chicago, Ill.
315 Mr. John Routh, Pittsburg, Pa.
316 Mrs. Routh, Pittsburg, Pa.
317 Mr. Wm. Ryley, Kansas City, Mo.
318 Mrs. Ryley, Kansas City, Mo.
319 Mr. Burr Rumsey, Ithaca, N. Y.
320 Miss Helen B. Runyon, New York.
321 Mr. Whitfield Russell, Paducah, Ky.
322 Mr. Hudson Samson, Pittsburg, Pa.

323 Miss Sara Sands, Manistee, Mich.
324 Miss Flora May Sands, Manistee, Mich.
325 Col. Geo. Sanderson, Scranton, Pa.
326 Mr. Jas. R. Scanlan, Elgin, Ill.
327 Dr. R. Schiffman, St. Paul, Minn.
328 Mrs. Schiffman, St. Paul, Minn.
329 Miss Minnie B. Schiffman, St. Paul, Minn.
330 Miss Florence A. Schiffman, St. Paul, Minn.
331 Rev. John L. Scudder, Jersey City, N. J.
332 Mrs. Scudder, Jersey City, N. J.
333 Miss Addie Scudder, Jersey City, N. J.
334 Miss Alice Scudder, Jersey City, N. J.
335 Mr. W. H. Schuette, Pittsburg, Pa.
336 Mr. Geo. E. Sebring, East Palestine, Ohio.
337 Mrs. Mignon L. Selden, Micanopy, Fla.
338 Mr. Cyrus Spaulding, Webster, Mass.
339 Mrs. Spaulding, Webster, Mass.
340 Mr. R. G. Severson, Burlington, Vt.
341 Mrs. Severson, Burlington, Vt.
342 Mr. B. F. Shattuck, Boston, Mass.
343 Mrs. Shattuck, Boston, Mass.
344 Miss Kate M. Shaw, Lexington, Ky.
345 Mr. T. B. Sheldon, Red Wing, Minn.
346 Mr. Wm. E. Sheldon, Boston, Mass.
347 Miss Sheldon, Boston, Mass.
348 Mrs. Adelaide E Sherry, West Point, Ind.
349 Mr. Albert Sherwin, Leadville, Col.
350 Miss Susan Sherwin, Leadville, Col.
351 Mr. W. W. Sherwin, Elgin, Ill.
352 Mrs. Sherwin, Elgin, Ill.
353 Miss Susie D. Sherwin, Leadville, Col.
354 Mr. Nathan Shoemaker, Philadelphia, Pa.
355 Mrs. Edward Shortell, Ridgefield, Conn.
356 Rev. R. E. Shortell, Ridgefield, Conn.
357 Rev. W. B. Slutz, Carthage, Mo.
358 Mrs. E. McPherson Smith, Detroit, Mich.
359 Master Wm. McPherson Smith, Detroit, Mich.
360 Mr. E. S. Smith, Seattle, Wash.
361 Hon. Samuel T. Smith, Waterloo, N. J.
362 Mrs. Smith, Waterloo, N. J.

363 Mrs. Louise Palmer Smith, Glenburn, Pa.
364 Miss Edith P. Smith, Glenburn, Pa.
365 Mr. Francis H. Smith, Washington, D. C.
366 Mrs. Smith, Washington, D. C.
367 Miss Margaret A. Smith, Mahoningtown, Pa.
368 Dr. L. P. Smith, Washington, D. C.
369 Mr. Geo. P. Smyser, York, Pa.
370 Rev. Samuel P. Sprecher, D.D., Cleveland, O.
371 Rev. N. F. Stahl, Scranton, Pa.
372 Mr. Wm. Stahler, Norristown, Pa.
373 Rev. William E. Stahler, Lebanon, Pa.
374 Joseph A. Stan, New York.
375 Gen. D. S. Stanley, Washington, D. C.
376 Miss Blanche H. Stanley, Washington, D. C.
377 Mr. Jos. A. Starr, New York.
378 Miss Mary L. Starr, New York.
379 Rev. J. T. Steffy, Dawson, Pa.
380 Dea. Edward Sterling, Bridgeport, Conn.
381 Mrs. Sterling, Bridgeport, Conn.
382 Mrs. Juliette Stewart, Buffalo, N. Y.
383 Mr. J. R. Stewart, Buffalo, N. Y.
384 Miss Stewart, Buffalo, N. Y.
385 Mrs. M. F. Stires, Jersey City, N. J.
386 Hon. James S. Stocking, Washington, Pa.
387 Mr. S. R. Stoddard, Glens Falls, N. Y.
388 Hon. J. W. Strevall, Miles City, Mont.
389 Mr. Reed Stuart, Detroit, Mich.
390 Mrs. J. F. Studebaker, South Bend, Ind.
391 Hon. John M. Stull, Warren, Ohio.
392 Miss Edith Symington, Baltimore, Md.
393 Mr. M. C. Swift, New Britain, Conn.
394 Miss Bertha H. Swift, New Britain, Conn.
395 Mr. H. M. Taber, New York.
396 Mrs. Elizabeth Talmadge, Westfield, Mass.
397 Mr. Edward Taylor, New Haven, Conn.
398 Rev. W. T. Thompson, D.D., Charleston, S. C.
399 Rev. F. L. Tobin, V.G., Pittsburg, Pa.
400 Mrs. M. S. Town, Elgin, Ill.
401 Rev. E. W. Trautwein, Johnstown, Pa.
402 Mrs. W. G. Trunkey, Franklin, Pa.
403 Rev. C. E. Tucker, Bradford, Penn.

404 Miss Mary S. Van Beuren, New York.
405 Mr. H. S. Van de Carr, Stockport, N. Y.
406 Mr. Edward Van Dyne, Troy, Pa.
407 Mr. H. N. Van Keuren, Newburgh, N. Y.
408 Miss A. Helena Vreeland, Frenchtown, N. J.
409 Mr. Jas. H. Waite, Malden, Mass.
410 Mrs. Waite, Malden, Mass.
411 Miss Sophia G. Wallis, East Orange, N. J.
412 Mr. W. F. Walworth, Cleveland, Ohio.
413 Mr. Wm. T. Ward, Poughkeepsie, N. Y.
414 Dr. E. Warner, Worcester, Mass.
415 Mrs. Warner, Worcester, Mass.
416 Miss Mary Watson, Sewickley, Pa.
417 Mrs. Mary D. Watson, Allegheny City, Pa.
418 Miss Agnes C. Way, Sewickley, Pa.
419 Capt. T. J. Weakley, Dayton, Ohio.
420 Mrs. Weakley, Dayton, Ohio.
421 Major Joseph Weaver, Canton, Ohio.
422 Mrs. Mary Weatherbee, Worcester, Mass.
423 Miss Eliza A. Webber, Charleston, N. H.
424 Mr. Joseph T. Wells, Englewood, N. J.
425 Mrs. Wells, Englewood, N. J.
426 Mr. A. B. Westervelt, New York.
427 Mr. L. H. Wheeler, Boston, Mass.
428 Mrs. Wheeler, Boston, Mass.
429 Rev. A. B. Whipple, Pittsfield, Mass.
430 Miss Nellie L. Whipple, Pittsfield, Mass.
431 Miss Phila M. Whipple, Pittsfield, Mass.
432 Mrs. L. F. Whitlock, Flatbush, L. I.
433 Rev. Robt. K. Wick, Jersey City, N. J.
434 Mrs. John M. Wieting, Syracuse, N. Y.
435 Mr. Alexander Wildman, Danbury, Conn.
436 Mrs. Emma M. Wiley, Colorado Springs, Col.
437 Miss Susanne E. Williams, Cleveland, Ohio.
438 Miss Katherine M. Winton, Scranton, Pa.
439 Mr. Adam Wilson, Pittsburg, Pa.
440 Mr. James T. Wilson, Baltimore, Md.
441 Mr. Wm. A. Wilson, Kansas City, Mo.
442 Mr. Jas. B. Williams, Stamford, Conn.
443 Miss Williams, Stamford, Conn.
444 Miss Lulu Woolsey Brown, Jersey City, N. J.
445 Mr. Isaac Yohe, Jr., Monongahela, Pa.

INDEX.